Veso

VLG – Book Four

Vampires, Lycans, Gargoyles

By Laurann Dohner

Veso by Laurann Dohner

Drugged and kidnapped by Vampires, presumed dead by his clan, powerful VampLycan Veso must rely on a creature he dislikes almost as much as the suckheads who nabbed him if he hopes to escape— a human. But when Glenda proves more resourceful than most of her kind, he agrees to see her safely through the Alaskan wilderness. He'll have to fight an overwhelming attraction to the inquisitive beauty every excruciating step of the way.

Glen doesn't know which is worse: learning she's the distant relative of a Vampire who fancies himself a king (um...what?!), or the fact that said relative is trying to force her to birth his queen by mating her with a half Vampire, half Lycan. Veso is scary, has claws, but he's also key to her survival. She just wishes that she didn't notice all his muscles or the way her body responds to his. He has promised to keep her alive but she might lose her heart in the bargain.

VLG Series List

Drantos

Kraven

Lorn

Veso

Veso by Laurann Dohner

Copyright © February 2017

Editor: Kelli Collins

Cover Art: Dar Albert

ISBN: 978-1-944526-80-1

Veso - VLG – Book Four

By Laurann Dohner

Prologue

Veso snarled low, avoiding the lodge. He hated mating ceremonies. That would never be him, taking a mate. A scent caught his attention and his anger increased as he spun, spying movement along the path.

Brista hurried toward him, a smirk on her lips. "I knew you'd use the path farthest from the event to avoid running into people."

He didn't like her but tried to hide his distaste. She always annoyed him. "What do you need?"

She halted, her expression changing to one of frustration. "I thought we could go together. Please?"

"You know I hate those things. No."

"Come home with me then."

"I'm never going to test a mating with you. It's not personal." He turned away.

"We'd make a good match."

He turned back around. "I don't want a mate."

"I'm the clan caregiver, and you're as loyal to Decker as I am. Times have been difficult lately since he had to leave. I think he'd be pleased when he returns to find us paired together."

He studied her closely, wondering if she was testing him. Had he somehow shown his true feelings? He hated Decker and secretly worked with a few of his clan to take the bastard down. "Nabby has been boasting to his friends that if something happens to Decker, he'll take the clan. You're worried?"

"Of course not." Fear showed on her features though. "Decker will find a way to deal with Lord Aveoth and come back to us."

It was probably true. Decker was devious. The bastard wouldn't die easily or just go away forever. "I need to go on patrol. Kira is out there and she's useless."

"She should die," Brista hissed. "Isn't there any way you could get rid of her? I don't know what leverage Davis uses to keep Decker from outright killing her."

He somehow managed to force a smile. "I'm always looking for opportunities," he lied. "Go do your duty and represent the clan at the ceremony."

"That's what you should do too. It's why I sought you out. Nabby isn't doing us any favors. He's too immature and letting the power go to his head. He pissed off a few elders last night by ignoring their advice. I fear he won't want to step down once Decker returns. There are rumors he's plotting a coup. You need to lead us in his absence, Veso. Nabby fears you."

"Nabby is an idiot but he's not that stupid. Decker would bury him. You're worried for no reason."

"Fine. At least rid us of Kira. Do that and it will endear you to the loyal."

"I'll think about it."

He spun, hurrying away before he snarled at her. Brista was a bitch. There was no honor in wanting to kill Kira. She was mostly human, and she'd never betray her VampLycan father by exposing what they were to the world. She had also been in love with his friend Lavos's older brother for years, and Lorn felt the same for her. The VampLycan threatened anyone who looked at Kira wrong with dismemberment and death. Of course, it was forbidden for him to be with her. Decker would see them both dead before he allowed them to mate.

Veso headed toward the section they were assigned to patrol and picked up the scent of smoke, as well as humans other than Kira, and he swiftly unleashed his claws, climbing the nearest tree to get a better view of the area. He spotted the smoke and kept to the trees to get closer.

He shook his head, staring down at Kira and the male humans who'd breached VampLycan territory. She was too soft to kill them. Instead, she threatened them. They didn't attack her though. He'd have leapt down from where he remained hidden in the trees if they had, ripping them apart with his claws. Instead they grumbled and whined.

"It's about two miles to where the fence was," one of them protested. "It's almost dark."

"Then I suggest you pack up fast and jog. Did you forget about the other rangers on their way? Smoke travels for miles. They aren't as easygoing as I am, boys. We've dubbed one of them Ranger Rage. He gets super angry over idiots starting fires." Kira waved a hand toward the flames. "That will set him off big time. Do you know how dry it's been? Forest fires are a real hazard. He kind of beat the living shit out of the last guy who started one. He said it was worth the three-day suspension because he got

9

to break the guy's jaw. It amused him, thinking about that poor sucker needing a straw to eat from for a few months."

Veso grinned. Ranger Rage? He had a feeling she was referring to him. He'd been furious when he'd been assigned to train the little human'ish, but she'd earned his respect.

She got the group of humans packed up and moving in short order. He stayed in the trees, jumping from one to the other, following to make certain they didn't turn on her. Humans were deceiving that way. Kira stopped following the hunters but he kept with them right until they climbed over the fence. He remained there for a while, watching until they were totally out of sight.

He sighed, taking a seat on a branch. No matter how many times he'd lectured Kira on how to handle trespassers, she didn't have the heart to kill. Innocent humans didn't ignore signs to breach their territory. They always brought guns. That meant they were poachers, murderers of animals they shouldn't hunt. Some of the clan felt she was too dangerous to allow to live. Idiots.

He leaned back, resting his head against the trunk and watching the sun go down. Kira would be cleaning up any evidence of the invasion of their territory. He didn't feel like yelling at her, lecturing yet again about how she should have killed instead. She'd just peer up at him and wait until he was done, then roll her eyes. He'd heard her excuses too many times before. She'd claim they were morons, but they didn't deserve to die.

He'd also have to report the trespassing if he made Kira aware he knew about it. Which would only make some of the clan more riled about Kira. He didn't want to get her into trouble. Nabby had appointed himself

Decker's replacement since their leader and his most trusted enforcers had fled to avoid the wrath of Lord Aveoth. He didn't trust the stupid son of a bitch not to attempt to kill her.

It would blow Veso's cover if he ripped off Nabby's head. Everyone needed to believe he was loyal to Decker.

An odd sound had him lowering his gaze, staring over the fence. His mouth dropped open as he watched some dirt lift, bodies coming out of the ground. He recognized their faded heat signatures.

Fucking Vampires. What the hell?

They climbed out of the earth, then took a minute to hide the traces of where they'd buried themselves. Six of them jumped the fence, entering VampLycan territory. The stupid bastards passed right under him but then they stopped. He wondered if they would look up, aware of him after all.

"I smell human," one of them softly rasped.

"Me too."

Shit. Kira must still be at the campsite. The wind is coming from that direction.

One of them giggled. "I'm hungry."

"Let's go feed. We can go hunting on a full stomach."

They took off, moving in the direction of Kira.

Veso dropped out of the tree. He landed with a thud and the bastards turned, hearing him. He snarled, tearing off his clothes to get them out of the way.

The Vampires gawked at him, either surprised he was stripping or maybe just that he was there at all. He half shifted to unleash his claws and fangs, attacking while he still had surprise on his side.

The closest one froze, terror on his features. Veso ripped his head off, the bastard turning to ash. He lunged at another but that Vamp avoided getting his throat torn out. They could move fast when motivated. He spotted two of them turn tail and run. They weren't heading back to the fence though, going toward Kira instead.

He needed to kill them all fast and get to her. She'd be no match for Vampires. He'd trained her well but she lacked their strength and speed.

One of the Vampires came at him from the front, the other two moving to his back. The bastards never fought fair but that was fine. The odds weren't in their favor. Three against him almost made Veso laugh.

He went after the one in front of him, grabbed hold, and punched the son of a bitch in the throat with his claws. They tore through and he twisted his wrist hard, removing the bastards head. Solid body turned to ash and he spun, snarling again.

The guns pointed at him pissed him off. "Cowards," he spat. Bullets would hurt but they wouldn't take him down. He rushed at them and they fired, then jumped out of the way to avoid his lethal claws.

The pain was less than he'd expected and he glanced down, stunned at the sight of darts sticking out of him.

They fired again, this time hitting him in the arm and in his side. He snarled, ripping out the darts.

To his horror, his knees gave out. He crashed to the ground.

Drugs. It sank in fast. The suckheads had shot him with tranquilizers or poison. He wasn't sure which but it hit his system hard.

Another dart imbedded into his ass. He tried to howl out a warning to Kira but his mouth wouldn't open. His entire body refused to move when he attempted to push up, needing to attack.

One of them bent over him. "That was easier than I thought to find and capture a half-breed."

"Our two dusted companions would disagree."

"Better them than us. Damn, he's big. Who gets to carry him?"

"I'm older. You do it."

"That makes you stronger."

"We'll both do it."

Blackness took Veso.

Chapter One

Noise alerted Glen that something major had happened. The usually eerie silence was broken by excited hisses. She shivered, knowing it didn't bode well for whomever or whatever excited the creepers. She walked to the door and peered out into the hallway through the one-inch bars on the small window section of the door.

Candles had once been a romantic symbol but watching the flames flicker from the wall sconces in the rock tunnel had become her only source of light. Her mind blanked when she tried to remember how long it had been since she'd seen daylight. Everything had blurred until her sense of time had been lost. It could have been days or weeks since that horrible night when she'd been kidnapped from her apartment.

The hissing grew louder, the noise scarier than usual, with a menacing quality. She almost backed away from the door but fought the urge out of curiosity. The thick door kept her locked inside the tiny room, but it also protected her from the creepers. They wouldn't be able to break through the two-inch-thick locked door.

Wheels squeaked and movement drew her attention. A creeper walked backward, pulling a gurney. She hated the sight of those pale, hideous creatures that hissed threatening words and revealed sharp, dark-stained fangs when they came to torment her outside the door. Sometimes they would just scratch at the metal, trying to get inside. She refused to think of them as human.

A large man had been chained down on the mobile table. He was the reason the creepers hissed, which continued as he was wheeled past her door. She got a good enough look at his massive bared chest and his biceps as he strained and fought the shackles that held him. Long black hair hid his features with his head lifted, chin to his chest. He tried to kick at the other creeper by his restrained ankles. They had a blanket thrown over his middle section.

"Sssstop," that one hissed.

"Fuck you," the guy snarled.

Glen gasped, jerking away from the door. He hadn't sounded human with that animalistic grumble. He sure wasn't a Vampire, his skin too tan. The noise faded and she closed her eyes, fighting tears. She just wanted to wake from the nightmare but that wouldn't happen. It was all real.

Keys jingled sometime later and she slid along the wall to the far corner, praying the person would just pass right by her door. They'd already fed her the crappy meal she got every day. She was only allowed a bath once a week, when she was taken down the tunnel, but that had already happened the day before. It wasn't time.

The footsteps stopped right outside her door.

"My dear, dear Glenda," the singsong voice taunted. "It's time to meet someone."

She squeezed her eyes closed, wanting to avoid looking at the thing she'd learned to hate most. She refused to call him a man.

The key twisted in the lock, metal creaked, and she figured her life was finally about to end.

"I see you," the son of a bitch chuckled.

She opened her eyes, glaring at Vlad. It was highly doubtful that was his real name. He was rail thin, his skin so white it seemed to glow from the candlestick he held aloft with one boney hand. Hatred battled fear inside her as she stared into a pair of sinister dark eyes.

"Leave me alone."

"It's time for you to learn what your purpose is."

"I already know what you're going to do to me. I've heard the screams from other people and their sobbing afterward. One of the women in another cell told me that you monsters bit her and took her blood." A chill ran down Glen's spine. "I'm assuming you killed her, since she never came back after the last time."

He tilted his head at an angle that made it seem as if his neck were broken, really giving him an evil, inhuman appearance. "Not you, beloved. Your bloodline has assured you won't be cattle to feed the masses. It's why you are given food and are cleaned occasionally. We don't want you to die."

"What does that mean?"

"Come with me." He waved his hand toward the door.

Glen hesitated. She hated the dank room where they kept her prisoner, but leaving it was far worse. Creepers always littered the tunnels, hissing when she passed them to reach the room where they allowed her to bathe, where the tub resembled a cow trough with tepid water. They were always waiting, their dirty clothes stinking of death and unwashed bodies. Vlad had kept them from attacking so far, but she feared they wouldn't listen to him at some point.

"Ticktock, beloved. Hurry your step. You don't want to anger the master. He has been patient long enough."

The master. She'd watched enough movies to know he would be the one in charge. The romance novels she read implied Vampires were sexy and charming. That hadn't been her experience so far. It would be revolting if Vlad touched her or sank his yellowed fangs into her neck.

She took a few deep breaths, attempting to calm her racing heart. At least it will be over soon, she concluded. Don't go out with a whimper. Die with dignity. Her shoulders straightened as she pushed away from the wall, jutting her chin out. Fuck these assholes.

"After you, unloved. Why don't you lead the way?" She was proud of how steady her voice sounded.

His eyes widened. "Excuse me?"

"There's no excuse for what you've done to me and all the others."

A smile curved his lips, the coldness of it enough to make her almost regret her change in attitude. "There's a spark of that spirit I saw when you were first brought here and demanded your freedom. It was disappointing to the master when I reported that you seemed broken."

"It's called being in shock, asshole. I'm over it." She'd love to break a chair and stake the master, but especially Vlad. Does that really work? A stake to the heart? Holy water? Too bad I'm not religious and don't wear a cross. To press one against the awful freak and watch him scream out in pain would have made her smile.

"Walk," he hissed.

She kept her chin up and shoulders straight as she stepped into the tunnel.

"Go to your left."

It was the direction that the creepers had just taken the large tan guy. She had a really bad feeling as she walked fast enough to keep Vlad from bumping into her. She didn't run away, even though it was tempting to try;

17

she knew more creepers were somewhere ahead in the flickering candlelight. Additional sconces hung on the endless tunnel walls, about twenty feet apart, but they didn't put off a lot of light.

"Turn right."

Glen followed directions and saw brighter lights at the end of the tunnel. They passed more metal doors and she picked up a few sounds of distress. A cell on the left couldn't contain a woman's sobs, the distinctive noise soft but clear.

A chill ran up her spine. Vlad had to be lying, and she was about to become dinner to some bloodsucking monstrosity.

Images of old Vampire movies flashed through her mind. The master would probably be some ancient being with horrible features, who would be even less human than what she'd already seen. She slowed her pace, but Vlad's bony hand shoved against her shoulder to push her forward and right into a large room where the metal door had been left open.

She couldn't help but gawk a little at the creepers hovering near a door on the other side of the room. They appeared far worse in brighter light than in the dim tunnels. They weren't just pale, but had thin black veins showing all over their exposed skin. Their eyes were bloodshot, the whites of them almost completely red.

One of them smacked his lips and she glared, daring him to try to bite her. Her hands curled into claws as her muscles tensed, preparing to fight. No way was she going to be a chew toy without trying to tear his evil eyes out.

A young blond man in all black clothing stood in the center of the room. He wasn't as pale as the creepers or Vlad, but not by much. He smiled, revealing smooth white teeth. His hair was trimmed short and pale blue eyes regarded her. She glanced down his body. He wasn't more than twenty, if she were to guess, and the modern slacks and shirt made her wonder if he was another kidnap victim.

"You're pretty." He took a step closer, staring. "Isn't she, Vlad?"

"Yes, Master."

Shock reverberated through Glen. "You're the master?" She couldn't hold back the stunned observation. "You can't be."

"Why not?" He slightly bowed at the waist and used his hands to make the gesture a little flamboyant. "Am I not what you expected?"

"No." She wasn't about to mince words. "You look barely out of high school."

He smiled again. "You're a brave young woman."

"I'm a pissed-off young woman," she corrected. "How dare you kidnap me and the others. We're not cattle." She shot Vlad a glare. "You should be feeding this one cheese because he definitely looks like a rat."

Vlad hissed, showing those foul fangs of his.

"Enough," the master chuckled. "She's got fire. I knew she would."

"She cried a lot when she first arrived," Vlad muttered.

"Stop speaking before I rip out your tongue," the master threatened.

Vlad closed his mouth and stepped back, effectively blocking the door so she couldn't escape. Her gaze returned to the master. He didn't look monster-like but instead kind of innocent and youthful, except when he opened his mouth to speak.

"You're not here to be anyone's blood donor."

19

That made her feel slightly less fearful. "What do you want from me then?"

He stepped closer, examining her face. "I see the family resemblance. The curly blonde hair, the perky nose, the delicate features. You remind me of my sister, except you have brown eyes. She had blue. I knew you would be the perfect host to fulfill my legacy."

"What family resemblance? Legacy? What are you talking about?" Her stomach rolled a little, and she prayed they weren't really related in any way, that he didn't plan on turning her into a Vampire.

"I'm your..." He waved a hand. "I forget how many generations...but I'm a distant relative."

"No, you're not." She instantly balked.

"Oh, but I am, my dear. Trust that I double-checked your ancestry carefully to make certain we are linked by blood."

She really didn't like being associated with him in any way. "Like a fifth cousin?"

"No." He walked around her, studying her from head to foot. "You're from my sister's birth line. That would make me a great, great..." He shrugged, a sign of impatience. "Enough. We're related."

It took a lot for her to hold still. He gave her chills when he examined her that closely. It freaked her out. "Why am I here if you don't plan on feeding me to your, um...creepers?"

He laughed when he stopped before her, way too close for her comfort. "I'm a king."

She blinked, unsure how to respond to that.

"I need a queen."

"Excuse me?"

"I need a queen, someone worthy of ruling my empire by my side."

Glen had to lock her knees to keep standing as horrible suspicions filled her head. "Don't look at me. You just said we're related."

"Royal bloodlines should marry."

"That's sick. Incest is wrong."

"Don't you know anything about history?"

"You mean how some royal families married cousins? I'm aware and it's still wrong."

He grinned. "Fortunately, your opinion doesn't matter."

She took a step back. "Stay away from me. I'm not marrying you. Ewww!"

"Don't, Vlad," the master ordered.

Glen twisted her head and realized that Vlad had inched closer to her, so she stepped sideways, keeping both of them distanced.

"You're not the one I want."

"Thank God." She relaxed slightly. There are worse things than being bitten on the neck, she thought. One of them would be him wanting to get me naked. That tops the list any day.

"It's your child who will become my queen."

Her mouth fell open. "I'm not pregnant." She was sure of that.

"Not yet—but you will be soon."

She frantically shook her head. "Hell no. Not a chance." Her gaze darted to Vlad. "Kill me now if he's the one you think is going to knock me up. I'd rather die."

"Not him." The Vampire master had the nerve to laugh.

Glen glared at him, terrified and horrified at the same time. "Not you either."

The master smiled. He did that a lot, and it never reached his eyes. There was something cold about them, emotionless and scary. It made her wonder if he even had a soul.

"Humans and Vampires can't procreate life."

That's good news. It meant neither of them planned to rape her.

"We can, however, impregnate Werewolf females under the right conditions. I considered having you turned into one but the likelihood of death is far too great. I rejected that option." He paused. "It would also give you the ability to control your reproductive cycle. I won't have you denying ovulation. You're the last of my line who is female, of breeding age, and carries a family resemblance. I can't take the chance."

The master scowled. "Besides, it's a brutal business, turning into one of those nasty creatures." He opened his mouth and snapped his teeth. "Too much blood loss when they tear into you." He paused. "There's also the fact that I want my queen to be strong. I desire her to be an equal. It's not really possible considering how old I am, but I do want her to be as close as I can design her. That means she'll need to be sired by something I don't like..."

Glen didn't know what to say, so she just kept silent, glancing around, looking for an escape but not seeing one. Werewolf? Did he just say that? He did. Shit! Vampires exist and now Werewolves. What's next? Witches and demons? I don't want to know. Vlad still blocked the door behind her, and the one on the other side of the room wasn't an option, since two creepers stood in front of it.

"I've decided to breed you with one of them."

She glanced at the creepers. "No way!"

"Not my pets." He chuckled. "I doubt they even have a sex drive or remember what a woman is for except to feed from." His voice lowered. "They aren't very bright."

"I'm not allowing anyone to touch me."

The master suddenly lunged, and she gasped when he captured her jaw. His hand was icy cold to the touch. She tried to jerk away but cried out from pain when he tightened his hold, his fingers digging into her tender skin.

"You have no say in the matter." He eased his grip and let go. "Pay close attention if you wish to know what I expect from you—and you do want to know."

No, I don't. She kept silent though, afraid he'd put that clammy hand on her again.

"Vampires and Werewolves can breed under certain circumstances, which I have already stated. Half-breed children were born of such unions, and the man I've chosen for you is one of them."

She let that sink in. "Some half Vampire, half Werewolf? Is that what you're saying?"

"Isn't that what I just told you?" He shook his head, a disgusted look twisting his features. "She's pretty but not very bright, is she, Vlad?"

"No, Master."

"Hopefully her daughter will be more intelligent. I'll be in charge of her education once she's born. We'll make certain she is an exceptional student."

"Yes, Master."

Kiss-ass. Glen shot Vlad a dirty look before turning it on the Vampire master. "You want me to let some halfling monster guy touch me? Not in this lifetime."

"In your lifetime, to be exact. You will be locked inside a room with him until you produce a daughter."

She gaped at him. The guy was insane.

"With luck, the first attempt will work. I'm hoping you don't birth a boy."

"They make for good blood donors," Vlad piped up.

Glen was horrified. "You'd suck blood from a baby? It would die!"

"Shut up," the master snapped. "The boy would be a relative of mine, and therefore I would put him to work for me. I could use any boys as day guards." He glanced at her stomach. "I prefer the first one you have to be my queen. I don't want to have to wait too long to claim her. I'm lonely."

"You have your brides," Vlad whispered.

"Brides aren't my queen," the master hissed at him. "Silence!"

"Brides? Plural?" Glen had caught that.

The master arched an eyebrow and frowned. "I have five of them, but not one is worthy of me. They serve my physical needs, but my queen will rule at my side."

He's bat-shit crazy, she decided. Oh God. I hope he can't turn into a bat. That was a disturbing thought.

"I'll introduce you to the VampLycan. He's vicious, so try to keep far from his mouth when you breed with him. He won't willingly agree to this."

"I don't agree either," she reminded him.

"As I said, your wishes are irrelevant."

Glen stared at him, her mind working. "Let me get this straight. You want me to have a baby so you can marry a relative and this...whatever...doesn't want to touch me either, but you expect us to have sex?"

"Exactly."

Glen blinked a few times, letting that information sink in, then had to lock her knees to remain upright. "No."

"I'm not asking. He's being cleaned right now. I didn't think you'd find blood appealing, and you'll need to be in the mood. He'll be chained down flat, so just climb on. I'm aware you're not a virgin." He shook his head. "Young women these days are so promiscuous. You even lived with a man for two years. In my day, your parents would have disowned you for such shocking behavior, but at least I won't have to instruct you on the mechanics of getting pregnant."

The guy had nerve. "You expect me to just climb on some poor guy and, um...do him? No way in hell. You're crazy!"

Her pale relative grinned. "He can't hurt you if he's the one chained down. You'll do it—or I'll wait for him to go into heat. They do that, you know. It's disgustingly crude, but it will serve my purpose. You'll be the one tied down, naked, at his mercy. And they have none. He'll rut on your body

25

until he no longer has the need. That's when he'll decide to kill you, but I'll stop him before his cycle ends. You'll hopefully become pregnant. I just don't know what shape you'll be in after a few days of taking his lust."

Vlad chuckled. "He could crush her bones. They aren't gentle in heat. But she isn't his mate, so how do you plan on getting around that? They can only impregnate a mate, from what we've learned."

"I've thought of that."

The master snapped his fingers and the creepers suddenly lunged.

Glen screamed and tried to twist away but they were on her in a heartbeat, taking her to the floor. Her back hit the dirt so hard, it knocked the air from her lungs.

The master was suddenly straddling her hips, and she watched, horrified, as he withdrew a big syringe. It was full of something dark, looking suspiciously like blood.

Then she screamed again in terror as he buried the needle into the skin of her left breast, right above the edge of her low-cut shirt. "What is that? What are you doing?"

"It's the VampLycan's blood." The master finished injecting her and withdrew the needle. He lifted it to his lips and licked the tip. "Mmmm."

"How long?" Vlad hovered over them.

"A few minutes." The master continued to sit on her while the two freakishly pale creepers held her arms down. "Did I properly introduce myself, my dear? I'm King Charles Borrow, at your service."

Her maternal grandmother's maiden name had been Borrow, a hint that he must come from that side of the family. "You're insane! I'm going to die now. Have you ever heard of people going into shock by being given the wrong blood type?"

"Human blood, but not VampLycan." He used one hand to withdraw an old-fashioned timepiece from his pocket and used his thumb to lift the lid. "Right now his blood is mixing with yours." He leaned in close enough for her to smell his breath, not a pleasant thing. "What does it feel like?"

She was petrified and a little lightheaded but that was from the fear. Those horrible creepers were too ghastly to look at, their cold hands on her wrists what she guessed it would feel like to be held down by corpses. They were animated though, real freak shows. Her relative wasn't much better. Part of her hoped the blood would kill her. It beat living in the hellish nightmare her life had become.

"I asked you a question. What does it feel like?"

She took some deep breaths and tried to ignore everything but her body. Her heart raced and the lightheadedness was more pronounced. "I think I'm going to faint."

"Don't crush my amusement." He suddenly jabbed the needle into the other side of her chest, again just over her breast.

Glen screamed out from pain once more, tried to struggle but couldn't get away as he dropped his other hand on her rib cage to hold her down. She watched helplessly as he used the dirty needle to draw her blood. It filled the large syringe.

The pain dulled when he withdrew the needle and eased his hand off her ribs. She sucked in another breath, blinking back tears. His weight lifted off her middle as the crazy Vampire master rose to his feet.

"Now it's his turn to be given your blood. It's a bit barbaric but it will fool your bodies into thinking you're truly mated, at least long enough for you to get pregnant. Get her on her feet."

The creepers yanked her up and released her. Glen spun away, putting as much distance as she could between all of them and herself. There wasn't anywhere to really go except to press against the rock wall.

Vlad bent to retrieve the forgotten watch and return it to his master.

"Now what, Master?"

The blond handed over the filled syringe. "Inject him and shove her inside his cell." He glanced at her. "Go near his mouth and he'll kill you. He could drain your blood or just tear you open enough for you to die of blood loss. The only way you'll walk out of here alive is if you produce a girl for me. I give you my word as a gentleman that you shall have your freedom then."

She didn't trust him as far as she could throw him. Not that she'd ever want to touch the man.

"I had to call in a lot of favors from friends to have this VampLycan captured and brought here. Some of them died in the process. I'm that determined in this endeavor. I'll even reward you with money if you don't give me any headaches. But disappoint me, and your life will be a living hell. Do what you modern whores do, and make me my queen."

Chapter Two

The lit candles in caged lanterns hung high on the walls, making the room brighter than anything she'd seen since being kidnapped. And Glen couldn't help but stare at the huge man chained down on the gurney.

It was the same man who'd been rolled down the hallway outside of her cell. The blanket she'd seen draped over his middle had been removed and wasn't within sight. They'd chopped off his long hair and given him a bath of some sort. He currently lay naked, secured by his ankles and wrists. The snarls and vicious sounds he made kept her by the door.

Muscles bulged aplenty as he struggled. She'd seen bodybuilders before, but never so much of one. Her gaze avoided his midsection, since she'd hate to be stared at if she were in his vulnerable situation. Her chest still hurt from the two holes that had been jabbed into her by the needle. The lightheadedness had faded but she was starting to get a headache.

"Could you please stop?" The noises he made were making it worse.

He ignored her.

"Please?"

An earsplitting howl almost sent her crashing to her knees as she covered her ears.

"STOP!"

It cut off and she lowered her hands. "Thank you." She darted a glance his way. Whoever had cut his hair had done a decent job at least. It was jet-black in color but his eyes freaked her out a little. They didn't appear human; they were golden-brownish but showed a lot of yellow. She'd had a cat once with eyes similar in color.

He still struggled against his bonds, and she saw blood near one ankle.

"Listen." She tried to use reason. "We're both prisoners here. My name is Glen."

"Stay away from me!"

His voice was deeper than any man's she'd ever heard, and she totally wanted to obey that command. "No problem."

"I know what they want. I'll kill you if you straddle me."

She sat down on the hard-packed dirt, putting her back to him as she studied the metal door. It was locked; she'd already tried to yank on it. No other openings were in the room that, like the other, looked as if it had been carved out of stone. "No worries there. I've never raped a guy before and don't plan to start now."

He grew quiet, and she almost missed his growls. It was eerily silent, reminding her of what she assumed a grave would be like. She reached out and touched the rock wall. Then she lowered her hand and dug in the dirt until she found more rock.

"I don't suppose you have claws that can dig through rock, do you?"

He said nothing.

"I was told you're like half Werewolf. I don't know anything about them except what I've seen in movies. Do you have super-strength that can knock down a metal door?"

His continued silence irritated her.

"I'm trying to think of a way to escape."

"I can't dig through rock or break down that door."

His softer tone was kind of nice and husky. It beat him snarling. She resisted the urge to turn her head to glance at him. The whole naked thing made her uncomfortable, and probably him too.

"I was hopeful."

"Why do you have a man's name?"

The question surprised her. "That's what you want to know? Really? Out of all the things to ask me, you choose that? It's short for Glenda. But I hate it. Kids teased me growing up."

"It's a good name."

"Glenda the good witch. It sucked. I told them it's spelled differently but kids don't care about actual facts. They just want someone to torment."

He growled. "You're a witch?"

"No!" She did look over her shoulder then, seeing his face turned her way. He was shockingly handsome, with masculine features and full lips. His expression was still scary though. "Don't you watch movies? Never mind. Are witches real?"

He said nothing.

"Forget I asked. I don't want to know. Ignorance was bliss. I really wish I didn't know Vampires were real, or Werewolves, but I'm sure this isn't some nightmare. I would have woken up by now if it were."

He sniffed. "You're human."

"And you're not." She got to her feet and brushed off her skirt, examining the lock on the door. "I wish I'd been wilder as a teen. I might have been able to figure out how to pick this. It looks old."

He kept quiet.

"I was kidnapped from my apartment, and apparently, I'm some distant relative of the master."

"I was told why we're here and what they want."

"Then you know I'm not here because I want to be."

"Yes."

"We're both in a hell of a lot of trouble. I don't suppose you have a pack like Werewolves do in the movies, and they'll track you down to save us?"

"Doubtful."

"Great. There goes that scenario. We're on our own."

"Just stay away from me."

As if she had to be told. Glen muffled a snort. "Did you hear me the first time? I'm not a rapist, and I sure as hell don't want to go near you. I'm not even looking your way."

She kept close to the walls with her gaze averted away from him. The chains of the handcuffs made little noises, so she assumed he continued to struggle to break free.

Glen ran her fingers over a crack in the wall, trying to see if it had any give to it. Some loose chips of rock broke off. She looked up, studying the ceiling. There were blast marks, which meant that the room had probably been carefully made. "The room they kept me in was much older. I'm sure we're in an abandoned mine. I saw wood beams where I was kept and they appeared to be rotting. This section is newer. They used metal braces in the tunnels here. What do you think?"

"We're definitely in a mine."

She almost forgot he was naked and barely stopped herself from turning around. "Do you know what location we're at? Like a guess? I have no idea. I was taken and knocked out. I woke up here."

"Not really. They drugged me and I woke right before they brought me inside. It's boarded up from the outside, they had to lift a section to drag me in. Who gives a shit where we are?"

"I do. I don't know if it's night or day, how long I've been here, but I'd like to figure out where I am in case I can find a way to escape."

"Pay attention to when you don't see the soldiers. They'll be sleeping during the day. That's how you can tell the passage of time."

"Soldiers?"

"The ones with the red eyes and the veins showing on their skin. They are soldiers."

"Creepers. I call them that because they're as creepy as hell."

"You can call them whatever you want. Vampires make them and use them until they become too insane and unstable to control any longer."

"How do you kill one? Do you know?"

"Take the damn head off."

"What about a stake to the heart or crosses?"

"Total bullshit. You have to take the head off to keep them from healing and getting back up."

She filed that information away. "Where's a machete when I really need one?"

He made a snorting sound. "As if it would do you any good. You're human. The only way you're going to be able to kill one is if you attack it while it's sleeping during the day."

She didn't like the sneered tone. Someone sounded prejudiced against her kind. He'd said "human" as if it were an insult. "Like you could kill them either."

"I could if I were free."

Her heart sped up. "You could?"

"I have claws. I could rip their heads right from their bodies. They wouldn't have gotten me if they hadn't cheated by drugging me."

"I've counted at least nine of the creeper things, plus the master and Vlad. Those two don't have red eyes or ugly skin veins like the creepers do."

"Soldiers," he corrected. "That's how you can tell what they are."

"Okay. You think you could win a fight against that many of those things?" She wasn't sure.

"I'm strong and fast. I could take out the soldiers and Vlad. He's a younger bloodsucker but a full one. The master would be harder to kill, but I could win if I were able to destroy everyone else in the nest first. They wouldn't be able to swarm me."

"Swarm?"

"They would all attack at once to bite and claw me. The massive blood loss would weaken me enough for the master to have a chance at winning."

Glen slid a glance his way, taking a quick peek. He did appear really big, even lying down. He was also very muscular. She could try to free him but then he could become a threat to her. She retook a seat on the dirt, trying to weigh her options.

34

"What are you doing?"

"Thinking."

He mumbled, "I'll kill them all. They'll have to let me up at some point."

"What makes you think that?"

"I have to piss, and I'm going to start smelling after a week or so if I can't bathe."

She wrinkled her nose at the thought of that, then felt sympathy. "You have to pee right now?"

"Yes."

She'd hate being chained down. The poor guy would have to urinate where he lay. She glanced around and only spotted a bucket in the corner. It was a poor man's version of a camping toilet. Shit.

She rose to her feet and hesitated, trying to form a plan.

"What are you doing now? Keep away from me. I'm not breeding you."

"Stop being paranoid. I'm not going to jump your bones. I'm trying to come up with a way to help you out."

"You don't have keys for these chains. There's nothing you can do."

He had a point about not having keys. He was restrained to a gurney table though. She snapped her fingers. "I'm going to go under you. Don't freak out."

"What?"

"I'm going to investigate that bed you're on. I bet it has screws or something. Maybe I could take it apart enough to free you. At least it means you'd be off the table and able to move around."

"Go ahead."

She hesitated then faced him, keeping her gaze locked on his face. "How do I know you won't kill me? You obviously don't like me, but I'm a prisoner here too. I just want to survive and go home."

His lips twisted downward as he scowled. "Try to set me free."

"Are you going to hurt or kill me if I manage to do this?"

His chest distracted her when he sucked in a deep breath, watching it expand. She darted her gaze back to his face. He was grimly staring at her. "I give you my word. I won't harm you."

"How do I know you're not a liar?"

Anger glittered in his eyes. "I'm honorable. I'm a VampLycan."

"And that means what, exactly? I know jack shit about you except you're super pissed, don't seem to like what I am, and you're supposed to be some kind of half Werewolf-slash-Vampire. Maybe you'll go for my throat and suck my blood."

He growled low. "Fine. I need you to escape. Do you believe that?"

"You said you could kill them if you're free. It doesn't sound like I'm of much use since I can't kill them."

"I need you to draw them in here," he stated softly. "It will get them to open that door. That's honest enough. I won't hurt you."

"Why would they open the door?"

"You're important to their master. They'd rush in here to save you if they thought I'd gotten free and might kill you."

"Will you take me with you if you get out of this room?"

He hesitated.

"Don't be an asshole."

He surprised her by smiling. It reached his eyes, and he actually seemed amused. "Fine. I swear on my life to not harm you, and I'll take you outside. You're on your own after that."

"Okay. I guess that's a good compromise."

"Get over here and see what you can do with this damn table."

"We have a deal. Don't forget that." It was tough to approach him and not look at his lower body. She lifted a hand and used her fingers to block her view until she was close to the gurney. She ducked down, then gripped the edge of it to help keep her balance. It was shadowed beneath the table, so making out the details was tough.

"I'd kill for a flashlight. Those lanterns are too high for me to reach and take one down."

"Human eyesight," he grumbled. "Great."

"I'm not the one strapped to a table about to have an accident," she muttered. She dropped to her knees and reached up, feeling the underside of the table.

She closed her eyes since they didn't do her much good anyway. "This thing is an antique. I can feel rust."

"Just get me free."

"I'm trying. I found a lever thing. Let me see what it does."

She had to wiggle it a lot of times to get it to move. It was stuck. She gasped when it did move, and part of the table collapsed. She threw her body back, narrowly avoiding being struck. Her butt hit the dirt floor hard and the lower half of the table drastically tilted. "Um...okay."

"What are you doing?"

"Do I look like I know medical equipment? I don't." She stood up—and realized her mistake as she stared right at his bare lap.

She spun around. He wasn't aroused, but she'd seen way more of the man than she'd meant to.

"Get me free!" he demanded again.

"What's your name?"

"What does it matter?"

"Just tell me your name and stop being a dick." She instantly regretted calling him that, the image of his still in her mind.

"Veso."

She hesitated, and then reached for her skirt, shoving it down. He snarled from behind her but she ignored him, stepping out of the skirt. Her shirt fell long, hiding her panties. Glen held the material out and stepping forward. She covered his lap and tucked the bottom and top of her skirt under his butt, careful not to touch skin. She stepped back fast.

"Better."

He openly examined her legs. "Don't think of breeding with me."

"Give me a break! I just was covering you up. I have underwear on, which is more than I can say about you." She rounded the table and crouched down by his head. "I have an idea. You aren't going to like it but I need better lighting."

"What are you going to do?"

"Just stay there." She chuckled at her own joke. It wasn't like he had a choice.

"I asked you what you're goin—"

She found the matching lever on the other side and pulled. It wasn't rusted. The front dropped, the legs totally collapsing. It left him inches from the floor with the wheels under him.

"That." She took a deep breath and crawled to the side of the gurney, gripping the edge of it with both hands. "I'm going to roll you over."

"Don't!"

"It's dirt. It shouldn't hurt. I need to see the bottom of this thing. Do you want to be free or not?"

He glared at her. His eyes were intense and kind of pretty in a strange way, if she could look beyond the anger.

"Do it."

"Okay. Here we go."

He weighed a ton. She strained to lift one side. He threw his weight in the opposite direction as much as he could. It helped, and the gurney tore from her fingers, flipping him over the rest of the way to land with a hard thud. Now the gurney covered his back and he lay face down.

"Are you okay? Can you breathe?"

"Now you ask that?"

She grinned and bent forward. "I'll take that for a yes. I can see everything better. There are screws. I think I can take it apart."

"Just the wheels or where I'm chained?"

"I'm not sure." She tried to use her fingernail to twist a screw. It wouldn't budge. "Shit."

"What?"

"They won't move."

He sighed loudly. "I guess I won't have to worry about you mounting me now. You're too weak to flip me back over."

"Shush. I'm thinking." She glanced at what little clothes she had left and grimaced. "I have an idea. Can you see me at all?"

"No. My face is in the other direction and I'd have to lift this up a bit to turn my head."

"Good." She reached back and shoved up her shirt to reach her bra. "We're in luck, I think. These are old flat-head screws. It just means I need something straight and rigid to turn them."

"What's good about that? You don't have a screwdriver."

"No, but I have underwires in my bra." She removed the garment and pulled down her shirt, studying the lacey material. "Vlad didn't take it away from me." She found where the underwire rested and used her teeth to bite the thin material. "These damn things tend to break through at some point, so I end up removing them. It's annoying how that always happens...but not this time. It's going to work in our favor."

She caught a glimpse of plastic through the black bra, and continued gnawing the threads until the tiny hole was just big enough to start pushing the capped metal out of one side of her bra cup. "Bingo. We have one." She tossed the bra on the floor and fit the straightest part of the wire against the screw. It started to turn.

"I'm a genius!"

He muttered something she didn't catch.

"What?"

"I'll think you're smart if you get me loose."

"Would you be grateful enough to actually get me to a city or a house with a phone when we break out of here? I can't imagine an abandoned mine is close to anything."

He refused to answer. She got one screw free and worked on another. "Ingrate."

He growled.

She ignored him, hoping her plan would work. She had no idea what she was dismantling, but she'd remove every screw, and hopefully the gurney would just fall apart. That would leave her cellmate free to move around, even if he had to drag a section of metal with him.

Veso fumed. He'd been kidnapped by Vampires. It was humiliating enough to acknowledge that a weaker species had gotten the better of him. He would have turned them into dust if they hadn't cheated. They never would have captured him if they hadn't shot him with darts that drugged him into sleep. Cowards!

But his rage burned hotter as he thought about why it had happened. The Vampire who'd hired others to drug him planned to force him to breed with a human. It was like adding insult to injury. They'd even shorn his hair, as if he were a scruffy dog that needed grooming. Their clammy fingers had touched his scalp as they'd chopped away his hair until if felt very short. The degradation had grown when one had produced disposable razors to remove his chest hair.

His current position of being flat on a dirt floor with a table strapped to his back didn't do anything to defuse his temper. He was at the mercy of this human to help him escape.

41

He was going to kill every damn Vampire he came across once he was freed.

He'd keep his bargain with Glenda though. He wouldn't hurt her and he'd take her to the surface. He'd even help her get to a safe location, but he'd have to wipe her mind afterward. She had been captured too and brought into the mine against her will. She was an innocent.

"Yes!" Glenda sounded excited.

A second later, one of his arms came free. He lowered it. The handcuff was still attached to his wrist but the other side wasn't hooked to metal anymore. He glared at the offensive restraint. Once he got home he'd be able to get them off, or perhaps he could find tools at the house he took her to so she could call for help. He would need to think up a story to implant into her mind to tell the human authorities.

"One down, three more to go," she announced.

He clenched his teeth and refused to thank her. He was going to save her ass, and it really irritated him that his freedom depended upon her.

Humans were nothing but trouble. They feared what they didn't understand and would want to attack his people if they ever discovered others existed. Her kind would never change. Only their weapons advanced with time. Villagers had once hunted Vamps and Lycans with pitchforks and swords. Now they had guns and bombs.

He focused his anger on the master who had decided to capture and breed a VampLycan. His keen hearing had picked up most of the conversation Glenda had with the supposed Vampire king. He stifled a snarl. As if any daughter of his would end up the companion of a suckhead. Veso sure as hell wouldn't fuck a human, either. They were too weak and

42

fearful. She'd probably run screaming the first time he shifted forms or flashed a little fang.

"Almost there," she whispered.

Something dropped a few inches from his face, and he stared at the screw that landed in the dirt. She was literally taking the gurney apart. He had to give her credit for intelligence. He was curious as well, if he had to be honest. Was she really using a piece of her bra as a tool? And then there was her show of bravery. Most humans would be frozen with terror at being locked up inside a room with someone like him.

Metal popped and his other arm was freed. He had a set of handcuffs attached to each wrist but at least he could move. He wanted to push up his chest and throw the gurney off him but held still so she could free his legs.

"Two down, two to go."

"I'm aware. I can count."

Does she think I'm dense? She probably does; humans believe they're the only intelligent life on the planet.

He clenched his teeth and tried to be patient. He focused on a plan of escape while he waited. She told him she'd counted nine soldiers, one full Vampire, and then the master. The odds weren't in his favor since he could still feel drugs in his system, but he had rage on his side and determination. He had a real chance to fight his way out of the nest.

"So much for being thankful," she muttered. "Did anyone ever tell you that you're kind of a grump?"

She reminded him a little of Kira, who was the result of a VampLycan mating with a human, taking mostly after her weaker mother. He'd been

43

ordered to train her to fight. At first it had been a pain in his ass but he'd tolerated her well enough, despite her human tendencies. "Yes. There's a woman where I live who says that often."

"She's right."

"I'm having a bad night."

"I've had a bad few nights or weeks. I lost track of time but I've been down here way longer than you, buddy. You don't hear me growling and grumbling or being rude."

She had a point. He wasn't going to admit it though.

"And I'm the one who doesn't have claws," she went on. "I keep questioning my sanity over letting you go. Don't you think I'm aware that you could be lying? You gave me your word but I don't know you from Adam. You could be a big ol' liar. You'd better not be."

He had to give her credit for taking a huge risk. He wasn't so sure he'd be as willing to trust a stranger if he were in her position. "I won't harm you, Glenda."

"Glen."

"You're a woman. I refuse to call you by a man's name."

"Veso is a weird name but I'm not refusing to call you that. The name is Glen. Please use it. I told you, I got teased about being a movie witch, so I prefer just Glen."

He wasn't going to argue with her over a name. "Fine, woman."

"You want to play it that way? I'll just call you big and scary."

He actually smiled. She had spunk.

One of his legs dropped away from the table. "I know what you're going to say, Glenda. Three down, one to go."

She sighed. "Almost done, scary dude."

It surprised him when the urge to laugh surfaced. It wasn't the appropriate time to find humor but she amused him. "Dude?"

"I'm originally from Southern California. I grew up by the beach."

"Where do you live now?"

"Oregon. My job transferred me there about eight years ago."

She was a long way from home. "Where do you think we are?"

"Somewhere in Oregon."

He didn't correct her. It might distract her from freeing his leg. "How were you taken?"

"I was sitting on the couch after work, eating dinner and watching a show. It was about eight o'clock." She sucked in a sharp breath. "Ouch."

"What happened?"

"Nothing. The wire is getting messed up from fighting with these stupid screws. Some of them are rusty." She paused. "Anyway, I was eating dinner and minding my own business when I heard a window break in the bedroom. I thought one of the neighbors' kids threw a ball, since I live on the second story. That happened once last year. I ran in there to try to see who did it, but Vlad and two of those creepers were climbing inside. I tried to run but they're too fast. Vlad tackled me and I hit the floor. He shoved something stinky over my face and it knocked me out. I woke up here." She laughed humorlessly. "So much for that bullshit about how Vampires can't enter your home without permission. I sure didn't invite them in."

45

"That's not true. It's a story humans tell each other to feel safer."

"Like the myth about wooden stakes through the heart? You said it doesn't kill them."

"It will hurt them and give you time to run away if you pierce their hearts. They have to heal enough to get their heart pumping, yank it out, before they can move around much."

"What about silver bullets and Werewolves? Is that bullshit too?"

"It hurts like hell but silver is just another metal."

"Fantastic. So what kills Werewolves?"

"Are you thinking about trying to kill me?"

"No." She sighed. "I'm just passing the time. This is all new to me. Wouldn't you be curious?"

"Yes," he admitted. "Werewolves can die if you cause enough damage to make them bleed a lot. They heal faster than a human but not like a Vampire. Beheading them works every time."

"I'm starting to see a theme here. 'Off with their heads' must be your motto when you fight."

He grinned. "Yes."

"Almost got it." She dropped another screw in the dirt. "This last one is really tough. The top of it is mostly stripped."

It took long minutes, with Glenda grunting a few times, but his leg finally dropped to the ground. He lifted up a little and turned his head, spotting her on her knees. He rolled, tossing the gurney in the opposite direction. The skirt she'd tucked over him earlier lay on the ground, so he grabbed hold of it and stood, clutching it against his groin.

Glenda sat down on her legs and stared up at him. He saw fear when she glimpsed his full height. He glanced at the black silky material fisted in his hand. It was tempting to just toss it aside, since nudity didn't bother him, but she was a woman not of his kind. It would probably send her into hysterics. That was the last thing he needed.

He breathed through his nose and caught the scent of blood. He lowered his gaze to her hands curled together near her knees. A small stain of red showed on her fingertip. "You're bleeding."

She lifted one hand, revealing her index finger. "I cut it. It's no big deal unless you're thinking I'm dinner. I'm so not."

"I don't drink blood. I'm mostly Lycan."

"Thank goodness." She seemed to recover but her gaze kept darting to his chest and arms. "You're like a house on legs."

He wasn't certain what that meant and frowned.

"You're huge. What are you? Six foot four? Five?"

"Does it matter? I'm strong and a good fighter. We need to lure them into opening that door." He turned his head, glaring at it. It appeared too solid to knock down. Part of it was metal around the edges with thick wood in the center.

"Are you like, talking to them with your mind? Calling to them?"

He looked at her and scowled. "No. Stop comparing me to whatever movies you've seen."

"Just checking," she muttered, climbing to her feet. She sucked on her injured finger and turned her back. "I won't look. You said you had to pee. They left a bucket...how medieval of them. Put the skirt on after you're

47

done. It's got an elastic waist. It's not going to be the manliest look, but it beats flashing me your goods."

He couldn't help but stare at her legs after she faced away from him. She had nice ones. The shirt she wore fell just a few inches lower than her ass. The ass didn't look bad either. He glanced down at the skirt and sighed. "I guess it will work until I can steal something better." He quickly relieved his bladder.

"Maybe we can find your clothes down here."

"I wasn't wearing any when I was taken."

She twisted her head, gaping at him. "Did they grab you in the shower or something?"

"No. I was on patrol."

"You walk around naked?"

"I wasn't in skin when they drugged me."

She paled and her eyes widened.

"I'm a shifter. You must know what that is, don't you? I have a television and movie collection too. I change forms, Glenda. I tore off my clothes in case I wanted to transform to have four legs to fight them. And fur is harder to tear into than skin."

"Oh shit." She faced away and actually grabbed hold of the wall. "I'm so going to need therapy if I survive." She paused. "No. Cancel that. They'll lock me up in a mental ward and think I'm nuts if I tell anyone about this."

Veso grinned. She did amuse him. "You'll be fine." He'd wipe her memory and replace it with something less traumatic. He put on her skirt then bent, cutting off some of the length with a claw so it didn't confine his movement around his knees.

"I hear that! That was my favorite one," she muttered.

"I'm covered."

She turned and glanced down his body. "So what do we do now?"

Chapter Three

Glen tried not to gawk at the giant muscled guy. He had shredded the bottom of her skirt so the ragged ends covered his groin area and down his thighs about a foot. She'd teased him about not looking manly but with that body, he could have worn one of her dresses without losing his appeal. His inhuman eye color helped that masculine image in an odd way. He screamed supernatural being to her.

"We'll draw them to the door so they open it." He seemed to be assessing her.

"How?"

"I won't hurt you. Remember that."

What is that supposed to mean?

He suddenly lunged at her, snarling. His hands opened and his fingernails grew into sharp claws.

The scream tore from her throat as she tried to run. She slammed into the rock wall, forgetting in her terror that it was even there.

His big body pressed up against hers. His skin was hot, and she squeezed her eyes closed, waiting for him to tear into her skin with those sharp nails.

He didn't. He just snarled.

Glen peeked—and saw fangs. His mouth was open and his eyes were terrifying. They were pure yellow and glowing. All the brown in them seemed to have totally disappeared.

She shoved with her hands, slapping them on his muscled chest. Another shriek tore from her.

He twisted his head and stared at the door. He had her pinned against the rock wall and those claws of his were inches away from her sides. He threw his head back and a roar of rage nearly deafened her.

She screamed again, terrified. She sucked in a lungful of air, ready to let another cry loose, when he backed off.

"Stay put and don't move," he growled low.

She looked down her body, expecting to see blood. There wasn't any. Her shirt was intact, not torn to shreds. Her ribs didn't even hurt from having his chest pressing her tight against the rock wall.

He crept silently toward the door and moved to the side, leaning against the wall.

Keys jangled and the door was torn open. Vlad rushed inside.

His eyes widened when he saw what was left of the gurney. He was already pale, but Glen swore he turned even whiter. His mouth opened, revealing those yellowed fangs. He shrieked like a terrified little girl and turned, probably planning to flee, but Veso suddenly blocked his path and fisted the front of Vlad's clothes, shredding material. The big man threw his other arm forward, seeming to slap the Vampire hard.

Something warm and wet splattered Glen. She automatically flinched away when she felt it on her cheek. She saw drops of red across her arm. It took a second to realize it looked just like blood.

She lifted her chin and became confused. Vlad was gone, and something like dust billowed in the air near the floor. The dirt floor between her and where the Vampire had been was marred with dark spots. Parts of his clothing remained, still clutched in Veso's hand.

"Where did he go?"

Veso scowled when he looked at her, then dropped the material in his hand and bent. He went through the clothing and produced a key. "I removed his head. Vampires turn to ash when they die." He unlocked each handcuff and let them drop to the floor. "Let's go. Stick close to me. I don't have time to baby you. Be brave or die."

Veso was a man who didn't mince words, that was pretty clear. Glen had fantasized about escaping, and she finally had a chance to do just that. She rushed after him. The big, scary dude wearing her skirt charged out into the darkened tunnel and she wanted to stay right on his ass. He didn't seem the thoughtful type to wait for her to get over her trauma.

She hoped he could see with those weird eyes of his because she could barely make out anything but his bulky, shadowy shape. The ground tilted upward as they walked. She was pretty sure she'd have noticed that much difference in the rise of the floor, so they were headed somewhere she hadn't been before.

They approached some lit sconces on the wall and she almost regretted being able to see better when two of those creepers suddenly came hauling ass toward them. They were white-skinned freaks wearing all black. One made a high-pitched screeching noise.

Veso stepped back and slammed into her. He threw his arm out, knocking her into the wall. It hurt, but she realized why he'd done it when a pale hand tried to reach around him to grab her.

Veso snarled and snatched both of the things by their throats. He lifted them, putting them closer to the burning candles. It gave her a good enough view to see that he'd literally embedded his claws into their flesh. Blood poured out of their throats and over the backs of his hands. The

52

creeper with long, raggedy locks got a little too close to the flames. His hair caught fire.

Veso flung that one down the tunnel and slashed at the other still held by his claws. Glen managed to suck air into her lungs, but wished she hadn't when the stench of burnt hair almost choked her. The one on fire shrieked and rolled on the floor about six feet away. The flames had spread to his clothes so a secondary unpleasant smell followed.

She glanced away from the creature in time to witness the horrific sight of Veso removing the head of the other creeper. The body hit the floor but the thing's head remained in his hand, where he held it by the hair. He tossed it and stormed forward, going after the one who'd just managed to put out the flames.

Glen couldn't move, glad the rock wall was holding her up. Her knees wanted to give way as she watched Veso bend, slashing one claw-tipped hand at the downed creeper trying to get up. Its head rolled one way, the body dropping in place.

Glen opened her mouth, not sure if she was going to puke or scream. A noise came out of her, reminiscent of a squeak.

Veso looked back at her, his golden-yellow eyes bright in the darkness. "Don't freeze up. Keep moving!"

Her entire arm shook when she pointed at the body in front of her. "You said they turn to ash. That's not ash!"

He snorted. "These things leave bodies behind if they were recently made. They were newer. Step over it. There are at least seven more. Don't forget that."

She shoved away from the wall and almost tripped on the body she had to step over. "Shit. Okay. I'm moving. Don't leave me."

He growled, a look of disgust on his features. "Humans," he huffed. "Don't look at them if it bothers you."

She had serious doubts about trusting a man who'd just done that to two... Not people, she reminded herself. Creepy things. Bloodsucking murderers deserve to die. Move your ass. Scream or puke later.

"I'm right behind you." She had to glance down though to avoid stepping on the second body. She made it past and rushed forward, sticking close to the big guy wearing her skirt and sporting razor-sharp claws that had grown from the tips of his fingers. I'm glad he's on my side. The floor grew steeper but she trudged onward.

"There are people down here. We need to save them." She was proud she could think around her fear and manage to remember the other victims.

"Not my problem."

She grabbed at his arm. "Wait!"

He didn't look at her, watching the darkness ahead of them. It made her pause, staring too. She couldn't spot anything, but what did he see?

"Are there more of them?" she whispered, trying to keep her voice as soft as possible in case they hadn't been seen yet.

"No. It's clear so far. We need to go."

"What about the other prisoners?"

He twisted his head and glared down at her. "My people are going to come in here and clear this nest out. They can save the survivors, if there are any. I'm getting out of here to tell them about this place. You can come with or stay behind. Pick." He tore his arm out of her hold.

She opened her mouth, ready to argue with him.

"We can't rescue anyone if we're recaptured, damn it," he rumbled. "We need to get out and send help back for the others. You're already slowing me down as it is. Move or stay. I'm out of here." He spun away, stomping forward.

It was growing darker without any wall candles lit nearby and she reached out, finding his back. She kept her hand there, afraid she'd lose him since she couldn't even make out shapes anymore. He stopped and she bumped into his back.

He growled low. "Why are you touching me?"

"I can't see anything."

"Fuck." He nudged her with his elbow. "Here. Get a good grip."

She blindly found his forearm and clutched on.

"Let go if I say to. I need to be able to fight. Just find a wall and hug it. I'll get you when I'm done."

It wasn't as if she had a choice. "Got it."

He turned a corner and she scraped against rock. Glen grit her teeth. He wasn't doing a very good job of being her eyes, since he hadn't even tried to stop her from accumulating scratches. She just hoped that was the least of her worries. She really didn't want to have to let go of him and prayed he wouldn't abandon her in the dark. Those creepers would grab her without her ever being able to see them coming.

"That's why," he muttered.

"What?"

He paused and sniffed loudly. "Dawn."

"What?" she repeated, keeping her voice low.

"I smell it. That's why we've only come across two. We're close to the entrance."

"Dawn has a smell?"

"It does. Most of the newer ones have probably gone to their day rest. The two soldiers I fought were a bit weak and that explains why. They're usually harder to kill." He reached out and closed his hand over hers, trapping her fingers against his arm.

His own fingers were wet, and she wanted to jerk away, realizing it had to be blood. She didn't feel claws though. "What exactly does dawn smell like?" She was curious and it helped distract her from being afraid.

"Come," he ordered, ignoring her question. He moved fast, taking her with him since it was walk or stumble.

The sight of tiny cracks of light ahead helped motivate her to move to his side instead of letting him lead. The closer she got, the more she understood what she was seeing. Old timbers blocked a hole at the end of the tunnel. Faint light peeked in through the gaps.

"Dawn," he rumbled. "I told you." He stopped gripping her. "Stand back."

"Okay." She let him go and moved to the side until she touched hard-packed dirt walls. It wasn't rock in that area, a good sign.

Veso moved forward and she could make out his shape with the help of the light. He lifted one leg and kicked. Wood snapped and big gaps appeared. He kicked again, higher, making the hole bigger. She smiled.

They were about to be freed. She could shower and eat real food. Freedom!

The sound of loose rocks skittered behind her and she turned her head, her heart racing. It was dark...but she swore something moved near the floor. "Um, Veso?"

"Almost done."

"Veso?" She let her panic rise her voice.

"What?" He turned. "Shit." He lunged forward. "Go!"

He'd broken enough of the boarded-off area that she saw the pale hand when it reached the light. The creeper's face came into view next as it crawled forward. More movement showed behind it. The things were coming at them from the floor, moving on their bellies.

"Go," Veso snarled again.

She didn't need to be told a third time. She spun, rushing to where he'd kicked apart the boards. The hole was only waist high, but she had no qualms when it came to dropping to her knees and crawling out. She didn't look back, not wanting to see how many of those things were in the tunnel.

Dirt and grass met her as she shoved her hands outside and realized there was another problem. Six feet from the opening was a drop-off.

Glen froze, glancing around. She was on little more than a wide, grassy ledge. Sheer rock rose to her right and left. She inched forward, staring down.

"Fuck me," she muttered.

She was outside though, in the faint light of the sun that had just risen.

Something slammed into the boards behind her and she rolled to the side, bumping into a big boulder to get out of the way. But it wasn't Veso who came flying out of the hole, along with a few broken pieces of boards. It was a creeper. It hit the ground and rolled right over the edge, screaming.

She leaned out to watch it fall. It hit the rocks far below. The screaming stopped. It seemed to be burning but there was no smoke. The skin was turning black, the shape kind of crumbling inward, and then the body was gone. It had turned to ash and the wind blew it off the rock.

"I need a big fucking drink," she muttered.

More boards broke and she turned her head. Veso bent forward and he stepped outside of the tunnel.

"We have a problem," she informed him.

"I just threw it into the sun. That was probably the oldest soldier in the bunch, since he was pretty strong."

She hesitated. "Um, this really isn't the outside. It's more like they blasted a hole in the wall and found a big drop-off."

He came forward and looked over the edge. The grimace on his face said it all. He turned his head, glancing right and left, then turned around, staring back where they'd come from. "Just my luck."

Glen glanced at the hole he'd made for their exist. "We have to go back in there, don't we?"

He shook his head. "No. The soldiers are weak but still conscious. I killed one of them but more managed to crawl toward us. They're about ten feet or so back. The only thing keeping them from coming closer is the sun. But the master won't be feeble. I don't know how strong he is, but most masters can withstand daylight and move around well as long as they aren't directly in it. I'd rather avoid a fight if I can. There could be more full-blooded suckheads, and they might attempt to drug me again. I can't see any master only keeping one true Vampire in his nest, besides himself. He'll want strong ones to help defend him." He turned back around and stared down. "I'll take my chances climbing."

"We don't have any rope." She worried that she even had to point that out. He should have already thought of that particular problem.

He lifted both hands and unleashed his claws. "I don't need any."

"What about me?" She glanced at her hand. "No claws."

His eyes had returned to a golden brown and he seemed amused when he grinned. "Those soldiers are lying just a dozen feet inside. You can climb with me or wait until the sun lowers. They'll come out here to get you, if their master doesn't first."

She turned, staring at the hole he'd made in the timber. It scared her knowing those things were lying on the floor, just waiting for the sun to go down so they could move around again. She looked over the edge. It was at least a two hundred foot drop to a bunch of rocks and vegetation below.

"Shit."

He chuckled. "I promised I'd get you out of there. I did. Now you can remain here or go with me to safety. Your choice."

She pushed up, standing. Her legs felt shaky. He could have just left her there. She appreciated that he even offered to help her climb down. "This is so going to suck ass if I fall to my death after all this." She wiped her hands on her shirt. "What do I do?"

He stepped closer, looking her over. "You're totally helpless."

There was that disgusted look that she was starting to hate seeing on his smug face. "I got you free. Don't forget that. Please don't leave me here. Is that better? Just tell me what to do. I don't have shoes and rock climbing was never on my bucket list."

He sighed. "I'll have to carry you, rather than you climbing beside me. You'll fall otherwise."

She gritted her teeth. The guy could be an asshole. She took a deep breath and blew it out. "You don't have to sound so disgusted."

He surprised her when he grabbed her hips. She gasped, afraid his claws were going to puncture her. No pain came, though. Veso lifted her off her feet.

"Hold on and wrap tight around me. Understand?"

She hugged his broad shoulders. He was really warm. His hands shifted, getting a better hold on her.

"I said wrap around. That means your legs too."

She lifted her legs and muffled a curse when he grabbed her ass with both hands, hiking her up his body more. It made her very aware that her shirt had lifted and she only wore underwear. He had her high enough that her thighs were just above the waist of the borrowed skirt he wore. It meant her pussy pressed against his belly, only a thin layer of cotton separating skin from skin. She adjusted her arms, wrapping them around his neck.

He tipped his head back, staring into her eyes. "Close your eyes and hold on. Do not scream or whimper. I need to focus on climbing. No distractions."

"Got it."

He let go of her ass and she tightened her grip so she didn't slide down his torso. He reached up and cupped the back of her head, none too gently shoving it against his shoulder.

"And don't move your head. I need to see."

"Okay," she muttered against his skin.

She stared over his shoulder as he turned and began to climb the boulder to his left, her right. Her back brushed rock but he was careful not to crush her. She squeezed her eyes closed when they started to move higher and away from the ledge. One glance down assured her they'd plummet to their deaths if he fell.

She'd gone from one terrifying experience to another kind of hell.

Veso dug his claws into the crack in the rock. It was a little painful with the extra burden of the woman but it could have been worse. She wasn't too heavy and he was grateful for her smaller size. He normally liked to keep his chest closer to the surface when he climbed but she was in the way.

He reached up, finding another hold, and pulled, rising another twelve inches.

Glenda kept quiet, something he was grateful for. Her breathing against his neck tickled though. He hated being aware of the feel of her against him when he paused, looking for each handhold. She had soft thighs that were pressed against his sides. Her heels were dug into his ass muscles. The heat from her sex was noticeable too. It reminded him that he needed to get laid if a human was making him a bit horny.

He flexed his hand and dug his claws into another crevice. He blindly felt with his feet, finding a solid place to anchor with his toe claws. He pulled, staring up at what he hoped was the top about sixty feet above.

He distracted himself by plotting what his next move would be. The nest had at least one vehicle. They'd driven him to the mine. He'd woken when they'd dragged him out of the back of a truck. He'd have to steal it and figure out how far they'd taken him from VampLycan territory. It could have been a short ride or hours. The drugs they'd given him had kept him unconscious for an unknown duration of time. The view he'd seen from the ledge wasn't of any familiar landmarks.

The woman would have to be dealt with after that. He'd find the nearest human dwelling, wipe her mind, and send her to their front door. He still needed to think of a cover story to replace her real memories. He remembered seeing a report on the news about how a human man had kidnapped a woman and stolen her to be his bride. He could tell her something similar, and that the male had been killed by falling over a cliff.

He chuckled, glancing over his shoulder. She probably feared falling herself, not knowing how well he could climb.

The sun rose higher, warming the rocks around him. Sweat began to bead on his skin and when he pulled them up another foot, the woman slipped a little down his body. Her hold around his neck tightened and she sucked in a sharp breath but didn't speak.

He stifled a growl, realizing he couldn't let go to reach down and adjust her higher up his body. He pushed her against the rock though to take a moment to rest. It made him acutely aware of her new position. Her sex was right over his groin.

His dick responded, and she obviously felt it too, because she sucked in another breath. He tried like hell to ignore the hard-on he sported. At least the tightness of the woman's skirt kept his shaft from pressing too much against her body. That was the only highlight of the hellish experience. He reached up, finding another handhold.

"We're almost there," he informed her.

Glenda didn't answer, and he grinned. She was either too terrified by his current aroused state or she was following his instructions. He didn't like where that second thought led, wondering if she'd do anything he demanded. A few ideas came to mind that made his dick even harder.

I don't fuck humans, he reminded himself.

It didn't help. He imagined Glenda on her hands and knees in front of him. She was an attractive woman, for a human. Too small...but big enough.

He growled, irritated with himself and her. He wouldn't be thinking about fucking her if she wasn't riding him. He took a deep breath and swiftly regretted it. Her scent was stronger now, between them sweating and with her throat so close to his mouth. She smelled good.

Veso focused on climbing, finally seeing the top. The line of trees assured him there was space above him that would be more than another ledge.

"Almost there." He wasn't certain if he'd repeated that for her, or to assure himself that he'd be rid of her soon.

She liked to use a man's name. He refused to call her that. It was best if he kept her angry. "Did you hear me, Glenda?"

"I heard," she whispered. "You said not to talk."

He reached the top and found a good place to brace his toes. "This is the difficult part. I have to find something to hold on to that won't slide off the side. Just hang on."

He blindly reached up, feeling grass. It was loose when he dug his claws in, and he had to duck his head when it rained down on them, hitting their bodies. She clung to him tighter and he dug his claws in deeper, finding something solid under the dirt. It felt like rock and he pulled hard, seeing if it would come down too. It held.

He climbed a few inches higher and hoped her added weight and bulk wasn't going to be an issue. He got high enough to peer over the top, seeing forest and trees. The opening to the mine where he'd been taken inside loomed, but the truck wasn't parked near the entrance anymore.

It infuriated him as he reached down and hooked Glenda under her ass with his free arm. There was no way he could make the rest of the climb with her in front of him. His weight might snap her back when he dragged himself over the ledge.

"Listen to me," he demanded. "I'm tired and I won't argue with you. Do exactly as I say. Ready?"

"Shit. Yes."

"Lift your head up and look above us."

She did as she was told. "We're here."

"Almost." He braced his legs and moved the arm under her ass. He used it to reach up, finding another spot to grab that didn't crumble so both of his arms were pinning her in between the cliff and his body. "You can step on my thighs. Just stand up, brace your hands on my shoulders. Then turn and climb the rest of the way."

Her soft brown eyes widened and he identified fear. "What?"

"Would you prefer to climb around me and cling to my back with your arms while the rest of your body is just hanging?"

"No."

"Then do it. I'm braced. You won't fall. I'm not going to let you."

She swallowed hard and nodded. "Okay."

He almost felt proud of her as she eased her grip with her thighs and tried to follow his instructions. He bent a little, giving her more room to maneuver between him and the rock face. One of her feet found his calf after she wiggled a bit. It was hell since it meant her pussy rubbed against his erection trapped under the borrowed skirt. He silently swore to personally rip off the head of the master who called himself a king.

And so way would he return home in Glenda's skirt. He'd have to steal clothes first or he'd shift into his other form.

She managed to use his calf as a foothold, then lift herself enough to find purchase with her second foot on his thigh. She stopped hugging his shoulders and gripped them instead. She wobbled, reminding him of a baby moose first learning how to stand. He was amused watching her expressions. She was terrified but had a determined look on her face. He gave her credit one more for bravery.

Straightening put her breasts directly in his face. The shirt separated them from his view, but he was more than aware of those soft mounds as she moved around. The bra had been left inside their cell. He would have forgotten about that except her breasts jiggled when she trembled again, her balance unsteady.

He clenched his teeth. "Turn and climb now."

"Easier said than done," she muttered but she released his shoulder with one hand, throwing an arm out and finding something to grab. She looked down, moved one foot, turning it. "Are you sure you have me?"

"You're not getting any lighter, Glenda. Move your ass."

She turned and started to climb. He lifted slightly, giving her a boost. She bent over in front of him, her shirt rising up with her arms. It gave him a clear view of the silky black panties she wore. She had a nice ass, both sides of it clearly revealed with the cut of the small material.

He had the urge to lean in and shove his nose between her legs to take a sniff at her pussy. He closed his eyes after she wiggled her ass, almost teasing him with it. His dick suffered the consequences. He wanted to fuck her. He couldn't see anymore but the memory seemed imprinted onto his brain.

He growled when she lifted one foot off his thigh and he had to look at her to make sure she didn't fall back and land on him. She almost kicked him in the chest as she wiggled again, gaining more of her upper body on solid ground. He stared at her ass, suffering. She made it to the top and crawled away.

He used his fury to yank his body over the top—and froze when he made it all the way up.

Glenda was just a few feet away from him. Her ass was in the air, her chest against the grass. The woman seemed to be kissing the ground.

He arched his eyebrows but couldn't look away from her rear end.

Veso moved before he could stop himself, crawling forward until he was on top of her, his limbs bracing her into position.

She gasped and twisted her head, her eyes wide.

He froze again, realizing what he was doing. The urge to tear off the clothes between them and just take her was so strong, he battled with it.

"What are you doing?" She lifted her chest and it bumped her ass against his dick. She jerked away but her shoulders hit his arms that were locked in front of her, keeping him from crushing her with his upper body, his hands braced on the ground.

"Hold still." He needed to think around the desire to fuck her. It would be so easy to take her. That scrap of material she called panties was flimsy. The skirt he wore made him very aware when the breeze blew that it wasn't an obstacle, since every draft hit his balls.

She hunched her shoulders and tried to squeeze forward between his arms. He growled. He didn't like her trying to get away from him. She stopped, her gaze locked with his over her shoulder.

"What are you doing, Veso?"

"There could be guards." His mind started to work. He refused to fuck a human. He'd never live it down if any of his clan found out. "Hold still while I look around."

"Won't all the Vampires burn if they come out into the sun?"

"Sometimes Vampires have humans under their control."

"Oh. You didn't need to cage me under you. Just tell me not to move."

He wanted her to move. He'd like it if she dropped her arms and shoved her ass up in the air again to press against his groin. It would be simple to rip away those panties covering her pussy, jerk up the material covering his dick, and enter her from that position.

He forced his gaze away from hers, looking around. Think! He breathed through his mouth, a sad attempt to avoid her scent. The Vamps had let her bathe and wash her clothing. She didn't smell bad at all. He wished she did.

The truck was gone and no other vehicles were within sight. "The master must have left and took the vehicle with him. It explains why he didn't come after us." His anger at that suckhead helped him ignore the desire to fuck Glenda. "He must have a day place nearby though. He wouldn't go far from his nest."

"Is that good or bad?"

"Bad. We're going to have to hike out of here and find a road or a home."

"Great. Between us, we're almost dressed."

She had to remind him of how little they wore. He lifted up and straightened, adjusting his dick before she noticed. It was impossible to hide his erection though so he decided to ignore his lower half. He got to his feet and walked toward the entrance of the mine. He refused to see if she followed. It was safer for Glenda if he avoided looking at her.

"So rude," she muttered.

He hoped she didn't like him. It would mean she wouldn't come on to him. At this point, he'd fuck her if she did.

Veso let the entire situation sink in and the rage that surfaced helped to cool his desire for the human. He'd been drugged, taken from his territory, had to depend on a human to help him escape, and now they didn't have access to a vehicle.

He examined the tracks in the dirt. "There is only the truck. These were all made by the same one. We'll follow the tire tracks and it will lead to a road. Keep up."

"Sure. No problem."

Sarcasm. He remembered why he didn't like humans. The problem was, Glenda was growing on him. She hadn't burst into tears or acted the way he thought she would. It left him a little off balance. That has to be it, he decided. That was where the attraction had sprung from.

"What do we do when we reach a road? Hitchhike?"

"Yes." He wasn't about to tell her that he'd pull whoever stopped out of their vehicle and alter their memories. The person would never remember picking up two people or driving them anywhere. He wouldn't leave an innocent in the middle of nowhere.

She'd just find out what he could do, and possibly guess she might get her memories wiped too. He could always take control of her mind if she panicked and tried to run away.

Veso was careful not to walk too fast. She was barefoot but the dirt road wasn't rocky. He didn't want to tire her out too quickly. The last thing he needed was to have her in his arms ever again. She didn't complain as he led her forward, always watchful for anything that could be a danger.

They came across a house a mile down the road. He held up his arm to indicate she should stop, and then sniffed the air. "Shit. Stay here."

"What is it?"

"I smell death. The Vamps had to drive right past this place. They probably fed off the inhabitants."

"I hope not."

"It's what they do. Humans are cattle to feed from to them."

"Nice."

He glanced back, holding her gaze. "It's how they think. I don't have the same opinion since I don't drink blood. I'm going to look inside. Don't move."

"Like my feet are glued to the ground," she promised, crossing a finger over her heart.

He understood the gesture and shook his head. Silly humans.

He strode toward the house, hoping the master hid somewhere inside. He'd love some payback and ripping off his head would help. He was wearing a woman's skirt and it was all that prick's fault.

The back door opened at the twist of his hand on the knob. The smell of death didn't travel inside with him. It meant the body remained outside. He searched the one-story cabin, finding no trapdoor or life inside. He listened, sniffing again. There wasn't a trace of cooked food or that of the fireplace being recently used. He checked the two closets and even climbed up inside the loft. It was empty. He dropped down and exited through the back door. No vehicle was within sight.

He rounded the cabin and spotted Glenda almost where he'd left her. She'd moved off the dirt road to sit on the grass. He sniffed, following the smell of death.

He found where the human had been buried in a shallow grave behind a tall wood pile. The earth had been turned over but it didn't look too recent. Perhaps a week, maybe two. He couldn't tell how many bodies were down there but the interior of the home had appeared as if a single human had lived inside. He left the wood pile and whistled.

Glenda lifted her head.

"Come inside. It's safe."

"Nobody's home?"

"No." He didn't want to share what happened to the homeowner. It might make her leery. Some humans didn't like to enter the dwellings of dead people.

She followed him inside and immediately lunged toward the phone. He grabbed it from her but didn't hear a dial tone. It either wasn't connected, or the Vampires might have pulled a wire to the house before they attacked so the owner couldn't call for help.

"Give that back. I need to call the police."

"No." He wasn't certain how she'd take it if she found out it was damaged. It was possible she'd cry. He didn't want to witness that. He'd have to go out and see if he could fix it, but even if he were able to get it working, he still didn't want her to use the phone. The last thing he needed was a bunch of humans around.

Her mouth parted.

"My kind will handle this. Do you want more humans to die? Those soldiers would slaughter humans, even ones with guns. Do you understand? Go shower. There's a bathroom. I'll make the call."

She bit her lip. "You'll let me call the police later though, right? I'm sure they're looking for me."

"Yes," he lied, jerking his head. "Go shower." He wanted her out of the way, and some space from her would be good. "There's a propane tank outside. It means heated water."

He almost felt guilt at the longing on her features. "Okay."

He watched her go and waited until the bathroom door closed and the water came on. "Simple-thinking humans," he sighed.

71

He hung up the phone, searching for anything with a hint of their location. The human had bills in the top drawer of a desk. They were addressed to a post office box but he had a town name. That angered him off too. The Vamps had taken him farther from home than he'd estimated.

He walked outside to see if he could get the phone working and call his people.

Chapter Four

"He thinks I'm an idiot," Glen muttered, using the soap to scrub her skin where blood had dried from Veso killing Vlad and those other creatures. The hot water did feel heavenly as she stood under the spray.

He didn't want her to overhear his conversation when he called someone. He could have just said so instead of treating her like a child.

She rinsed the conditioner out of her hair and turned off the water when she finished. The towels were cheap, harsh ones she wouldn't have bought herself but they were nicer than anything she'd been able to use since her kidnapping. The few baths she'd been allowed to take had been miserable.

Something registered as she finished drying off. The cut to her finger hadn't hurt when she'd used soap.

She stared at where the cut had once been, noticing for the first time that it had completely healed. It stunned her as she touched the undamaged skin. There wasn't a mark on it anymore from where the underwire had sliced her fingertip.

"What the hell?" She planned to ask Veso how that was possible. First though, she'd have to get dressed.

She grimaced at the sight of her discarded shirt and panties. The last thing she wanted was to put them back on. She stepped over them, wrapping the towel around her body. The cabin probably had clothes she could borrow. She unlocked the bathroom door and stepped out.

Veso wasn't within sight. She took a few cautious steps into the living room, searching for him. The only other interior door was wide open, and she could see a bed. She crossed the room and paused there, looking inside. It was obvious a man owned the cabin. There was only the bed and one dresser. No knickknacks were in sight but a deer head hung over the bed. She turned away.

"Veso?"

He didn't answer.

Fear crept up. Had he just abandoned her? He'd gotten her out of the mine and found a cabin so he'd kept his promise. She hustled to the phone—only to come up short.

"You son of a bitch," she muttered.

He'd smashed it into half a dozen pieces, all of them strewn across the counter below where it had been mounted on the wall.

Anger came next. The bastard had broken the phone on purpose, stranding her in the middle of miles of woods.

She rushed to the front door in hopes of seeing another cabin or signs of life. Just a vast view of trees met her wandering gaze.

She clutched at the towel with both hands to keep it in place as she began to pant. It was rare for her to suffer from a panic attack but it was certainly the time for it. She was a city girl. Images of bears and wolves filled her head. She'd have to walk along that dirt road for who knew how far to find someone to help her.

Wood creaked from somewhere on the other side of the cabin and she spun, staring out the windows. Movement caught her eye near the back door, and she almost tripped on the bearskin rug near the fireplace as she dashed in that direction.

Glen halted at the door, and her mouth dropped open.

Veso hadn't left her after all.

He was totally nude and standing on the back porch. He held a garden hose over his head as he tipped it back, letting the water run over his face. Her gaze lowered, openly admiring his muscles and that broad chest of his. His eyes were closed so she allowed herself to peek lower. He wasn't hard anymore.

She was glad when he turned a little, presenting her with his beefy ass. It was as tan as the rest of him, proof that he didn't wear anything when he sunbathed. He shook his head, water spraying in her direction, but the door's big glass window took the hit instead of her. He lowered the hose and held it near his chest, using his other hand to wipe across his throat and lower.

She took a few deep breaths to calm down, now that she knew he hadn't taken off. But the phone still angered her, and she gripped the handle of the door, shoving it open.

He turned his head, opening his eyes.

"Why?"

He scowled. "You were in there a long time. I hate having dirt and blood all over me."

"I meant about you mangling the phone, Veso. Why did you do it? I wanted to call someone to get me!"

"I told you. No police." He adjusted the hose so the water ran down his back. "Come here if you're going to stand there. Be useful."

"Excuse me?"

"Scrub my back."

She glanced at the expanse of skin, from his neck to where his waist dipped right before it flared out at his ass. That was a lot of flesh to wash. "No thanks. Wash it yourself. You broke the phone!"

He shrugged.

"You said I could make that call."

"I told you what you wanted to hear to get you to do as I asked."

She fumed. "You jerk! You actually admit it?"

He dropped the hose, shutting it off when he released the clamp that allowed the water to flow. She locked her gaze on his face when he slowly turned around. The guy had balls, and he didn't seem to care that she could currently see them if she glanced down. He stalked closer and reached out.

"This is being a jerk." He fisted the towel and yanked hard, tearing it off her. "Thanks. I forgot to get one."

Glen was so taken aback that it took her a second to react. The guy had just stolen her towel. She threw one arm over her breasts, lifted her leg and twisted, trying to hide her body from him. She bumped into the doorframe with her shoulder and just froze.

He had the gall to chuckle and start drying his chest with the stolen towel. He also didn't hide the fact that he was taking in every inch of her as his gaze lowered.

"Don't worry, female. You're too small to fuck and not my kind." He stepped closer, his bigger body crowding her and rubbing against her side as he maneuvered through the door she partially blocked. "I'd break you."

Heat flooded her face and she was muted by a mixture of anger, outrage, and shock. He got past her inside the house and moved away. She turned her head, watching him wrap her towel around his hips as he entered the kitchen.

She frantically looked for something to grab, the curtains on the window the closest thing she could find. The rod snapped loose when she ripped it down and the curtain barely covered the front of her as she turned.

"You asshole!"

He ignored her.

"How dare you!" She recovered fast and moved to the left, pressing her bare ass against the wall. Anyone in the woods would be able to see the back of her otherwise. There weren't any neighbors but that was beside the point.

"Go in the bedroom and find clothes."

"Don't tell me what to do."

He opened the fridge and bent a little. "Don't then. Walk around naked. I still won't fuck you."

Glen forgot how to breathe while her temper raged. She shook a little from it and her shoulder brushed up against a frame hanging on the wall. She turned her head, seeing it was a photo of some bearded guy in fishing gear, holding what appeared to be a two-foot-long trout or some other kind of trophy catch.

He had a lot of nerve to say that to her. He probably thought he was a super-stud, and being kidnapped by her crazy Vampire relative to become some kind of supernatural breeder had just amplified his monster ego.

She reached up and lifted the picture off the wall. It was in a five-by-seven frame. She pitched it at the jackass.

Her aim was off and it slammed into the cabinet about two feet to his left, missing him. Glass shattered and the frame dropped to the floor.

Veso straightened and looked in her direction. His eyes were wide and she knew she'd surprised him.

"I'm sorry I missed. I was aiming for you thick skull. I do not want to have sex with you. How many times do I have to say that? Get over yourself!"

He took a step closer and his lips parted, fangs showing. He growled. "You came after me in a towel."

"I thought you left me here to die! I freaked out a little and then I was upset about the phone. You broke it and you lied to me. Excuse the hell out of me for not waiting to get dressed first to confront you."

He advanced a few feet and growled again. "Don't throw things at me."

"Don't be such an asshole and maybe I won't."

His eyes narrowed, the color of them changed. They went from golden brown to almost all yellow. His hands fisted at his sides and his upper lip curled. "Don't insult me, human."

She was over her limit of dealing with crazy freak shows after all she'd been through. "I am human, and guess what? I'm glad. You should see yourself right now. Your eyes are all weird and you have those messed-up teeth. What's next? Are you going to beat on me? Rip off my head? What a big bad jerk you are. I didn't ask for any of this! I didn't want to be kidnapped by some gang of sickos who drink blood and I sure as hell didn't sign up to be locked inside a room with you. You think you're attractive to me? Ha! I don't do dogs."

He tilted his head a little, glaring at her. He didn't growl again. She figured that was a plus. He also didn't come any closer. His hands remained fisted at his sides though and his body looked tense. She could see most of it since he was only wearing her towel around his waist. It looked a lot smaller on him than it had on her.

Long seconds ticked by and some of her anger faded. "I'm going to go get dressed now. We're in this together until we're not, so try to remember that I helped you escape. We did that working together. Remember? Please don't lie to me again or insult me. It's getting old when you accuse me of wanting to jump your bones. That was that creepy weirdo master's idea, not mine. Plus, I'm a bit freaked out." She held up her once cut finger. "It healed. The cut is gone. How is that even possible?"

He blinked but didn't move or say anything. She eased away from the wall. She had to walk sideways to avoid flashing him her bare backside. The curtain covered her breasts down to her mid-thighs. She was afraid to look away from him as she kept scooting closer to the bedroom door.

"We're both under a lot of stress," she reminded him. "So just chill out. Sorry I called you a dog. I was mad. You have a tendency to do that to me. You're very abrasive."

He moved his head to keep tracking her. It scared her a little. She had no idea what he was thinking or if he was still pissed. His expression had blanked but those yellow eyes reminded her of a predator. The dog comment had been a little out of line but justified. Still, she wasn't about to admit that aloud to him.

She made it to the bedroom door and relaxed a little. He blinked again and she backed into the room, reaching out to close the door between them. Her fingers brushed the wood and she pushed, hoping there was a lock on it.

Veso lunged, coming right at her. A table was in his way but he just shoved it aside.

A scream caught in her throat and she only had time to suck in air before two-hundred-and-whatever-he-was pounds slammed into her.

It threw her off her feet and backwards. She expected pain but she hit something soft instead. Her body bounced once on the mattress before she was pinned when Veso grabbed her wrists, jerking them above her head. He leashed them together between his finger and thumb. Their faces ended up being inches apart and she couldn't look away from his sharp fangs.

"What are you doing? Get off me!"

His eyes glowed a brighter shade of yellow. They were eerie, yet entrancing. They really did remind her of a cat's, only the shape was wrong. It was the inhuman quality of them.

Her heart was pounding and she felt fear. Would he hurt her? She didn't think he would. Sure, he was a jerk, but he hadn't left her inside that mine. He could have. He'd even taken her up that cliff. A cruel person would have just abandoned her on that ledge to face the coming night where those creepers could get her.

"You piss me off too," he snarled.

"You lied to me and broke the phone. You treated me like a moron when you told me to shower. You just didn't want me around when you made that phone call. I played along because a hot shower did sound good. I also didn't want to argue with you again."

His grip on her wrists lessoned a tiny bit but not enough for her to jerk them free. She tried to no avail. His skin was a little chilled from the cold water he'd dosed himself with from the hose outside. He was big, and she was more than aware that he could crush her, but he'd braced his elbows on the bed to hold most of his upper body weight. She felt small and helpless under him. It was a reminder that he wasn't anything like her. Being half Vampire and Werewolf was a pretty terrifying concept.

He didn't respond and she continued, trying to calm him down.

"You get pretty condescending, Veso. I've been through a lot. I know you have too, but you were just taken to that mine. I was there for a while. I didn't know about Vampires or creepers." She took a breath. "Or about what you are. It's all new to me and it's kind of been a nightmare I wish I hadn't experienced."

Some of the brightness of his eyes toned down to a softer shade. It encouraged her.

"You keep accusing me of wanting to molest you. It's insulting. I don't know what your world is like but in mine, the men usually pursue the women. Not the other way around. I don't have any trouble getting dates if I want one. I don't have to take advantage of drugged men. Do you see how your accusations could push someone's buttons? It would be like me accusing you of getting kidnapped on purpose so you could be locked in a room with me. Hell hasn't frozen over, has it? You say I'm not your type. Well...Ditto."

"What is your type?"

The question surprised her. "What?"

"What types of humans do you fuck?"

She wasn't sure how to respond. Part of her wanted to tell him it was none of his business, but she was still floored that he'd even asked.

"I bet they're scrawny and weak."

"I..." She didn't know who to be more insulted for. The kind of men he thought she dated or herself. "Please get off me."

"Answer. Describe your last lover."

"No."

"Because he was scrawny and weak."

"You really are an asshole."

He growled.

She swallowed, regretting those last words. "Please get off me? Is that better?"

"Why the hell do you smell so good?"

"What?" He threw her for a loop again.

He sniffed at her, and she gasped when he buried his nose against the side of her throat. "You smell so fuckable to me."

Her heart raced. "It's the blood. Remember? They stole our blood and injected us. They gave you some of my blood and forced your blood into me. That master guy said something about fooling you into thinking we were mated or something like that."

His mouth was compressed into a tight line when he raised his head. "Right. That's how your finger isn't cut anymore. My blood healed you."

"That's possible?"

"Yes." He eased some of his weight off her upper body but didn't let go of her wrists. His gaze lowered to her chest. "You've still got bruises that haven't faded yet. They must have been pretty severe to still show."

"He jabbed two needles into me." She swallowed hard. "That's so weird. The blood thing, that is."

"You wouldn't understand."

"Do you already have a mate?"

"No. We can only take one. I wouldn't feel affected by you if I was already taken." He grumbled a little, his chest vibrating. "I still want to fuck you."

She had no words. She just swallowed hard and stared at him.

"We're not mated. My mind knows it but my body isn't listening."

"Make it listen to reason then," she suggested.

He glanced away, seeming interested in studying the room. He finally looked at her again. "The Vampires ripped out the line going into the house. I managed to connect it again but it didn't work. Then I realized where we are after finding some mail the human had in a drawer. I'm farther from my territory than I should be, so no one will be looking for me here. It means they kept me drugged for at least one full day before I woke. I lost my temper and broke the phone."

"Oh."

"We're going to have to stay together longer, until we can find a connected one so I can call my people. I would leave you here but it isn't safe. The master will return to his nest at nightfall and he passes this cabin. I didn't go to all that trouble to rescue you only to allow you to be recaptured. It would just mean he'd attempt to drug and kidnap another

VampLycan to breed with you." He growled, his gaze lowering to her breasts.

"And that makes you angry?" He appeared furious.

He held her gaze. "Yes." That one word was snarled.

"Me too." She was glad they had something in common.

"No one else is going to fuck you if I can't."

She hadn't expected him to say that. It left her mute once more. He leaned in and sniffed her again. She held still since it was impossible to get him to move off her until he was ready to.

"Damn," he rasped. He suddenly buried his face against her skin.

Glen gasped when he nuzzled his nose against her neck and licked the skin right under her ear. His hot breath fanning her flesh tickled a little. She didn't struggle, too afraid he was going to bite her. He'd admitted he was part Vampire. Maybe he did suck blood.

"Don't eat me. I'm not food," she said in a shaky voice. "I'm a person. Remember?"

He groaned. "Don't give me ideas."

"Please, Veso?" She recalled reading that using someone's name helped somehow if she found herself in a bad situation with another person...or was she supposed to tell him her name, to remind him? She had a hard time thinking when he ran the tip of his tongue along her neck again.

"Be quiet. I want to test something."

"That doesn't sound good." She realized she spoke that thought aloud.

He suddenly nipped her with sharp teeth.

He didn't break skin, but there was no question that he had fangs. She could feel them against her throat. The bite didn't hurt but it did startle her. A jolt shot through her body. It wasn't fear. She wasn't sure what it was, but it made her aware of her fast heart rate and how warm he now seemed to be on top of her.

He growled low and nipped her again. The second time didn't come as a surprise—but her response did. Her entire body started to tingle, almost as if a limb had gone numb and she'd tried to move it, forcing blood to circulate. She'd never experienced the feeling on such a massive level.

"What are you doing to me?" She tried to free her arms. She wanted to touch him for some crazy reason.

He nuzzled her with his face and picked a spot lower on her throat, almost at her shoulder. He bit her again, that time a little stronger. His fangs didn't hurt but she did close her eyes, totally focused on his mouth. Her nipples beaded tight and she shifted her legs, spreading them a bit to alleviate some of the heat that suddenly seemed to flood her lower body.

"Answer me! What are you doing...?"

He wedged one thigh between hers and tilted some of his weight. He moaned, nipping her again. Glenda closed her eyes and fisted her hands. An awareness began and she identified it quickly. She was turned on...and it was growing stronger.

"Why are you doing this? You don't even like me."

He paused exploring her skin with his mouth and teeth. "That's the problem. I'm starting to." He lifted his head away from her throat, panting. "I'm just...seeing if I can turn you on."

Glen opened her eyes and was mesmerized by his. They were beautiful and surreal with how yellow they had become. It was a reminder that he wasn't human but for some reason, it didn't matter as much. She lowered her gaze, studying his face. He was so handsome, whatever he was. He moved his head and his gaze caught her attention again. She couldn't look away.

"I'm attracted to you."

"This can't end well," she blurted.

The brightness of his irises dulled a little. "I know."

"Let me go."

He glanced down at her mouth and she could almost guess his thoughts. He was considering kissing her. He had fangs. They were displayed when he ran his tongue across his lower lip. Part of her was tempted to lean up a little and meet him halfway.

"I can't mate a human, but I can fuck one."

Anger stirred inside her. It wasn't reasonable but it upset her off all the same. "You think I'm not worthy of you. God, you're such a jerk! Get off!"

He suddenly rolled away and released her. The bed shifted as he left it and stood, keeping his back to her. "Put on clothes."

She sat up and grabbed at some of the bedding, hiding most of her body since the curtain wasn't enough. Her hands trembled. "I will when you leave."

He didn't move. Long seconds ticked by until he finally spoke. "It's just a trick because I've been given your blood and you've been given mine."

"I pointed that out, remember?"

He slowly turned, and she couldn't stop her mouth from dropping open when her gaze lowered to the towel wrapped around his waist. He was hard and fully aroused. There was no missing that when his cock was straining against the material. He was big all over.

"Glenda," he rasped.

She forced her gaze up to meet his.

"Get dressed or I'll take you."

She sealed her lips and took a deep breath through her nose. She swallowed, avoiding glancing down his body a second time. "Are you going to make me do it in front of you? A little privacy would be nice."

"Right." He didn't budge.

"That means you should walk out of the room and close the door."

"I know." He still didn't move.

They studied each other and he finally turned, walking to the doorway. She took in his broad back, then the outline of his ass through the towel. He had an amazing body. He came to a halt at the door and clutched the frame on each side.

"Could you close the door?"

The wood creaked and she saw his fingers whitening. He had the frame in a death grip. A low growl sounded.

"Fuck it." He spun, staring at her. His eyes were bright yellow again. "I want you. I know it can't end well. I can't mate a human but I need to find out what this is between us. I want you too badly."

She yanked the covers up higher on her chest, almost to her throat. "No."

He cocked his head and his nostrils flared. "You want me too."

She conceded that, yes, he affected her. She was more than aware of the signs her body was suffering from sexual desire. "We're a train wreck, Veso. Do you know what that means?"

"What?"

She paused, debating her words. "We're not even the same species but I guess I could get pregnant if we have sex. That's what that master creep said. I do not want that to happen, and you don't want that either. You'd probably kill me."

He scowled. "I wouldn't do that."

"I don't know you well enough to be certain you wouldn't. Just walk out and let me get dressed."

He paused then gave a sharp nod and turned back around, snagging the door handle on his way. He slammed the door closed between them.

Glen sighed and eased her hold on the covers, slowly getting out of bed.

"Shit," she muttered, walking toward the dresser. Talk about a close call.

Chapter Five

Veso paced the living room and clenched his fists. He was furious at the master Vampire who'd put him in this mess. He kept glancing at the closed bedroom door and fighting the urge to go after Glenda. He still wanted her. His dick felt rock hard and her scent drove him insane.

The phone wasn't working so no help would be coming. He'd have to take her with him to keep her safe until he found a working phone or a vehicle to steal to take him back into his territory. He was half tempted to wait until dark and set a trap for the master. He'd like nothing better than to rip that son of a bitch to shreds.

He quickly discarded the thought. He had no idea of the numbers he'd face. It would leave Glenda vulnerable if there were too many and the nest could steal her away while he fought. He also wasn't about to forget how they'd captured him the first time. The cowards used darts.

He calculated again where he estimated he was and felt more rage. They'd taken him almost eighty miles from home. He knew all the roads around his territory. The Vamps would have had to carry him for at least six miles to reach one of the old roads. They were in bad repair from years of neglect and it would have slowed them down. The sun would have risen before they reached the mine. It meant they must have kept him drugged, and had hidden out somewhere closer to his territory during the day, then the drugs began to wear off when they were taking him inside the mine.

Had they done anything to him while he slept? Bitten him? Used him as a food source? His injuries would have healed within hours.

Glenda opened the door, wearing some human's clothes. They were huge on her and obviously belonged to a man. The long sleeves of the button-down shirt were rolled at her wrists so her hands weren't lost in the material. She'd borrowed jeans and had used a belt to keep them up since the waist was too baggy. The bottoms of them were rolled to reveal her bare feet.

She looked absolutely adorable—and that pissed him off too.

"My turn," he grunted, storming past her and slamming the bedroom door.

The scent of her lingered in the room so he breathed through his mouth as he examined the cabin owner's clothing. Nothing fit him right. He settled for a pair of sweats that only reached to his calves. He tried on a shirt but it wouldn't button over his chest. He bent a little to look down his body and the tight arm sleeves ripped at the seams near his shoulders. He snarled, digging his fingers into the tears and yanking the sleeves off entirely.

There was a mirror and he stepped in front of it. "I look ridiculous." His people would laugh if they could see him.

"Are you okay in there?"

"No."

"What's wrong?"

He stalked over to the door and jerked it open. He wasn't sure what he'd do if she laughed, but she frowned instead when she saw him. Her gaze traveled down his body. "Oh. You're kind of big."

"Kind of?"

"You look like the Incredible Hulk, minus the green skin."

"What the hell does that mean?"

She glanced down at the sweat bottoms. "Um… Let me find scissors. They'll look better if we turn them into shorts. I'll cut them just above the knee."

He appreciated her helping him as she went into the kitchen and started opening drawers. She located what she wanted and came back to him. "You should stay in the bedroom and hand them to me through the door. They'll be easier to fix if they aren't on you at the time."

He hesitated. "Thank you."

She smiled. "You're welcome."

He stripped off the sweats then opened the door to find her inches away, waiting. She accepted them and strolled back into the kitchen. He watched through the slightly open door as she removed the bottoms of the sweats. It didn't take much time before she handed them over.

He closed the door and pulled them on. They now reached just above his knees. He went to the mirror to take a look. The sweat shorts looked better but the shirt still irritated him. He left the bedroom.

"I have a job for you, Glenda."

"Okay."

"Find and make us something to eat."

She frowned. "Why me? Because I'm the one with the boobs?"

"Fine. I'll make us food and you go search the outer shed for anything we can use."

She sighed, her expression softening. "I'll take kitchen duty."

She amused him. "Good. I eat a lot. We need our strength. The Vampires wouldn't have touched the human's food so there should be some in the pantry. We could be miles from anything. We'll take some supplies when we go in case we're out there all night. I'll be right back."

He walked out the back door and circled the shed. There didn't seem to be any traps, and he had to snap the lock to gain entry. There wasn't much inside except gardening tools.

His thoughts kept returning to Glenda. He'd overheard most of her conversation with the Vamp. She was some distant descendant of the master. The asshole seemed hell bent on forcing her to birth a daughter. It meant she'd remain in danger of being taken again as long as the bastard still lived. At first he hadn't really cared what her future held. He'd planned to warn the other clans that they were at risk of being kidnapped the way he had been. They'd change security procedures to prevent it from happening.

But Glenda's future bothered him now. It infuriated him, thinking about her being in danger. The master would change his plans once he realized he wouldn't be getting his hands on a VampLycan again. He could decide to breed Glenda with a Lycan, then breed her child with another master Vampire, to get his so-called strong-blooded queen.

Just the thought of some Lycan rutting on Glenda had him snarling under his breath. He'd hunt the mangy mutt down, tear him apart, and make a rug out of the Lycan's fur for Glenda to walk on in front of his fireplace.

Wood snapped and he looked down, realizing he'd broken the hoe he'd been trying to fashion a weapon from. He dropped it and reached up, rubbing the tense muscles along the back of his neck. He had actually pictured Glenda inside his cabin, his home.

It's the blood exchange, he reasoned. It accounted for the possessive way he felt about her. He'd never heard of a mating bond forming by injecting blood into a couple. It should be temporary...but what if it wasn't?

He closed his eyes, letting that possibility sink in. He would be mated to a human. He'd have to take her home to his clan.

She'd be treated badly as his mate, at best. He'd have to fight to keep her safe and protect her at all times from enforcers like Nabby. That mean bastard would kill her on sight. Hell, if Decker returned to power over their clan, he'd order Glenda killed, and every VampLycan in the clan would be forced to try to take her life. Decker hated everything human.

"Son of a bitch," he snarled, opening his eyes.

All the scenarios played out in his mind. He'd have to track and kill the master Vampire. The nest he'd been taken to hadn't held any of the Vamps who'd attacked and drugged him. It meant there might be a larger nest to deal with. It was possible that the old mine had just been a holding facility for their prisoners. He didn't want Glenda in danger, but he also wasn't about to leave her alone while he dealt with the problem. She wouldn't be safe unless he was around to protect her. The only other option was...

Shit. I have to take her to my den.

He tried to imagine how she'd respond to being locked underground and left there while he hunted down the Vampires. She would probably try to escape—and that would leave her smack-dab in the middle of VampLycan territory. Best case, they'd capture her, wipe her mind, and send her home. The master would recapture her if Veso hadn't killed him by then. Worst case, someone from his clan would kill her. It was a hell of a situation.

He left the shed after packing a few things that would help them survive in the woods and entered the house. The smell of beans and corned beef had his stomach rumbling. The sight of her cooking made him pause. She turned her head and smiled.

His dick stiffened. He wanted her more than food. Just from the simple domestic sight of his woman preparing him a meal.

"Whoever lived here really liked refried beans and corned beef hash. They were stockpiled. I used three cans of each," she informed him. "I hope that's enough."

He managed to nod and set the wrapped bundle down next to the door, closing it behind him. She faced the two large pans she had cooking on the stove, stirring them with a wooden spoon. The urge to stalk closer and pull her into his arms surfaced. He resisted.

"Almost everything in the fridge is expired, including the milk. I hope you don't mind beer, water, or soda. Those are your only drinking choices. Oh, and I found a shotgun. I didn't touch it. I don't know if it's loaded or not."

That got his attention off her ass. "Where?"

"In the pantry. It's leaning up against the wall in there. How weird is that? There's a box of shells on the floor next to it. That's an odd place to keep a gun."

He stomped over to the narrow door she'd pointed to and yanked it open. He leaned in and spotted the shotgun. He grabbed it and checked. "It's loaded. The poor bastard never even got off a shell."

He bent and scooped up the box of shells, studying the other shelves. There weren't any spares. He carried the weapon and box to the small table, putting them down.

"What does that mean? What poor bastard?"

He found Glenda frowning at him. She turned off the flames under the pans.

"The owner of this cabin is dead. He either wasn't able to reach his gun to shoot at the Vampires before they attacked or they caught him unaware before he knew he wasn't alone anymore."

"How do you know that?"

"That death smell I picked up? Someone is buried behind the cabin."

She paled.

He regretted telling her but they were leaving soon. "I haven't smelled any blood inside the cabin. They probably killed him outside. There wasn't any damage to the doors but I doubt he locked them. It's a remote location."

She just stared at him.

"What?"

"You sound so cold. You're saying a man died, yet you're wearing his clothes and about to eat his food."

"Life can be harsh. So can death. I didn't kill him."

"You suck." She spun away and opened the cupboards, lifting out two plates. "That poor man."

"Let's just eat and get going or we might be recaptured. Those bastards already shot me with drugs once. I don't want to give them the opportunity to do it again."

That seemed to calm her. She dished out a huge plate of food and served him at the table. "What do you want to drink?"

It didn't matter to him. "Whatever is cold. I don't care."

She yanked open the fridge and removed a soda, bringing it to him. She returned with a big spoon. "There you go."

"Thanks."

"I'm glad you at least know that word," she muttered, stalking back to the stove to fix her own plate.

"I have a lot on my mind."

"Don't we both." She came to the table with her plate and got another soda from the fridge, finally sitting across from him once she'd retrieved a second spoon. "It's hot."

He dug into the food, rather than lunging across the table to take her to the floor. He wanted her bad. His dick remained hard and the urge to strip her naked again was stronger than his desire to eat. He lifted the spoon and dug in, substituting one hunger for another.

"What's next?"

"We pack some supplies and get going. It's best if we put as much distance as we can between us and that nest. We still don't know where the master sleeps."

"You're sure he wasn't at the mine?"

96

"He would have come after us if he'd been there. I don't think he was though. The truck they drove me in was gone. I'm guessing he took it. He'll be close, since he needs to keep control of his soldiers. I'm more worried about how many other Vampires are with him in the other location."

"Aren't they stronger if they stick together?"

It was a good question, proving to him that she was smart. "A lot of Vampires don't trust soldiers. They do go crazy after a while and prove harder to control. They've been known to turn on their masters. Vamps will sleep apart from them during the day just as a security measure."

She ate, seeming to ponder his words. He glanced at her repeatedly, not enjoying the hints of fear he spotted.

"It's going to be fine. We'll cover a lot of ground before night falls."

"I'm going to slow you down." She held his gaze. "It would be faster if you left me here, wouldn't it?"

It would but the idea of her being in danger didn't sit well. "No," he lied. "Then I'd have to backtrack to get you before darkness when I did find a vehicle. There are socks in the bedroom. I want you to put a few pairs on your feet to protect them from the ground. We stick together."

She looked relieved. "Okay."

"I keep my word, Glenda. You helped get me out of that mine. I won't leave you to die." He motioned to the gun. "Have you ever fired one before?"

"No."

He smothered a curse. "Never?"

"No. I never had the desire to own one. I was raised in a pretty decent neighborhood. I have deadbolts and live on the second story. I never

97

thought Vampires were going to burst through the windows to come after me."

"Fair enough."

"Can I ask you something, Veso?"

"It hasn't stopped you before. You're very curious."

"Do you blame me? This is all new. Can Vampires fly? Turn into bats?"

"No."

"Good. So if I rent a place in a high-rise, like six or seven floors up, I'll be safe from them reaching my windows, right? For future reference."

"It would depend on the building."

"What does that mean?"

"They can leap about ten feet with ease. Possibly fifteen, depending on the Vampire. It's probably how they entered your apartment. Does this building you have in mind have balconies? They could leap from one to the next to climb higher."

"I don't know. I was just thinking I might want to move but I'll have to see what I can afford. I don't want to be kidnapped again."

"Worry about that later. Let's survive today."

"I'm just thinking about the future."

"Tall buildings won't save you from Vampires, even if there are no balconies. They can control human minds and get your neighbors to allow them inside the building you live in. They'd be able to kick in your door to get to you or even tear through the wall of a unit next to yours. Does that answer your questions?"

She sighed and dropped her chin.

"What did I say?"

She looked up at him. "Did anyone ever call you a buzzkill?"

"No."

"Well, I just did. You're bumming me out."

"I'm being honest. You're in danger. That master isn't going to just give up his plan until he's forced to. He seemed crazy. You'll need to go into hiding once you're returned home or he'll come after you again."

The more he thought about his own words, the less likely he knew it would be that he could effectively wipe her mind. She wouldn't be able to stay out of danger on her own if she couldn't remember what she needed to hide from. He studied her sad expression. It just reaffirmed that he'd have to keep her safe until the master was dead.

But a little fear might keep her from trying to run away from him.

She bit her lower lip.

"I heard what he wants from you. He could breed you with a Lycan, then use your daughter to breed with a Vampire to get what I am. He'll want to recover you. Breaking the treaty and entering VampLycan territory to drug me proves he's insane."

"What treaty?"

"Vampires have sworn to stay away from us."

"Why?"

He held her gaze. "We're bad news to anyone who fucks with us. Few are stupid enough to try."

"Oh." She took a few bites. "Why are you bad news?"

Her questions began to irritate him. "We got the best qualities from both Vampires and Lycans. We're stronger, but without their weaknesses. Eat and stop talking. We don't have a lot of time. I want to be long gone from here before nightfall."

Glen ate as much as her stomach would allow then stood and walked to the sink, turning on the water.

"What are you doing?"

"Dishes."

Veso snarled.

She looked at him. "What is your problem now?"

"Leave them."

"No. It's rude."

"The owner is dead. He doesn't care if we leave a mess. Go put on socks and find some spare clothing. Perhaps a jacket. I believe I saw a backpack in the corner of the bedroom. Put those things inside but leave room for food."

She turned off the water. He was right. "Fine."

"Hurry up. We're out of here the moment I'm done eating."

She fled into the bedroom and located the backpack. It wasn't overly big. She packed a few extra pairs of socks, put three layers on her feet, and tried to find them each a spare set of clothing. There was a choice of jackets inside the closet. She found a lightweight one and shoved it inside. Lastly, she remembered to grab a roll of toilet paper. It might be a long day if they didn't find another house soon with a working phone.

Veso had finished his food when she reentered the kitchen. He had stacked some cans of food and bottles of water on the counter. "I'll be outside. Pack those."

"Pack those," she muttered, right after he left the cabin with the wrapped tarp he'd carried in earlier. "So bossy."

She did what he'd asked though, and then walked out the door wearing the backpack. Veso waited, his gaze tracking her, his golden eyes shining. Overall, he might be scary, but she had to also admit he was attractive.

"Let's go. We need to put distance between us and here."

She jogged down the steps and toward the road. Veso walked quickly with his long legs, the tarp under one arm, the shotgun in his hand. He turned off the road in front of her, into the woods.

"Where are you going?"

He stopped and gazed back over his shoulder. "Do you want to make it easier for the Vampires to find us?"

"We'll get lost if we leave the road."

"It will make it more difficult for them to track us. Most Vamps are lazy bastards. I was in this area some years ago. There's an abandoned mining town close and I believe that road will lead to it. Some of the buildings might be standing still, and that's the first place the Vampires will look. I want to be where they aren't hunting for us."

"Buildings mean someone might live in them, and we need help."

"I didn't realize how remote this area is until I found an address inside that cabin. Humans are something we'll want to avoid. The Vampires will have located where all of them are for feeding purposes and are probably in control of them. It means they'd try to capture us and hold us for the Vamps. Humans stick by roads—so we're leaving it."

"We won't be stuck out here if we find someone with a car. They'll have a cell phone too. Everyone does. We can call the police. You're big. Even if they've bribed people to do bad things, you could just punch someone."

Veso took a few steps in her direction but then stopped, scowling. "It's not up for debate. You have no idea what you're dealing with but I do. That nest looked pretty established to me, and they had time to add doors to make cells. It means they've been in the area for a while. Don't make me carry you, Glenda. Follow me or I'll toss you over my shoulder. What do you know about Vampires?"

"Not much."

"I know everything. I'd like to avoid being captured again. Those bastards are using drugs. Humans put us in danger, so it's best to avoid all of them. We're going to my people."

"The police—"

"Are fucking useless against Vampires! They can be mind-controlled. Humans would hand you right over to that master. Now stop stalling and follow me. You either walk or I carry you. That would slow me down. Stick close." He turned away, stalking into the woods.

"Damn," Glenda hissed. She followed him though. No way did she want to be left alone on some dirt road in the middle of nowhere.

She put on the backpack and tried to ignore the fact that the socks made her feet hot. They did protect them from hurting as she walked over

102

dirt and dry leaves. The trees grew thicker as they walked. One glance back assured her the cabin wasn't within sight anymore, nor the road.

"He's going to get us both lost," she predicted aloud.

"Stop your complaining."

"I just think this is a bad idea."

"I don't care what you think."

"I figured that out already since you refuse to listen to anything I have to say."

He came to an abrupt stop in front of her and she almost bumped into his back. He glared at her over his shoulder. "Can't you be silent? Do you always feel the need to argue?"

"Only with jerks."

His eyes narrowed. "At some point we'll find a place to hunker down before the sun sets. We'll be enclosed in a very small space to hide our heat signatures from the Vampires if they scatter and try to locate us. Remember that. You are slowing us down with your talking. Stop it and just walk."

He turned his head forward and took off, increasing the pace.

Glen gritted her teeth and trudged after him. The heavy backpack didn't help her mood but he carried whatever he'd taken from the shed under his arm and the shotgun, so she couldn't complain that he'd made her the mule of their trek.

The terrain became rougher when they reached an area where trees had fallen over and a lot of debris had accumulated. It surprised her when Veso turned, helping her climb over and get through some of the worst of it.

"Landslide?"

"Flood," he corrected. "Probably from when the snow melted at the end of winter." He lifted his chin, seeming to study the sky. "I don't see any indication of rain but I want out of this area. We need to reach higher ground."

"More climbing. Woohoo."

He actually cracked a smile. "At least we have rope now."

She glanced at the bulky tarp. "Inside that?"

"Yes."

"What's your plan? Just stay out here in the middle of nowhere until you think the Vampires have given up on searching for us?" The idea horrified her.

"They won't do that. The master has a plan for you. Did he come across as the type to easily change his mind?"

She would never forget the crazy bastard who claimed to be a relative of hers—or why she'd been kidnapped. "No. He's a lunatic."

"We'll keep going in this direction until we find a very remote home with a phone or a vehicle. It's possible the Vampires are unaware of some of the antisocial humans who live miles from others and don't use paved roads. Then we'll either get to call my people to come get us or we'll drive to them."

"I still think we should just go to the police. They can protect us."

"Foolish Glenda," Veso muttered.

She decided not to respond. He bundled the shotgun with the tarp, reached out, and gripped her arm with his free hand when the incline became steep. He might be a jerk but he kept her from stumbling as she struggled to climb the hill. The trees thickened again, the flood-damaged area left behind.

"I'll keep you safe."

She glanced at him, grateful.

He didn't look at her, instead scanning the woods. "Move faster. You're slowing us down too much."

Chapter Six

Glen didn't think there was any part of her body that didn't hurt. Her shoulders ached from the weight of the backpack digging into them all day. Her back felt too tense and her calves throbbed. The socks on her feet hadn't protected her from feeling as if she'd gained a few more bruises after traveling for miles on rough terrain. Sharp pains radiated from her stomach since their breakfast had been the only thing they'd eaten all day. Veso had refused to take a break, pushing her constantly to keep on the move. The only rest times they'd had were for a few drinks of water and bathroom breaks that hadn't lasted more than a couple minutes.

"This is a good place." He finally stopped at the top of a ravine, peering down.

Glen moved next to him, gaping at the jagged line where the earth just dropped in front of them, leaving a hundred-foot gap in the ground between them and the other side. "Shit. A good place for what? To die? There's no way we can climb down and up that. It would be suicide." She leaned forward a little, staring at the bottom. A lot of rocks sat below. "It looks really steep."

"It is. I'll lower you on a rope, and then haul your ass up on the other side once I climb it. You'll slow me down though, doing that, so we'll sleep here and tackle it in the morning. I don't want to be caught at the bottom during the night. This is a strategic place to defend."

Glen just shook her head. "How do you figure that?"

"Vampires can't fly. I toss them over the edge if we're attacked. The fall won't kill them but that landing will be a bitch. They'll break bones and bleed a lot. It will take them time to heal enough to come at us again. The sun will rise at some point and they'd need to find shelter far enough away to feel safe from me hunting them down while they sleep. That means if one falls, it won't attack us twice in one night. They won't want to die."

"We're going to get killed instead if we try to climb down and up that. Why don't we just head in a new direction and try to get around this?"

"I'm not backtracking. VampLycan territory is in that direction." He pointed over the ravine.

"You're insane."

"Determined. Learn the difference. I want to get home."

"Even if it kills us?"

"I can climb. You've seen me do it."

Veso drove her nuts. She walked over to a big rock and took a seat, removing the backpack. She decided to change the subject to avoid a fight. "I wish I could take a hot bath right now."

"You can have one when we reach my home."

That surprised her. He dropped the tarp bundle before walking the area. Glen bent forward, gently removing the layers of socks. Her feet ached and she soon discovered why. Bruises really had formed, but at least there were no cuts to her skin.

"We have perhaps an hour before the sun goes down. That will give us time to eat and dig in for the night."

She massaged the most tender spot on the ball of one foot. "I'm starving."

"You'll have to eat the food cold from the cans. A fire is out of the question."

"Why?"

"The smell of burning wood would carry for miles and help the Vampires locate us."

"Fantastic. Cold beans and corned beef hash. Yum. It's a good thing I'm so hungry. I don't even care at this point." She dropped her foot and watched Veso as he knelt and unwrapped the tarp.

He had a big rope coiled inside, a weird shovel, and the box of shells. A sealed bag had her frowning. "What is that?" She pointed.

"Emergency blanket. It's thin and lightweight but will help retain your body heat."

"And why did you lug a shovel?"

"For digging, and it makes a good weapon. I mentioned we need to hide our heat signatures."

He wasn't making much sense to her. He stood with the shovel and walked over to a few large boulders huddled together. He did something that extended the handle of the shovel, then crouched there and began to dig.

"What are you doing?"

"It faces the ravine. The rocks will hide our bodies from anyone approaching in the same direction we came from, and I'll dig a bit so we're hidden if a Vampire comes at us from the other side. They can see body heat, so I'll dig down far enough to make us invisible to them."

She unzipped the backpack and removed a can of corned beef hash. "Shit. I forgot to pack a can opener."

"Not a problem. Bring it here."

She stood and approached him. "You'll get dirt in the food if you use the sharp part of the shovel, now that you've been digging with it."

He dropped the shovel and twisted his body a bit, opening his hand and holding it out to her. She passed the can over. Her mouth fell open when he grew claws with his other hand and used the tip of one to circle the lid. Her mouth dropped open wider when she realized it actually worked. He managed to cut through the lid after a few passes. He handed it back.

"Eat."

She accepted it and backed away. "Thanks." Her gaze locked on his hand as the sharp nails shrank, disappearing into his fingertips. "That's handy." It was the only thing that came to mind to say.

"I'm not like you. Don't forget it, Glenda."

"Would it kill you to just call me Glen?"

He picked up the shovel, digging once more. "I refuse to call you by a man's name."

"Do you want something to eat?"

"I'll go hunting for something fresh after I've prepared camp. You eat the canned stuff."

She took a seat on the rock and used a little bit of their water to wet her fingers, using her pants to clean them as much as possible. She'd also forgotten to pack silverware. "You said you couldn't start a fire. How are you going to cook whatever you catch?"

He kept digging.

109

"Am I talking to myself?" She waited but he didn't respond. "No, I don't think I am. I'm pretty sure I'm talking to the guy with the shovel."

He growled low and turned his head, pausing with his task. "I'll shift and hunt something live. It's not my favorite thing to do but it won't make me sick. Your digestive system might repel raw meat from an animal. Mine won't. Any more questions or can I finish preparing us a safe sleeping space before the sun goes down?"

She swallowed hard. "I'll just shut up now."

"Good."

Glen wondered if he'd allow her to see him shifted and tried to picture him as a wolf. He'd be huge, for sure. All the movies she'd ever watched on Werewolves replayed through her head. Whatever he ended up being, she'd have to keep her cool and pretend he didn't scare the crap out of her.

"Can I ask one more thing?"

He growled and stopped digging, glaring at her. "What?"

"You will know who I am after you do this shifting thing, right? Like you won't think I look like dinner?"

He shook his head and went back to using the shovel. "I'll know you. You'll be in no danger unless you keep talking."

She sealed her lips. Veso had to be the grumpiest person she'd ever met. He had no compassion when it came to her curiosity. He might have known about humans all his life but she had everything to learn about his kind.

She ate the cold, greasy corned beef hash and tried to imagine it warm. Hunger helped her choke it down and she swallowed a little water afterward.

Veso kept digging and she hated that the shape of the hole began to remind her of a grave. He was also crazy strong. She watched the muscles in his arms flex as he kept tossing dirt into the bushes. He finally must have thought it was long and deep enough because he collapsed the handle on the shovel and set it aside. He stood, went to the tarp, and dumped out everything inside it. He lined the freshly dug hole with the thick material and turned.

"I'll be back. Stay far from the edge of the ravine and don't leave this area." He glanced around.

"What are you looking for?"

"Just checking to make certain no one is around." His nostrils flared. "I've never smelled any humans except you but that doesn't mean the master doesn't have some slaves."

"Slaves?"

"Servants. Is that a better, kinder term for you?"

"People don't own people anymore."

"You're so naive. Vampires can rip apart the minds of humans and force them to their wills. That's what I meant earlier about humans being under the control of Vamps. After enough exposure, they completely lose their self-awareness, surviving only to serve their master. They'd die and kill for him. Vampires have the ability to brainwash your kind and turn them into day guards."

"That sounds horrible."

"It is."

"That jerk could have done it to me."

"He probably would have if you'd fought him to the point that you annoyed him."

"Can you do that to me?" She hated to even ask, in case it gave him ideas.

"Rip into your mind and force you completely to my will? I could, but I never would. It destroys a human forever if it's done by someone ruthless. They're damaged and there's no way to fix their minds. They usually commit suicide if the one who controls them dies. They lose the will to live."

She sealed her lips, appalled.

"I'm going hunting. Stay put and away from the edge. The ground could be unstable."

"I'm tired. I'm going to sit right here."

"I'll return before dark."

She was tempted to ask him to shift forms in front of her but changed her mind. They would be sleeping together in that hole he dug, which meant very close quarters. She wasn't sure if seeing him turn into a wolf would terrify her so much she'd be unable to lie next to him.

"Be careful."

He walked away, quickly out of sight as he disappeared between the trees. She turned her head, gazing at where the ground abruptly ended. Tomorrow morning he wanted to climb down the ravine to get to the other side. Veso was a crazy bastard but he had saved her ass. She couldn't forget that. He'd also kept his word. He hadn't left her behind.

"Out of the fire but I'm still in the frying pan," she mumbled. "I just need to survive."

112

Veso refused to go far and kept on alert for any scents that could warn him of an attack. The Vampires who'd stolen him used drugs. It meant their human guards, if they had some, probably had access to them as well. He stopped when he felt safe Glenda couldn't see him and stripped, carefully placing his clothing off the ground to keep them cleaner. He bent, shifting fast.

He shook his entire body once the transformation completed. Time had rid him of the drugs in his system but his skin felt sensitive.

He caught the scent of a squirrel. It was easy to track it. The creature moved fast and tried to climb a tree but hunger drove him to climb after it, his claws scarring the trunk. The poor thing hadn't expected something like him to be able to follow, and he probably confused it enough to be able to capture it easier than normally. It died fast, painlessly, and he leapt out of the tree to eat it on the ground.

Glenda would be appalled if she could see him. He tried to imagine what she'd say, and none of it would be good.

He dug and buried the remains of his kill when he finished eating, rubbed his muzzle on the grass to clean off the blood, and returned to his clothes. He shifted back and dressed.

The desire to protect Glenda drove him to nearly run back to their temporary campsite. He refused to allow her to be recaptured. It riled him to the point of wanting to roar when he even imagined that Vampire master getting ahold of her again. She might not be his real mate, but his instincts didn't seem to care that it was just a trick of being injected with each other's blood. The feelings were real, despite the logic.

He found her still sitting on the rock but he knew she'd gotten up, since she'd moved over a few feet. He also faintly scented blood. "What did you do while I was gone?"

She turned her head, holding his stare. "I peed. Is that okay? I went behind that tree." She lifted her arm and jerked her thumb toward one. "Right over there. Did you find something to eat? That was fast."

"There's a lot of game in this area since humans aren't around to overhunt them." He stomped toward her and sniffed. "You're bleeding."

She lifted her hand, showing off a scratch. "I used a tree to brace my weight when I squatted and the bark was rough."

"God...you're so human." How could she get hurt taking a leak?

"What's your deal with hating my kind?"

He no longer like her thinking that way but couldn't honestly deny her accusation. "History."

"What does that mean?"

"Humans have always tried to kill what they don't understand and can't control."

"Is that why nobody knows Werewolves and Vampires are real?"

"Yes. Some would try to become what we are, thinking it would gain them great power. Others would try to capture our kinds and use us for experiments. We live much longer lives." He drew closer to her. The scent of her bleeding made him semi hard but he tried to ignore the reaction. "Some outright fear us and just want us dead. We're monsters to them."

She seemed to mull that over. "I get it."

That surprised him. "You don't want to deny it, or maybe argue about what good our blood could do for humans?"

"I watch alien movies. They're usually gory and always depict aliens being killers. Most Werewolf movies are horror too. That's probably why humans would want to kill or dissect first, ask questions later. Vampires have been frequently romanticized but after meeting real Vampires, even I want to kill them all."

"Most of them are pretty bad. They see humans as cattle, the way you humans see actual cows. Food sources."

"I do love my hamburgers and steak but now I'm feeling guilty."

He spotted real emotion in her eyes and approached her, taking a seat a foot away on the rock. "You wouldn't kill it if it begged for its life, would you?"

"No. Of course not. I doubt I could actually kill one, even I was hungry. I buy my meat in packages at the store. I can't even stand to look at the fish. Some of them have faces. It depresses me."

She was so tenderhearted. He thought that was cute, but then remembered the animal he'd just eaten. He changed the subject in case she asked what he'd had for dinner, focusing on her hand. The sight of her blood bothered him in more ways than just the thought it might cause her pain.

"Give me your hand." He held out his own.

"Why?" She peered at him with a frown.

"I can fix it. Infection can easily set in out here. It won't hurt."

"What are you going to do?"

"Lick it."

"Ewwww."

"Don't be squeamish, Glenda. Give me your hand."

"I'll pass."

He reached over, curled his fingers around her wrist, and turned to face her more. She wasn't able to prevent him from lifting her hand to his mouth or sucking on her skin. He stared into her eyes as he cleaned the scratch with his tongue. It clearly horrified her but he didn't care.

"That's really unsanitary."

He continued to hold her hand close and allowed his fangs to grow. Her eyes widened and she paled.

"Easy. I'm going to bite my tongue, not you. My blood will coat your scratch and heal it."

She seemed speechless and afraid. It hurt a bit to bite down but he didn't do much damage, just nicking his tongue with a fang to cause minimal bleeding. He put her hand against his mouth again, making certain his blood covered her scratch.

Glenda tried to tug her hand away a few times but she wasn't strong enough to free her wrist. He waited a full minute before he pulled back. Then he turned his head, spitting to be certain he didn't swallow any of her blood. "See? I didn't bite."

"You have really big fangs." Her gaze locked onto his mouth.

"I'm a big man."

She lowered her attention to his chest, then shifted her head in another direction to stare at anything but him. "Can you let me go now?"

116

"No. You'll try to wipe my blood off and it's not healed yet." He focused on her palm, waiting a minute or two, then wet his thumb with his spit enough to rub across the area to clean off his blood. "There. See?"

She turned her head and he watched her face. Shock was easy to read as she got a glimpse of her hand. "It's gone!"

He let go of her wrist. "I told you. My blood heals. Remember your cut finger? It was a small injury and you'd been injected by that master with my blood." He sniffed. "I don't smell any other cuts on you. Do you have any? I'm serious about infection. You're a species prone to getting ill."

"I'm good." She inched over on the rock, almost falling off.

"Don't fear me, Glenda." It bothered him that she did.

Her gaze held his. "Could your blood cure cancer and stuff?"

He shrugged. "I've never tried that. It's possible."

"You really could save so many lives if you donated blood to humans."

His anger stirred and it reminded him why he didn't like her species. "And we would become the cows. Or more like rats. Hunted, trapped, and used to death. They wouldn't care how many of us died to save their own. We'd become extinct. Your kind kills countless animals in laboratories and for what? So your perfume doesn't give you a rash? So you can see if the drugs you make will kill you? You cause yourselves harm and innocent creatures pay the consequences."

He stood, storming away.

Chapter Seven

Glen kept replaying his words in her head. Veso had a point. If anyone found out about his ability to heal with his blood, she doubted many people would care if he were willing to donate or not. They'd want to capture him and just take it. She watched him hide the rope and the other supplies they'd brought in bushes around the area, placing them out of sight.

"What are you doing?"

He didn't look her way. "What does it look like?"

It was a dumb question but she just wanted him to talk to her. "I'm sorry. I didn't mean to imply your life meant less than others. It just came as a surprise and that's the first thing my mind went to."

He faced her. "There are billions of humans on this planet and so few of us. We keep our numbers low to hide our existence. Our survival is based on secrecy to prevent your kind from wiping us out."

She rose to her feet and tried to hide the grimace when her ass and legs protested. "I said I'm sorry. This is all new to me. I'm going to blurt things out before I can think it all through."

Veso inclined his head. "I understand."

"Thank you."

"It doesn't make it any less annoying."

She actually smiled. "Probably not. I babysat three kids last summer for a cousin of mine and took them to the zoo. It amazed me what lame things they asked but they were all between the ages of four and seven. He's a widow and works too much to take them to too many places. I guess I'm like a child to you. Why is that monkey in the tree and why do they put those tigers behind glass so we can't pet them? Why? Why? Why? That was one word I really came to hate by lunchtime."

He grinned.

"I'm just so curious," she admitted.

"I'll try to be more tolerant of your questions."

"And the stupid shit I blurt out?"

"That too. If it makes you feel any better, most deadly diseases that kill humans are something that could only be cured if a Vampire turned them into one."

She opened her mouth, wanting to know why, but then didn't speak.

He seemed to guess her thoughts. "A small amount of blood can cure injuries that aren't too severe. Cancer mutates cells, from what I understand, as well as a lot of other human diseases that kill. Genetics also play a big part in most diseases." He stepped closer. "Humans would have to be completely changed over to combat something like that. Think of a world full of Vampires. They have laws so they don't turn even their own friends and families. If they all did, the Vampires would hunt humans to extinction just to survive. It would be the end of your world, and eventually theirs, since once the blood was gone, they'd eventually die out from starvation."

She understood what he was trying to say. "They'd kill all the people, then feed off the animals, until nothing would be left except bugs. Those would be hard to drink from."

He nodded. "That's a worst-case scenario. Think of the issues from using their blood to heal. Some would want to cure dying children with Vampire blood. Imagine being trapped in the body of a four-year-old forever. I've heard stories of ones like that, and all of them went massively insane. They had to be hunted and killed. They were cold-blooded killers without remorse. They mature in their minds but not in the flesh, denied adult needs because they're trapped in the bodies of small children. It depraves them until only utter madness remains."

She shivered, horror movies flashing through her head that she'd seen involving child monsters.

"You've had to deal with Vamps while you were captured. Most lose any sense of humanity when they're turned. It's in the Vampire nature, so they can feed without remorse, but they're smart enough to wish to survive. That means following basic rules to hide what they are from your kind. Ones who don't are considered rogue and killed to protect the others. You believe your world is harsh now? Imagine what it would be like if Vampires ruled."

"I get it."

He turned away, staring at the setting sun. "We need to lie down soon. Go to the bathroom again if you must. You won't be moving around after it's dark. Your heat signature will glow to Vampire sight."

She was glad she'd already emptied her bladder. "I'm good."

"I'll be right back." He walked off into the trees.

Glen approached the grave-like hole he'd dug. It was lined well with the tarp so they wouldn't be lying on dirt. She swallowed hard, not prepared yet to climb in. Veso returned fast and stopped next to her. She turned her head and peered up at him.

"Don't worry. You're tired and will sleep. I'll keep guard."

"Do you really think we'll be safe?"

"We didn't travel as far as I'd wished, but we're a long way from the road. They'll have to really work for it if we're found."

That didn't ease her worry much. "I'll help you down. Try not to tear the tarp. We're going to need it to stay dry if the weather changes. It's that time of year, when rainstorms hit. We won't see one until it's almost upon us with these mountain ranges."

"My socks." She turned her head, staring at the rock where she'd left them.

"I'll get them. Go in first."

Her gripped her by her hips, lowering her with ease. He released her as soon as she stood on the tarp then returned to the rock. He collected the pairs of socks she'd removed and brought them back, dropping them into the hole.

She backed up, expecting him to climb in with her, but he moved away again, returning with the packaged blanket. He hopped into the hole he'd dug and opened the bag. "I won't need this but you might."

She accepted the blanket, looking down at the tarp. "I wish we had a sleeping bag with padding."

"It's the best we can do for now."

It would make for a hard, uncomfortable bed. She lay down on her side, shoving her back against the tarp-covered wall he'd dug. "This won't collapse onto us, will it?"

"I'll dig us out if it does. Don't panic by screaming. Sound carries."

"You were supposed to comfort me by just saying no."

He chuckled as he stretched out next to her. It was a tight fit and he twisted onto his side to face her. That helped, putting a few inches of space between them. "I'll remember that."

It surprised her when he helped her unfold the blanket and covered her with it. She wasn't cold yet but the sun was going down. "We'll be trapped if Vampires just suddenly appear above this hole. You know that, right?"

"I have good hearing and sense of smell. They won't see our heat signatures unless they're right on top of us. I'll know they're there before they find us."

"Then what?"

"You stay here and don't move. I'll fight and toss them off the edge of the ravine."

"That's not much of a plan."

He shrugged. "I'd have given you the gun but you said you've never fired one before. You'd probably end up shooting yourself or me."

"Har-har. Very funny."

He arched his eyebrows. "I wasn't kidding."

"Wow, okay."

"I'll train you how to use one after we're safe."

"How come you aren't using it? You left it up there."

"Like I said, sound carries. It would only draw the attention of more of them. Since I'll be the only one fighting, quiet is better."

She wasn't sure how to respond to that. His offer to teach her how to shoot implied he'd see her again once they found help. Glen highly doubted it.

Veso lifted his arm and used his biceps as a pillow. "Rest. It's been a long day and I know you're tired. You did well. I was impressed."

"Thank you."

She closed her eyes and tried to get comfortable. It wasn't possible. The tarp was poor protection against the unforgiving dirt under her body. She mimicked what Veso had done and used her arm for a pillow. It helped slightly.

Time passed and she opened her eyes. It was much dimmer. Veso's face was close to hers and he'd closed his eyes. He really was a handsome man. She had to admit that. He breathed slow and steady, seeming to have already fallen asleep.

It figures. Men. She turned her head a little, staring up at the sky. The deep blue darkened until the stars came out. They were beautiful, but it also meant the Vampires were somewhere out there, looking for her and Veso. She shivered but it had nothing to do with the cold.

"Easy," Veso softly murmured.

She peered at his face but couldn't make out his features now that night had completely fallen. It made her startle when one of his hands curled around her waist and he gave her a gentle squeeze.

"I won't let anything hurt you. Sleep, Glenda. Morning will come soon enough and we have to travel a good distance."

She closed her eyes and liked the weight of his hand on her. It made her feel less alone. Veso had taken out Vlad before she'd even realized what

123

was happening and he'd dealt with those creepers they'd come across with ease. The big guy was a badass, and he'd promised to keep her safe.

Glen wondered how long it would take for them to reach where he wanted them to go. The idea of spending another long day walking didn't appeal to her. It beat being recaptured though.

Veso knew the moment Glenda drifted to sleep. He adjusted the blanket over her a little tighter and breathed through his nose, his senses on alert. He didn't smell anything alarming yet but the Vamps had to be hunting for them. He just wasn't certain how many of them there would be and if they'd waste time searching the human dwellings first.

The master Vamp would probably assume Veso had dumped Glenda off at the first opportunity and she'd head for something familiar, sticking to the roads. It wouldn't take them long to realize the truth. There weren't that many buildings in the vicinity.

Regret swamped him. He should have shifted forms and had Glenda ride his back to put them farther away from the search area. Instead he'd thought of her comfort, both physically and emotionally. He would hate for her to see him in another form and become absolutely terrified. Her mouthy comments might annoy at times but it would be worse if she became mute, reeking of pure fear.

His chances of getting back to his territory without another confrontation with the nest would be much better if he left Glenda behind. He stared at her sleeping features and that strong urge to protect her remained. She'd be helpless and quickly recaptured. He wouldn't allow that to happen.

124

He debated whether he should leave Glenda at least for a little while and seek out the Vampires. However many there might be, they'd have to spread out to search for the two of them if they wanted to be effective. It would leave the Vamps at a disadvantage, and he could attack them in smaller numbers, cut them down. The hunters would become the hunted.

Glenda made a soft noise in her sleep and he instantly discarded the idea. What if she had a nightmare and screamed? Humans tended to do that. The sound would carry and draw the Vampires right to her. She'd be alone.

He tightened his grip on her waist and pulled her closer, until she was pressed along the front of his body.

He inhaled her scent and his dick responded by hardening. Lust rolled through him and he stopped breathing through his nose. Having sex with the sun down and while they were vulnerable would be stupid. That was one thing Veso wasn't. He'd be damned if a bunch of bloodsuckers tagged him with their drugs because he was otherwise occupied and distracted.

Veso moved his arm, sliding his hand from her waist, up her back, to play with strands of Glenda's curly hair. His body had been fooled into believing she was his mate. The tender emotions surging through him had to be a result of the blood exchange forced on them. They might fade, he hoped they would, because he had no idea what he'd do if they didn't.

His clan would never accept her. Decker might have left with his most trusted enforcers but that didn't mean things had changed. At some point Decker would return, and he'd left enough of his devoted elders and clan members behind to assure someone would attempt to kill any human in their midst. They only tolerated Kira because she was at least in part VampLycan, and her father had some kind of leverage against Decker.

The desire to brush his mouth over Glenda's lips had him pulling back, pressing his spine tight against the side of the hole he'd dug. It would be a mistake to seduce her. She'd claimed they would be a train wreck. He hadn't enjoyed the comparison but he'd understood why she made it. They were from two different worlds and species. He wouldn't fit into her life and no one would accept her into his.

He thought of his father next and cringed, imagining his reaction if he introduced Glenda as his mate. Memories of his childhood still filled him with bitterness. He hadn't understood why his parents had argued so much and lived apart. Mates were supposed to be close and love each other. His tenth birthday had killed his youthful dreams of being part of a happy family. That's when his mother had told him the truth.

No. He needed to resist Glenda and avoid making the same mistake his father had. She would never purposely trap him, but the result would be the same if she got pregnant. He snarled, still enraged by his memories.

Glenda startled. He saw her eyes open and fear creased her features.

"It's fine. Sorry," he whispered.

"Vampires?" She breathed the word.

"No. I was just thinking of something unpleasant."

"What's wrong?"

"Nothing." It felt bad to lie to her. Mates were supposed to always be honest with each other.

It surprised him when she opened her hand on his chest and lightly stroked him through the ill-fitting shirt he wore. "Bad dream?"

126

He hesitated, listening. The woods had settled and he could hear small animals moving around. They wouldn't be if they picked up the scent of a Vampire. Their instincts would tell them they were in danger.

"Veso? Everyone has them. I do all the time."

"I was thinking about my parents," he admitted.

"You miss them?"

"It's just my father now in my life. My mother died."

"I'm so sorry." She stroked him a little more firmly.

"I'm not."

Her hand stilled.

He could just imagine her bad thoughts about him for saying that. He didn't like her thinking the worst of him. "She lost her true mate when she was a youth, before they matured. Her name was Parma and she was raised in the clan I was born to." He swallowed, unsure why he was sharing the story with her, but he wanted her to understand.

"She pursued my father from another clan. He said she was beautiful. She was very aggressive about it and he was flattered." The words got easier to say. "She seduced him." His anger probably sounded in his voice but he kept his tone soft. "My kind doesn't conceive unless they're mated, but my mother was mostly Lycan. You wouldn't understand this, being human, but Lycan's can control their bodies and their ovulation cycles. My mother did that, and tricked my father into getting her pregnant."

"Why?"

"Decker, he was her leader, asked all clan women to breed strong sons to help strengthen his position. More fighters assures a clan's survival. She didn't actually want a mate, since she'd lost her true one, and none of the

127

men in her clan trusted her with their seed." Bitterness sounded in his voice but he didn't hide it. "They must have known how cold and calculating she really was. They'd seen her grow up. She hid her scent from my father by lighting scented candles and was naked in his bathtub when he got off shift. She'd let herself into his home. He couldn't pick up that she was ovulating."

He closed his eyes, unable to withstand seeing pity in Glenda's face, if that was her reaction. "She got what she wanted from my father and ended up pregnant. I was born to gain favor with her beloved leader.

"My father learned of my existence because she grew tired of tending to a baby she'd never really wanted. She sent him a message that she needed help raising me. He begged her to mate him. He has honor. She refused. He also wasn't allowed to take me back to his clan, since I belonged to hers already. She'd sworn my life to Decker. My father gave up his status with his clan to live as her full-time babysitter. Decker allowed him to stay but he was never given any status in the clan until after her death. Even then, the clan leader never fully trusted my father."

She was silent for a while. He figured she was horrified.

"He must love you a lot."

Her whispered words soothed him a little and he opened his eyes. Glenda stared at his chest blindly, probably unable to see anything. "Yes. He gave up everything to raise me. We lived in a hut behind her home at first, until he built a cabin. He feared I'd freeze to death in the winter without a fireplace to keep us warm. He also had to leave me alone sometimes to hunt for food. She didn't want me in her house and my father didn't trust any of the clan with me."

"Why didn't your mother want you in her house?"

"She didn't want any responsibility for raising me."

"What a cold bitch."

Glenda's anger surprised him but he agreed. "She had no heart. Once she had birthed me, it proved her allegiance to Decker. She asked him to make her an assassin to help kill his enemies. Decker sent her after whoever he felt had become a threat or anyone who'd angered him. I was twelve when she didn't return. The killer ended up being killed instead."

Glenda's fingers fisted his shirt. "I'm sorry, Veso. That's so terrible."

"She told me when I was ten that I annoyed her with my need to touch and spend time with her. She spelled out why I had been born and the future she'd signed me up for. Enforcers never cry, they don't have any weaknesses, and I disappointed her with my love. I was born to become an assassin for Decker. She said my affection disgusted her. It was the first harsh lesson of many before she died."

Glenda rubbed her face against his shirt. "I'm so sorry. No wonder you're such a hard-ass. God. What did your father say?"

"He told me to ignore her. Of course I couldn't. He said loving someone wasn't a mistake but it could be very painful when they didn't return the emotion. He'd know. I think he tried to love my mother at first. The years changed that though. Then he began to warn me against allowing anyone to get close, because it could cause deep pain and open me up to betrayal."

"Is your dad loving?"

"He's loyal to me. He backed me when I refused to become an enforcer. I accepted guard duty instead."

"What's the difference?"

129

"It's complicated but it boils down to Decker couldn't send me to kill his enemies. I got my revenge on my mother by refusing to accept the position in the clan she birthed me to take."

"Well, I guess that's good."

"Do you have a strong bond with your parents? Siblings?" He knew nothing about her except she was a blood relation to a master, lived in an apartment in Oregon, and had annoying neighborhood kids who'd broken a window once.

"They divorced when I was four. My biological dad didn't want to pay child support, so he moved away. We heard he married someone else and started a new family. He tried to contact me in my teens but I didn't want someone in my life who'd just walked away the way he did. No thanks. My mom married my stepdad two years after the divorce. He wasn't exactly father material but he was okay. They had my brother when I was fourteen. We're night and day. I wish we were close but that's not how it turned out. I babysat him a lot when he was little but then I moved out at eighteen and hardly speak to them now."

"I got the impression human children tended to live at home until they marry. Do you have a husband?" The thought disturbed him so much so that he actually felt rage. He didn't like the idea of some human laying claim to what was his.

"No. I've never been married. I graduated high school and got a job. I felt like a burden living in their home, mostly. They had this tight family unit and I wasn't really a part of it. My brother got to call my stepfather daddy and I had to call him Mike. It was just awkward. I had a friend's sister who had a job where I work now, and she got me on the cleaning staff. It paid enough to get me a cheap apartment and I took night classes. I worked my way up and then transferred into a clerical position in Oregon. I talk to my parents on the phone at holidays but that's about it. I haven't been home for a visit in four years."

"Is there a man in your life?" He wasn't sure what he'd do if she said yes. There wasn't a scent of one coming off her and she wore no rings, but he didn't know when the Vampires had taken her. Time would have wiped away a human's scent and they could have stolen her jewelry.

"No. I work a lot. I'm going for a managing position that's opening up. It pretty much means I bust my ass to get there earlier than everyone else and I stay late. It's why I was eating at eight o'clock at night when I was kidnapped. I'd literally just walked in the door, kicked off my shoes, and opened the fast food bag when that window broke."

The wind picked up, rustling the trees. "We should rest. Morning will come soon and we need to travel a lot of distance."

"If you don't get us killed crossing that ravine," she murmured against his chest. "I still think we should go around it."

"It would waste an entire day. I won't let you fall," he promised. He'd get her down and up the ravine. It stood between him and VampLycan territory. The real problem would be what to do once he reached home. The clan would be upset if he returned with a human. They'd expect him to wipe her memories and send her back to her own people. He had no intension of allowing the Vampire to recapture her. That meant keeping her with him.

Glenda nodded against him. "You're warm."

God, she smelled so fuckable. He tried to think of anything else. Focusing on his mother helped. He'd never end up in the same situation as his father. He doubted Glenda would just hand over a baby to him and go back to her world if he accidently got her pregnant. And no way could she take his son or daughter into hers without him there to protect them both. He'd have to leave everything he knew for his child. It was best if he not risk a pregnancy. That meant controlling his urges.

"Sleep," he ordered. He just wished he could ask her to back away from his body but the hole he'd dug wasn't big. He'd been more worried about depth to hide their heat signatures than width to keep more space between him and Glenda.

Chapter Eight

"It's time to move."

Glen jerked awake to the sound of a deep, husky voice. She opened her eyes and stared up at Veso. He stood above her on the edge of the hole they'd slept in. Morning had come and they'd survived the night without being found.

"Go to the bathroom." He bent forward, offering his hand. "No time to waste, Glenda. I scouted at first light and found evidence that soldiers were within a mile of us."

She took his hand and he pulled her up, helping her climb out of the hole. Pain lanced throughout her body, sore muscles making themselves known. "What kind of evidence?"

"Dead bodies."

His response sickened her. "They killed more people?"

"Animals. They were savagely bitten and drained of blood, with multiple bite marks. I'd guess it was four or five soldiers. They got too close for comfort. We're putting more distance between us and them today."

She shuddered, feeling sympathy for the poor creatures who'd died. It also made her aware of what could have happened if those creeper things had found them in the night. She turned her head and stared across the ravine. It terrified her thinking of how Veso would get her to the other side, but there were worse things, like being recaptured by those freaks.

"Go to the bathroom and eat. I'm packing up our camp."

It didn't take her long to relieve her bladder behind a tree and Veso opened a can of beans for her. They were gross cold but she managed to get half of it down. Thoughts of real food taunted her but at least she wouldn't starve. Their meager supplies were better than nothing. Veso had packed up everything quickly and walked to the edge of the ravine, studying it at different angles.

Their conversation about his parents had changed the way she viewed Veso. It must have been difficult growing up without a mother who loved him. It explained a lot too. It would have messed him up being told he was the result of a power-hungry woman manipulating his father by having a baby she planned to use. Veso had been a tool to trade to get what she wanted. That's what it basically boiled down to. His cold-blooded bitch of a mom had rejected his love, and it sounded as if she'd slammed him pretty hard for even having emotions.

It also explained why he probably viewed women as the enemy. The fact that Glen was human would make it ten times worse in his mind, since he'd made his dislike for them known. Not that she blamed him for that either, after the few discussions they'd had on the subject. He'd be on a most-wanted list of every scientist and sicko in the world, something to hunt down and capture for whatever purpose they had in mind. None of it would bode well for his future.

Veso turned, scowling as she limped up beside him to peer down at the ravine below.

She assessed the situation. It was a long way to the bottom, probably a few hundred feet. "I don't think we have enough rope."

"I knew that. I thought I'd lower you as far as possible, have you cling to something, then climb down to you. From there, I'll lower you more until we reach the bottom. We'll do the same getting you up the other side. I'll climb until the rope ends, then haul you up until you have something to hold, and climb higher until we reach the top."

"Fantastic." She knew the sarcasm sounded clear in her voice. "It sounds super dangerous. Woohoo."

"You're hurting. I see the way you're moving. Did you lie about having cuts?" He sniffed. "I don't smell blood."

"I'm out of shape. That's all. There's nothing you can do about pulled muscles or bruised feet. I'll survive. Just don't expect me to run any marathons."

"Can you do this, Glenda?" He reached out and cupped her chin, making her gaze into his eyes. "Tell me the truth. I can tie you to my back if need be. We'll have to leave most of the supplies behind but we have to get beyond this ravine."

The solemn look on his face told her he meant every word. "I can do it. I don't want to end up back in that cell again."

He released her. "Put on your socks, multi layers, and let's go."

"You didn't eat."

"I had a snack before I woke you."

She didn't ask, afraid of his answer. He hadn't touched any of the cans. It meant he'd hunted his food. Instead, she did as he'd ordered and put on two pairs of fresh socks, covering her feet. Veso wrapped their tarp, the shovel, shotgun, and the blanket. It surprised her when he just pitched them over the edge.

"I can't believe you did that!"

He faced her. "What?"

"You probably broke the shotgun and the shovel."

"I threw them on a big bush. It will have softened the landing. If not, the tarp and blanket are all we'll need. Hand me the backpack."

He made little sense to her. "You're not throwing that too."

"No. I'll wear it on my back. Raw meat might sicken you and we can't light a fire. I won't risk the cans smashing open."

She passed over the backpack and watched as he slung it on. Then he crouched next to her, using the end of the rope to wrap around her waist. She lifted her arms out of the way as he tied a knot.

"Hold on tight and when I'm close to the end of the rope, I'll snarl. Find a good hold somewhere and dig in while I climb down to you."

She got the gist of his plan. "I still think we should try to go around and find another way across."

He sighed, his gaze locked with hers.

"Sorry. I felt the need to at least say it once more. But I'm starting to get to know you, and you're stubborn. You've made up your mind. I just hope it doesn't get me killed."

He stood fast. "I won't allow anything to happen to you."

The sincerity in his tone surprised her. "Thank you."

"It will be fine."

"Just don't drop me." That was a real fear.

He grinned. "I could lift a small car. You're nothing."

She studied him.

"I'm not human, Glenda."

"Right." She swallowed hard. "Okay. How do you want to do this?"

"Just go over the edge." He gripped the rope a few feet from her, the rest of it in a pile next to them. "I have you."

Holy shit. I'm doing this. She turned away, gripped the rope with one hand, and went to the edge. It was a long way down but Veso had a point. He wasn't human. He'd tossed that Vampire so hard it had busted through boards and made it at least six feet before sailing over the ledge at the mine they'd escaped from. That took a lot of brute strength. She was smaller than that creeper had been. I can do this.

Glen sat down on the edge, her feet dangling, and grabbed the rope with both hands. "You ready? I'll just slide off. Please don't drop me. I promise to try not to annoy you ever again." She glanced back to find Veso holding the rope with both hands, his legs braced apart, his gaze locked on her.

"We're wasting time we don't have. We have a lot of miles to cover."

"Fuck me." She closed her eyes and scooted, her butt leaving ground, and then she dropped a few feet. The rope dug painfully into her middle, the texture of it harsh against her palms, but she swung in the air instead of falling. He lowered her slowly, going about a foot at a time. She kept her eyes squeezed tightly shut for a few minutes until she felt braver. Then she looked down.

"I wish I hadn't done that."

"You're fine," Veso stated from above. "You're not heavy at all."

She hoped he wasn't lying to make her feel better. He'd lowered her about a fourth of the way down when she heard his snarl. It was time to find somewhere to cling to so he could climb down to her. She reached out, snagging a clump of bushes, found some rock to brace her feet on, and pulled her body against the side. Loose dirt gave way under her but she got a good hold.

Her heart pounded. What if she fell? What if the bushes she clung to ripped out of the dirt wall? She didn't like climbing. People were insane to do this kind of activity for fun.

"Okay," she called out. "I'm good but hurry."

"Don't look up," he warned from above.

She wondered why he'd said that until some dirt rained down on her. "Shit."

* * * * *

Veso felt great pride. Glenda had been very brave for a human. She hadn't screamed or lost her composure. He pulled her up the other side of the ravine, got her over the lip, and smiled. It had taken him longer than expected to climb down and then up but they'd made it. He helped her stand, brushing dirt off her.

"I need a bath in the worst way."

She looked sexy with messy hair. "We both do but we'll worry about that later. It's possible we'll reach the first river we must cross by this afternoon." He untied the rope from her waist.

She surprised him by gripping his shirt with her fist and stepping forward, staring up at him. "Tell me that's a joke. You're trying to be funny but failing at it big time, right? I imagine humor is a new concept so you just suck at it."

"What did I say?"

"Rivers to cross?"

"There should be at least three of them between us and VampLycan territory."

"Are there going to be boats? Ferries? Bridges? Those would be good. Even if they're those horrible swaying rope ones."

"We have to swim across."

She paled.

"What?"

"I don't know how to swim."

That stunned him. "You said you lived in California."

"I did but we were poor. My mom couldn't afford to pay for lessons. We didn't have a pool or access to one. I went to the beach sometimes with friends but I was terrified of sharks. Those eat people and rip limbs off. I laid out on the beach but never went into the water higher than my knees."

He had the worst luck, and the Vampire master couldn't have chosen a more ill-suited mate for him. She was his though, at least for as long as his instincts told him so. He reached out and gripped her hips, leaning in to stare deeply into her eyes. "We don't have time to argue. I'll get you across even if you're riding my back."

She bit her lip.

"I can do that. I could swim with you holding on to me. Let's go, Glenda. We have a lot of distance to travel before nightfall. I want to be beyond at least one river so we can get clean."

"Fine."

She impressed him by not arguing and he found himself smiling. "Good." He released her and began packing the rope in the tarp he'd

139

managed to get up the side of the ravine. His muscles were a little sore after all that climbing and lifting but he ignored the pain. Priorities demanded he keep them moving and make up lost time.

He kept the backpack on. Glenda's gaze went to it when he hoisted up the wrapped tarp and jerked his head in the direction he wanted to go. He spoke before she could.

"We're behind schedule. I need you to move faster today. That means making it easier on you."

"That's not fair though. I should take half the burden."

"Just say thank you and follow me."

"I have to pee first."

He sighed. "Hurry."

He turned his back, facing the ravine they'd just crossed as Glenda moved away. He scanned the other side, just for something to do. Movement caught his attention and he narrowed his eyes, focusing. There in the distance, between some trees, he spotted yellow.

The shape looked like a person and the color might be a shirt.

He turned, not caring about her modesty in that moment. It was more important to get out of the clearing. He was happy to see she'd disappeared into the trees. He followed fast, ducking behind one too.

"Glenda?"

"Shit! I'm right here. Don't come any closer. I'm squatting."

"I spotted a human. It has to be one working for the master. Hurry up."

He turned his head, peeking around the trunk. He didn't see movement again but he was sure that had been a human. It was possible that it was an innocent, but unlikely. The soldiers would have found and killed any humans who weren't Glenda. The bodies of those animals had shown a savagery that spoke of fury. No Vamp enjoyed animal blood over human. They'd taken their rage and hunger out on those poor beasts, making them suffer.

Glenda straightened a few feet away and he turned, watching her. Her cheeks were a little red. "I guess you heard me pee."

"I wasn't listening, and I don't even want to know why performing a normal body function embarrasses you. I'd piss in front of you if I had to go." He jerked his head. "Stick to the thick clumps of trees until we're farther away so that human doesn't spot us."

"What if it's a good guy? Maybe the police are searching for me."

He decided to be blunt. "It's too remote for them to reach this area easily from the time the sun rose. It means they were already out here in the night, and if the soldiers didn't tear them apart to take their blood, they are part of their tracking team."

"Oh."

"Move, Glenda. Now!"

She spun, doing what she'd been told. He followed her, keeping on alert. He was happy when she traveled at a faster pace without the weight of the backpack. Her balance was a lot better too, and he didn't have to reach out to keep her from falling as she climbed over rocks. She even stuck to the closely grown-together trees, just as he'd asked.

She might have potential as a mate after all.

That thought had him biting back a growl. His mind kept going there and it irritated him. The blood transfer had to be a temporary thing but he'd

141

hoped the effects would have faded after twenty-four hours. It had been longer and he still felt attracted to her, thinking of her in a way he shouldn't.

They were making good time. He stuck close to her, his gaze constantly moving, seeking a threat. The damn Vamp had day guards. It pissed him off. It meant they were being hunted around the clock and there was no safety just because the sun had risen. He'd also bet they had dart guns. The master was obviously insane but he would know humans posed no threat to a VampLycan unless they could drug him.

They made it down a slope and into another area ravaged by past flood waters. He didn't like being in the open but they couldn't bypass the area. He grabbed Glenda's arms before they left the trees and pulled her to a halt. He removed water and handed it to her.

"Catch your breath first. We have to run as fast as you can across this."

She stared at the destruction where water had taken down trees, left deep scars in the earth, and dragged rocks so they were partially covered. "We'll break our necks."

"One day guard means there are probably more."

She drank, handed the bottle back, and surprised him when she began to search the ground. She located a broken stick, then another, fisting them.

"What are you doing?"

She faced him. "I might not be Miss Outdoor Survival Champion but I've seen movies. These are good weapons. I dare any asshole to try to take me back to that mine. I'll stab him or her in the throat if they come at me. I'm not going to run and break my leg trying to get through that obstacle course."

"It's not that bad."

"It's uneven, rough ground, covered in rocks and trees and debris. I could fall and stab myself on one of these." She shook a hand, brandishing her stick. "I'm putting my foot down about this right now. I'm carefully walking across that area until we get to higher ground and the upright trees. Then I'll run again once we get past the clearing. Got it?"

"Glenda, you're not being reasonable."

"I'm human. You might be able to run across that without bodily injuries but not me. We're compromising on this. Deal with it, Veso."

He growled.

"Understood. You're not happy. How about you run and I'll follow at a slower pace to where you disappear into the trees? That way you can watch me and yell if you see anyone coming?"

That idea wasn't a bad one. She probably would fall and get hurt if he made her run. This way she'd only have to risk it if he spotted danger. He studied her. She looked tired. Walking would help her catch her breath. "Be careful."

"You too."

He hesitated, glanced toward where they'd come from, but felt certain no one was behind them. "Move as fast as you can and you run to me if I yell at you. Deal?"

"Like my ass is on fire."

He assumed that meant she agreed. He took off, not allowing his instincts to overrule his common sense to stay at her side. Her plan was solid, if not ideal. He dodged fallen trees, jumped over some of the larger rocks, and made it to the other side. He entered the trees, put the tarp down, and shrugged off the backpack. He climbed a tree, using his claws to tear into the bark. He got high enough to have a good vantage point.

Glenda had begun to cross the clearing. He checked her progress, ground his teeth at her extreme caution, then turned his attention elsewhere, looking for any movement that wasn't her. He spotted some wildlife but nothing human. He kept scanning, silently urging her to move faster.

He was able to glimpse the river when he climbed higher to get a better view. White caught his eye and he twisted, gripped another branch, and moved to get a better look. A low growl caught in his throat. Two humans were out there but far away still. They had large backpacks on, like hikers wore. He glanced from their location to Glenda. They wouldn't be able to see her unless they left the trees and rounded a bend where the flood trail had flowed.

He lost sight of them for a few minutes because of the density of the woods but then he caught another glimpse. They were heading toward the river. He swung back to the original branch he'd stood on and calculated how fast they'd have to move to avoid those humans. They could do it but Glenda would need to run.

Veso climbed down after feeling secure those two were the only threat. He waved to Glenda, using his finger over his lips to keep her quiet when he stepped out far enough for her to see him. She looked up, her mouth opened, but she said nothing. Fear showed on her face though. He nodded, dropped his hand from his face, and held up two fingers, then pointed in the direction of where he'd seen the men.

144

She picked up the pace and he hurried down the embankment, hauled her into his arms, and carried her back into the tree line so they'd make it there faster.

"Are you sure they're bad guys?"

He gently lowered her to her feet and put the backpack on. "I told you. It's a remote area. They'd have been food if they weren't working with the Vampires."

"That's not exactly what you said but point made."

"We have to run to get ahead of them to the river. Try to keep quiet and I'll lead."

She reached out suddenly and gripped his arm. "You're not lying to me, are you?"

"Why would I do that?"

"Because I might balk at the river but now I'm afraid, so I'll just do what you say when we get there, despite being worried I'll drown."

"I won't lie to you, Glenda. There are two humans and we need to avoid them."

"Okay. Let's go."

Chapter Nine

Glen had what she felt would be a permanent cramp in her side and her feet ached by the time they reached the river. Veso turned, staring down at her. It annoyed her that he wasn't panting too or covered in sweat. If she ever had doubted he wasn't human, no more. He'd kept her to a grueling pace between the clearing and the large body of water.

"I'll take you across first, then return for our supplies."

She bent, gripped her knees, and closed her eyes. "I need to catch my breath. You do that first and come back for me."

He growled. "I'd rather risk losing our supplies than you. I take you across first."

She lifted her head, staring up at him. "Give me two minutes. I bet you could swim across there and return in that time. You're a freak of nature."

He scowled.

"Do you want me to puke?" She collapsed, sitting down hard, and didn't even care if it was unladylike. She spread her thighs apart and leaned forward, bracing her hands there. "Give me at least two minutes. I should get bonus points for keeping up and not falling on my face. That had to be two miles I just ran."

"Damn it. Don't move."

He spun around, just trudging right into the water. She watched him as the water got deeper, until it reached his shoulders. He had the backpack on, the tarp locked under one arm. He swam as though he'd been born to do it, making it look easy as he used his free arm and both legs to maneuver

146

through the body of water. She saw stuff floating by him but he swam almost a straight line, seeming oblivious to the current.

"Freak of nature, alright," she muttered.

Some of the pain in her side faded and she slowed her breathing as Veso climbed out of the river on the other side, hiding their things, and then dove back into the water. He went under, and she tensed when he didn't come right back up. His head surfaced finally, almost mid-river as he took a breath, and then disappeared again.

"Iron lungs too. It's not fair."

Wood cracked, as if a twig had snapped, and she turned.

The sight of a man about eight feet from her had Glen grabbing for a rock as she struggled to her feet.

He was about twenty-two, wore a big backpack, and looked like some clean-cut college kid. He had just stepped out of the woods and his light brown eyes widened as if she'd surprised him too. She moved, backing up and hoping to draw his attention away from the river.

"Glenda?"

She hated when Veso was right. Though, the kid could be part of a search team from the police. It was possible someone had reported her missing. She swallowed hard, remembering there was supposed to be two of them. She anxiously glanced around looking for the other one.

The kid reached up and shoved off his backpack, taking time to remove something from a pocket. He held out a chocolate bar. "Here. I bet you're hungry. Do you want water? I have some. Come here."

She scowled. "Really? Candy? My mom taught me better than that by the time I was four." She gripped the rock tighter in her fist. "Who are you?"

He glanced at the rock and his features morphed to anger. "You try to hit me with that and it's going to get ugly. King Charles wants you alive but he didn't say I wasn't allowed to defend myself."

That was one question answered. She had another. "Why work for a Vampire? Are you stupid? Nuts? They'll kill you."

He shook his head. "I'm never going to die. That's why. King Charles promised to turn me."

"You're a moron. Have you seen those creeper things? Get off the drugs if think that's any kind of future." She glanced back, wishing she knew where the second one had gotten to and wondering where Veso was. She didn't dare look at the water in case the kid followed her gaze. She glared at him. "Why don't you take that candy bar and choke on it? That's a far better way to go out than being some insane jerk's puppet."

He lunged and she threw the rock, nailing him in the chest. It must have hurt because he dropped the candy and grabbed for his chest as he stumbled backward.

Instead of running, she dove forward, thrusting her elbow out and slamming into him as hard as she could. He grunted as they went down. She landed on him and used her other hand to claw at his face. He cried out as her fingernails raked his closed eyelids.

She sat up, jamming her elbow into him hard enough to hurt even herself, but she ignored the pain to snatch up another rock. She managed to grab one and started to batter him, using her thighs to brace herself when he tried to buck her off. She bashed him hard in the head. He tried to protect his face so she stopped using her nails on his eyes and went for his throat instead, still hammering him with the rock.

Someone grabbed her wrist and she was torn off the man under her.

She tried to throw her head forward, attempting to head butt the person, but she hit solid chest instead. A wet one.

She looked up at Veso, who just twisted, dropping her on her feet. He moved fast and she watched, mouth falling open, as he used his foot to step on the downed guy's throat.

"How many of you are there? Answer or I crush your throat."

The guy moved his hands, revealing the bloody scratch marks she'd put on him and a few cuts to his forehead and cheek from the rock. "Fuck you!" He flipped Veso off.

Veso looked at her. "Close your eyes now."

She did.

The sickening crunching sound had her spinning away, her stomach threatening to heave. Veso hadn't been bluffing. She didn't need to look to know that horrible sound had come from neck bones.

Something popped, a slight noise, and she gasped as Veso tackled her, taking her down. He twisted at the last second so he hit the rocky ground instead of her. Glen jerked her head up, staring at a metal dart that had landed by the river's edge.

Veso must have seen it too. He snarled. "Hold your breath and don't let go of me."

She barely understood him since the words came out so gruff. She gulped in air though and then they were rolling. Icy water almost made her gasp when they left the embankment and hit the water. She squeezed her eyes closed just in time and felt the current grab them.

149

The hold Veso had on her tightened to the point she felt he might break her ribs. She got her arms around his neck by feel and hooked her legs around his waist for good measure. He released her ribs and his body tensed, his muscles flexing.

They were under water and he was swimming. It didn't take long for her lungs to scream for air. Panic struck and she dug her nails into his skin, trying to tell him she was about to drown. He must have understood because in seconds their heads broke the surface and she gasped in air. He did too, and then the icy cold surrounded them again as he took them back under.

Something snagged on her shirt and tried to tear her away from him. It terrified her. What if they got separated? She really didn't know how to swim. Whatever tugged on her ripped free though and she just kept clinging to Veso's large, firm body. The current wasn't pushing at them anymore as hard as it had been when they'd first entered the water.

Glen was pretty sure she was going to die. She buried her face against Veso's chest and tried to keep calm. Drowning wasn't a good way to go. She felt air again and gasped, right before he went back under. It reminded her of videos of whales she'd once seen, taken from a ship. Veso would take them up for a second, then go back under.

How long could it take to reach the other side of the river? He'd crossed so fast the first time but it felt as though forever passed as he took her up for air about five more times. Maybe having her attached to him slowed him down. Whatever the case, when he finally took her up and wrapped his arm around her lower hips, hiking her higher on his body, she realized they stayed up, and Glen rubbed against his chest to clear the hair from her eyes. She opened them.

"We're downriver," he panted. "We've lost our supplies. I can't risk going back for them."

He hooked her around her rib cage, carrying her out of the water as he staggered up the embankment and into the trees. She used one of her hands to shove more of her plastered hair off her face.

"I can walk."

He ignored her, heading deeper into the trees until the river sounds faded. She didn't complain, instead just kept hold of him. He stopped after about five minutes and crouched a little.

"You can let me go."

She slid down his body and stood on trembling legs. The river had been cold and she instantly missed the heat of his body. Her soaked clothing felt really heavy and uncomfortable.

Veso pointed. "Climb inside that cave."

She spotted the small split in the rocks. "What if there's like snakes or something?"

Veso gripped her arm and growled low, his eyes flaring golden yellow. "Hide. I have to check the area. Be quiet and don't make a sound until I return."

They were still in danger. She lowered and remembered to just be grateful they were out of the water and she hadn't died as she crawled forward. It was a tight fit but she knew why he had chosen it. No sunlight reached beyond a few feet inside. She wouldn't see whatever bit or attacked her, if something else was already hiding there already.

Veso fumed as he stripped out of his clothes. His shirt was torn and useless. He threw it into the crevice he'd made Glenda enter and yanked off the shorts, tossing them out of sight too. He shifted, not caring if she were able to see him. He didn't hear her gasp so he figured she hadn't found room to turn around. He used his paws to shove dead leaves and foliage to cover their tracks from the tree line and peeked out at the river.

He spotted the other human pretty quickly, running along the other side of the river, searching for them. He lowered to his belly, keeping in the shade. The bastard had a rifle in his hand, the kind that shot darts. The backpack was gone but he knew it was the other so-called hiker.

It was tempting to go for their supplies but he wasn't willing to chance the human shooting him with a dart. He waited until the man disappeared around a curve and backed up, rose to all fours, and went hunting to see if there were any more of them on his side of the river. It didn't take long to discover they were alone, so far, at least within a mile. He returned to Glenda and shifted to skin, crouched down, and shoved his wet clothing forward to follow her inside.

The interior was damn tight, and he scratched his skin along the rock. It wasn't that deep. Maybe seven feet. His eyes adjusted and he found her along the back, where she'd come up against solid rock. She'd curled into a ball, her arms wrapped around her legs, head down.

"I'm here," he whispered.

She lifted her head and bumped it, softly cursing. "Is anyone out there?"

He reached out and put his hand on the back of her head to protect it from more accidental hits. She stared at him wide-eyed, blind. It was apparent to him that she couldn't see a damn thing.

"We're good for now."

"I'm freezing."

He could tell. "This isn't a safe location. Take off your clothes and wring them out while I'm gone. I need to find us a safer place for the night, away from the river. They know you'll slow me down."

"Fuck that," she muttered.

Her anger surprised him. He figured he was in for another argument but they couldn't stay where they were. They'd be found.

"Give me a minute until my teeth stop chattering and then I'll run. They're trying to tranquilize us, aren't they?"

"Only me. You don't pose enough of a danger to them."

"Tell that to college boy. I took his ass down."

He actually smiled. He had been impressed when he'd surfaced from the water and saw her straddling the male, beating on him. It had also infuriated him. She'd been attacked. "You did well."

"I might be small but I was raised in the city. I took some self-defense classes. Muggers and rapists target women all the time. Assholes expect women to run or just freeze up. They don't expect you to strike first."

"I'm proud of you." He gently rubbed her hair, his fingers tangling a little in the wet locks. "Stay here for a few minutes while I dress."

She tensed, then nodded. "Do I want to know why you aren't anymore?"

153

"I move faster on four legs than two and it keeps me lower to the ground, harder to spot."

"I'm going to have to see that sometime."

It reminded him of an earlier idea. "Ever ride horses, Glenda?"

"No. Why? Did you see some and think you can catch them? I could probably hold on to you though if you can ride in front of me. I seem to have that down pat. You didn't lose me in the water. I was like your second skin."

"You'd be holding on to me alright. As I said...I move faster on four legs."

Her mouth parted but then she closed it. A second passed. "Oh. You want me to ride you like a horse? That's kind of crazy. Is that a joke?"

"No."

She grew quiet.

"You're slowing us down. I don't have to worry about the supplies anymore. I can carry you on my back."

She closed her eyes.

"Glenda?"

She opened them and nodded. "Okay. Just tell me one thing."

"What?"

"You're going to know it's me, right? You won't go all murderish or something, will you?"

"Stop worrying about that. I'm still me in skin or fur. I won't have much of a voice though. My vocal cords change completely when I do. You'll need to climb on my back, wrap your arms around my throat, and use your knees to grip my sides. Just don't wrap your feet around my underside."

"Why? Will that make it tougher for you to run?"

"I don't want to be kicked in the balls."

"That's...um...fair. Okay."

"Don't be afraid of me, and do not scream when you see me. Just get on my back. Can you keep my shorts with you? I'll need something to wear later." He felt around, found them, and rung out most of the water. He pressed them into her hand.

She took them and nodded, shoving them between her shirt and her own pants near her hip. "I got it."

"No hesitation, Glenda. Our lives depend on this. Stay quiet and take my lead. I'll use my head to indicate if something is wrong or give a low growl. Understand?"

"Yes."

"Let's go."

"Now?"

"They're looking for us and the search grid has just been drastically condensed. They probably have radios. I would. We need to get out of here before they cut us off."

"Alright. Let's do this."

He released her head and backed away slightly, clenching his teeth as more rock scraped his skin. He shifted, hating that she'd hear it, but it helped him ease out of the tight spot by transforming his body. He made it outside, sniffed the air as he glanced around, and didn't see any threat.

He heard her coming and peered at the hole. She kept her head down, her chest close to the ground as she crawled out, probably to avoid the rock from digging into her back. Her head lifted—and pure terror showed as she met his gaze. He turned a little and lowered, watching her.

She only hesitated for a moment, then reached out, her hand shaking as she touched his side. "Shit!"

He used his head to jerk toward his back. He didn't have time for her to act so human. They needed to move. She got to her knees and gripped his back, rose up, and threw her leg over him. She eased down slowly.

"Fuck," she whispered. "I'm so going to need therapy."

He growled a warning and she grew quiet, leaned forward and wrapped her arms around his neck. She locked her fingers together and buried her face in his fur. "You're so warm."

He moved slowly, in case she threw herself off him when he rose to all fours and began to walk. She stayed on him and tightened her thighs just the way he'd told her too. He paused, wiggled his hips a little to put her in a more comfortable position, and then sniffed the air, taking in their surroundings. He decided to keep to the thickest parts of the trees and increased his pace. Glenda made a few low moaning noises but she didn't protest.

He was impressed with her once again. So much for her seeing him shifted and proving they could never be mates. She held on to him tight, as if it was fine with her that she was hugging a shifted VampLycan.

He focused on other things to take his mind off the feel of her as he ran, carefully scanning for any movement. They'd had to abandon their supplies. It meant feeding her would become more difficult. Her stomach

156

wouldn't tolerate raw meat well. Eventually it would weaken her. Of course, there was a way to obtain more supplies. Those day guards had been carrying packs. They needed human food to survive.

The human guards probably slept at night while the Vamps and soldiers hunted. He could sneak up and steal from them, if he could avoid the night hunters. It would also mean leaving Glenda unprotected for a time.

He'd keep moving until near dark, find them a secure location, and think over his options then. Right now, he needed to get them far from where they were.

Chapter Ten

Glen was riding the biggest dog she'd ever seen. Although to be fair, Veso didn't resemble some wolf or German shepherd. Any canine would take one look at him in beast form, piss themselves, and run for their lives. She could relate. It had been tempting to back up into that cave to cower when she'd first gotten a look at him with his scary black eyes, the long muzzle, four legs, massive paws with sharp claws, and a tail.

But he kept her really warm. Veso put off a lot of body heat, and his soft fur cushioned her body as he ran. He could probably move a lot faster but he wasn't. She chalked it up to him worrying she'd fall off, or maybe he felt as exhausted as she did. It was tempting to doze but every time she almost drifted to sleep, he leapt over something, making her cling to him a bit tighter.

They were covering a lot of ground though. He'd been right about that, and her feet weren't killing her. Riding turned out to be a lot easier than jogging to keep up with him. She wished she weren't wearing wet clothing. Her skin hurt in places she'd rather not think about from rubbing between his big body and hers. She tried to focus on other things, like imagining taking a warm bath or having an actual cooked meal. Once they reached safety, those things were a possibility.

He finally stopped and she lifted her head, searching for the cause. He lowered his body, turned his head, and bumped her with his muzzle. She stared at his sharp teeth, swallowed hard, and gazed into pure black eyes. The irises and pupils bled into each other. He glanced at the ground and she loosened her hold, climbing off.

She started to straighten but he gripped her wrist with his teeth. She froze, expecting pain. He released her fast and hunched down. She got the hint and sat.

He growled low, shot her some kind of look she couldn't read, and then took off, leaving her. She stayed still and silent. He might have felt they were in danger or he was looking for a place for them to bed down. She studied the sky, realizing it would be dark soon.

He returned about ten minutes later. He approached her, his focus on her middle.

"What?"

He crouched down, facing her, and began to shift. It amazed and terrified her at the same time as the fur receded to become smooth, golden-colored skin. He kept low when he was done though, hiding his lap. "Shorts."

"Oh." She pulled them out of her waistline and held them out, turning her head away to give him some privacy to dress.

He took them and soon spoke. "I'm decent."

She peered at him as he took a seat on the ground a few feet away. It was nice to be able to talk to him again. "Are we good here?"

"For now."

"I need to pee. I was too afraid to move while you were gone so I held still."

He lifted a hand, pointing to some bushes. "Over there. Don't go far or be long."

She got up and hurried. He hadn't changed positions when she returned. She sat down, a hundred questions filling her mind. She settled on the most pressing ones.

"How close are we to your home now?"

"We have a ways to go still. I decided it was time for us to rest. I scouted and found a place for us to bed down for the night."

"We're not going to keep moving?"

"We're settling in for the night. Humans are far easier to avoid than soldiers and Vamps."

"Why?"

"Humans don't see heat signatures, nor have super hearing or vision."

"Thank you for answering. I have a lot to learn."

He cocked his head, giving her an odd look.

"For when I go home. I don't want to be captured again."

"You wouldn't stand a chance of avoiding that without me."

He was probably right, and it scared her. "That's why I'm asking questions. To learn."

"I found a cabin with one human living inside very close to here. I am pretty certain he's working for the Vampires. I spotted him coming in from the woods with supplies on his back and gripping a dart gun, as if he'd been out searching for us all day. I think the best place for us to hide is in plain sight, where they won't think we'd go. I'm going to grab that human and we'll sleep inside his cabin tonight."

Her mouth fell open but she closed it fast. "Are you crazy?"

He hesitated. "He will have food and clothing, Glenda. Since this master has created soldiers, he'd want to keep the humans separated from them. I would."

"I don't understand," she admitted. "Why?"

"Soldiers are unstable, and can't be trusted around any blood sources while unsupervised by a full Vampire. It means if this master is reasonably smart, he's ordering the humans to lock in at night when the soldiers are hunting for us, to keep the day guards alive. Otherwise soldiers might attack and drain them. The master would have ordered them to avoid the homes of humans working for him. Humans need to be kept separated from soldiers or all bets are off. Got it?"

It made sense when he put it that way. Those creepers she'd seen probably would attack anyone, if given the chance. She nodded.

"The difficult part will be grabbing this human before he can get any kind of alert out to anyone. They're carrying cell phones. There must be a tower nearby."

"He might have to check in every few hours."

Veso shook his head. "That's not a worry as long as I don't have to kill him."

"It's not as if he's going to help us if he's working for the master."

"He won't have a choice. A Vamp was able to take over his mind already. I can ease into his head just as easily."

That disturbed her. "Mind control?"

Veso nodded.

It made her think about all the arguments they'd had. "Thank you for not doing that to me."

161

"VampLycans have honor, Glenda. I wouldn't do that to you unless I felt I had no choice. Life or death," he clarified.

"I still appreciate it."

He swallowed hard, staring at her. "You also were given my blood. It's probably out of your system but it's possible it gave you temporary immunity. Don't make a big deal out of it." He stood. "I'm going to need your help to lure the human out of his cabin. It might be dangerous but I'll be with you, just out of sight. We know the master wants you alive and unharmed. That's something we can use in our favor."

"I'm bait, aren't I?"

He grinned. "Yes."

"Fantastic." She got to her feet. "Before we do this though, I feel I need to say something."

"We have no time to waste. I can hear your stomach grumbling and you're shivering." Veso lifted his chin. "We need to be indoors before the sun goes down and the bloodsuckers begin to hunt." He met her gaze.

"What if you're wrong and this person is just some guy who lives in the woods?"

"Then tonight the Vamps will break into the cabin looking for food. It's a better defensive position than us out in the open. We'll have the element of surprise too, because VampLycans avoid humans. They won't expect us to do this, and would believe they're just attacking a human. I wouldn't harm an innocent, Glenda."

She couldn't fault anything he'd said, and she was starving. The idea of possibly sleeping in a bed, rather than on dirt, made her willing to agree to Veso's plan. "Let's do this. And hope the cabin has hot water. I'd kill for a shower. What do you want me to do?"

Veso rose to his feet. "I'm going to lead you to the cabin, then I want you to remain hidden, count to a hundred slow, and then rush to the door. Beat on it and yell for help, tell him you are being chased by a hungry bear. He should open the door right away for you. Jump back fast when he does and stay out of my way."

"You're hoping he won't see you," she guessed.

"He won't. Just get out of the way once that door opens. Fall back and go flat. Understand?"

She nodded. "Yes."

"Let's go."

Glen's anxiety rose as she followed Veso through the woods and they paused at a clearing. A small cabin had been built there, next to a stream. All the things that could go wrong played through her head.

Veso put his hand on her shoulder, stepped behind her, and ducked his head. "Remember to slowly count to a hundred. Then run as if your life depends on getting inside that cabin. Pretend I'm some deranged bear with paws larger than your head and I'm right on your ass. Got it?"

"If that's your version of a motivational speech, you're a scary guy."

He chuckled and backed away. She watched him circle the clearing, heading toward the back of the cabin. She counted silently in her head. Her heart rate increased, afraid of what she'd face when she ran across that clearing. The master did want her alive though, so her chances were good of not being hurt by whoever lived inside the cabin. Her worst fear was that there might be a surprise waiting. Veso had only seen one person but that didn't mean more weren't hiding inside.

Glen hit a hundred, sucked in a sharp breath, and sprinted forward.

"Help!" Her feet hurt a little as she ran but she ignored them, imaging Vlad hot on her ass. "Help me! He's going to kill me." She reached the cabin, ran up the five steps, and beat on the door with her fits, panting hard. "Is anyone inside? A bear's going to kill me! Help!"

A bolt slid from the other side and she backed up, quickly glanced around the narrow porch, then back at the door as it opened. The man who jerked it open was in his mid-thirties, clean-shaven, and had dark hair. His brown eyes showed his surprise.

Glen collapsed to her side, pretending to faint but using her arms to protect her head and ribs as she fell.

Motion from the top of the cabin caught her attention and she watched in amazement as Veso dropped from the roof and almost landed on the man who stepped out onto the porch. Veso's hand latched around his throat and he slammed him hard against the doorjamb.

Glen sat up and watched as Veso went almost nose to nose with the stranger.

"Don't move," Veso demanded.

The man he gripped held utterly still.

"What are your orders?"

"Find the woman, don't hurt her, and shoot the man with the darts I was given," the stranger stated. "Call in for help immediately."

"Did you call anyone when you heard the woman at your door?"

"No."

"Are you here alone?"

"Yes."

Glen stood, stepping closer to the cabin so she could see Veso's face. His eyes had turned a bright golden color. He glanced at her and she forgot how to breathe for a second. He raised his hand, blocking her from seeing his face. "Glenda, turn your back."

She hesitated.

"Do you want me to control you too? Do as I said now."

She spun away, curious but warned.

"Answer my questions. When did you check in last?"

"I did when I came home."

"When are you supposed to do it again?"

"King Charles said to call him if I see or hear anything tonight. Otherwise I must call him in the morning to let him know when I restart my search."

"Do you speak to King Charles or someone else?"

"Only to King Charles. It's a pleasure to serve him. I must shoot you with a dart and call him immediately."

"Forget about the gun. I want you to sleep until I tell you to wake. Do it now."

Long seconds passed and Glen glanced back. Veso was gone, so was the man, and the cabin door stood wide open.

She followed them inside, stopping right away. Veso had dumped the unconscious man on his back on the floor, a few feet from the door, and was yanking open a closet across the room.

She glanced around. The cabin had an open living space with a loft above on one side. A kitchen and bathroom had been tucked under it. The furniture was sparse and it had a rustic feel, with the exposed log walls. Her gaze returned to the downed man. He didn't move.

"Is he okay?"

Veso shut the closet, then took the ladder up to the loft. "He's alive and should stay down. Don't touch him or get too close until I find something to tie him up with. I'm not sure how deep his orders were planted yet. It's possible he could rouse if his mind is really messed up."

Glen kept distanced from the downed man by backing up. She turned, stared out at the trees across the cleared space, then closed the door. She locked it in case someone else showed up at the cabin.

Veso came down the ladder less than a minute later, empty-handed. He strode over to the backpack on the floor near her and dropped to his knees, opening it up.

"I should have checked here first."

Glen frowned at the sight of the old-fashioned shackles Veso withdrew. They were bulky restraints with about a foot of chain between the cuffs. "What the hell?"

"I'm guessing he got these from a Vamp. They're stronger than normal handcuffs." Veso turned, walked on his knees to the guy lying on the floor, and rolled him over. He shackled his wrists behind his back.

"They look a little rusty. Maybe we should find some rope or something else."

"If they were good enough for me, they are good enough for him."

Glen opened her mouth, then closed it. It wasn't worth arguing over. She'd heard every word exchanged and Veso had been right. The man was working with the master. He'd have shot a dart at Veso to knock him out and returned her to that horrible mine if he'd been able to. "I'm starving."

"Shower first. You're cold."

"Do you think there's hot water?"

"Probably. He's got solar panels and a utility shed in the back. It means there's a generator and possibly a water tank. I'm going to check out our weapons situation."

In other words, he wanted her out of his way. She didn't complain. At least he wasn't ordering her to cook him food this time.

Glen rushed toward the bathroom, grateful the cabin had electricity when she flipped on a switch and the light came on.

She closed the door and frowned at the crude bathroom. It had a shower stall and a toilet but no sink. It didn't matter though when she turned on the water and waited half a minute, running her fingers under the spray. It began to warm.

"Yes!"

Veso couldn't help but smile when he heard Glenda mutter that single word. He had been pretty certain the cabin would have hot water. It had been built sturdy for year-round use, not just some summer hunting shack. He located two guns in the cabin, including a shotgun, and then returned

167

to the sleeping human. He rolled him onto his side and knelt low, getting close.

"Wake and look at me," he demanded.

The human's eyes opened and Veso focused, pushing his power at the man's mind. "What were your exact orders about the woman?"

"King Charles wants her alive and unhurt. She's important to him."

"I bet she is." It still pissed him off thinking about the master's plans for Glenda. "How many other people are out working with you during the day?"

"There're eight of us."

"How many close to here?"

"Three more."

"Where are they?"

"Bob and Linda have a cabin two miles down the stream where it meets up with the river. Chuck is about four miles to the north."

"Describe them to me."

Veso listened, realizing neither of the men were the two who had attacked them earlier at the river. The human grew silent, staring at him. "Does anyone come here at night?"

"No. We're not allowed to go out after the sun goes down, until it rises. We're to ignore any sounds unless we think it's you or the woman. Then we're supposed to call it in but must stay inside."

It was just like he'd thought. The master feared his soldiers would kill his human thralls. "How do you get supplies?"

"I walk to Bob and Linda's place and pick them up."

"How do they get supplies?"

"They have a boat."

It wasn't what Veso wanted to hear. "Do you have a vehicle? Do they?"

"I have a dirt bike but I'm low on fuel for it. Bob owns the boat and a small backhoe. They're about to expand on their cabin. Linda is pregnant."

Veso felt pity for the humans. It wasn't their fault that they were helping the Vampires. The fact that the woman was pregnant made it worse. The master would dispose of them when he had no use for them anymore. "Go back to sleep and stay that way until I tell you otherwise. You're exhausted."

The human closed his eyes and his body relaxed. Veso gripped him, lifted, and went over to the closet. He jerked open the door, gently laid the man down in the confined space, and left him inside. He closed him in and blocked it so the human couldn't get out. Then he walked over to the cabin door.

Glenda had locked it but she hadn't noticed the secondary way to secure it. He lifted the two sturdy bars and shoved them into the brackets on each side of the frame. The human had probably had a few bears attempt to enter his cabin and had added the brace system to help keep them out.

There were solid shutters on the interior of the windows. He closed and barred the two on the lower floor and then checked the loft. It didn't have a window. Bears must be a big problem in the area for the human to have taken such measures. It was a good thing. It would make it harder for a Vampire to break into the cabin, and they'd have to put some effort into it. He turned on a light in the loft, a small lamp, then just jumped down to the main floor.

Veso glanced at the closed bathroom door, then entered the kitchen, flipping on the light. They both needed to eat. The human was well supplied on canned food. He used his claw to slice open the tops of two of them and dumped the stew into a pot. He scowled at the plug-in burner and figured out how to turn it on. The kitchen was as basic as it got and there wasn't a fridge.

The water turned off in the bathroom and Veso realized Glenda wouldn't have clothes, unless she put on her damp ones. He probably should return to the loft and get her something to wear but he remained where he was, using a spoon to stir the chunky meat and vegetable mix inside the pot. A smile curved his lips. He liked seeing her in a towel. He might even steal it off her body again.

His amusement quickly faded though when the bathroom door opened and she did step out in just a towel. Her skin was pink from the warm water, her hair wet, and the sight of her exposed limbs and the tops of her breasts gave him a whole new hunger. He wanted her. His dick stiffened and desire spread through him.

Shit. The attraction isn't fading. I can't want a human.

"That shower felt like heaven. There is hot water. I made sure I left some for you. I'm assuming it's limited, right? I mean, there's probably a really small water tank for this cabin. I looked in the cabinets. No new toothbrushes but he had dental floss and lots of toothpaste. I think I did a good job with my finger of getting my teeth clean. I'll never take that for

170

granted again." She smiled. "Did you see any clothes upstairs that we can borrow?"

"Yes."

She walked to the ladder, then froze.

Veso stirred the pot again but kept his gaze locked on her. She had such soft-looking skin. Delicate. Both pale and pink, so foreign to him. VampLycan women tended to be tan and really fit. Bigger. His dick didn't seem to care that Glenda wasn't his normal type or that she was human.

"Problem?" He guessed why she paused. She'd have to let go of her grip at the top of the towel to climb. It might actually fall off and expose every inch of her to him.

She looked into his eyes. "Um, why don't I finish cooking that and you go up there to find me something clean to wear?" She turned a little and stepped closer.

"I wouldn't do that if I were you," he warned.

She halted, her eyebrows arching. "Do what?"

"Come near me." He lowered his gaze, fixating on the tops of her breasts exposed over the edge of the towel.

She took a step back. "Don't even think about it. Your eyes are changing color again."

He jerked his gaze up to hers. "Don't wear so little around me then."

"There was nothing else in the bathroom to put on. Let's not go through this again. Train wreck, remember?"

"As if I could forget." He tore his gaze away to glare at the stew. "Get up there and find something. Do it now. I won't look."

Motion out of the corner of his eye assured him she followed his order. He wanted to peek but the last thing he needed was to get involved with her more so than he was already. The blood they'd been forced to share should have worn off by now. The fact that he still felt so attracted to her irritated him. Worse, it scared him. What if it wasn't just the blood link that drew him to Glenda? What if it wasn't a feeling that would pass with time?

"Goddamn," he snarled.

"Be careful. Did you burn yourself?"

He glanced up at the ceiling, able to track her by sound as she moved across the floor up in the loft. "Just put on clothes. The stew is about as warm as I'm willing to make it. I'm starving."

"Me too."

But again, he wanted her more than food. His anger grew. He couldn't mate a damn human.

Chapter Eleven

Glen put on an oversized T-shirt and a pair of boxers. The rest of the pants options she'd found were either dirty or jeans she couldn't fit into. The owner of the cabin seemed to have a limited choice on what to wear. She climbed down the ladder and found Veso placing two bowls on the tiny table. There was only one chair but he motioned her to it.

"Thank you."

"He only has water and booze to drink." Veso curled his lip. "I'm going to shower. Yell out if you hear the human moving around in the closet, got it? Don't confront him yourself or move the chair I used to lock him in. I'm sure he'll stay asleep but I'd rather be safe than sorry. His hands are secured behind his back but that doesn't make him less of a threat to you."

"What about your food?"

"I'll hurry and won't close the door all the way, so I can hear you if you need me." He left the small kitchen area and entered the bathroom.

Glen sat down and stared at the contents of the bowl. She usually didn't like stew but hunger made her change her mind as she lifted the spoon, blew on it, and took a bite. She closed her eyes, chewing. It was a bit too hot but she wasn't going to complain. It had been a long time since morning and it beat the breakfast she'd had.

She glanced around the cabin and remembered that the owner had a cell phone. It was tempting to find and use it. Veso would be pissed though, and she remembered how easily he'd seemed to take over the mind of the man he'd captured and put in the closet. His warning about the cops not being able to help her replayed as well, and she finally understood. A

Vampire could do the same to the police, take over their minds and control them.

"Damn." She finished her food and stood, taking the bowl and spoon to the small sink. She was about to wash them but instead just set them down. She'd wait until Veso ate and do them all at the same time.

Noise drew her out of the kitchen right as Veso exited the bathroom. The sight of so much of him wasn't getting old. He had the best body, and she hated noticing all those muscles as she scanned him fast before he caught her. He was staring at the door, as if to make sure she hadn't messed with it. She hadn't. He turned more and his gaze met hers.

"No problems?"

"Nope."

"The sun should be down enough for the Vampires and soldiers to be on the prowl."

That was a grim thing to say. "Fun."

He frowned, his lips twisting downward. "Sarcasm is never attractive, Glenda."

"How would you like me to react to you telling me that? Wring my hands and cringe? Cry? I understand that it's getting dark."

"It was a warning. And they have damn good hearing. A woman isn't supposed to be here. It's probably best if we don't talk at all."

She lifted her hand and saluted him. It was tempting to bend down three of her fingers and thumb to give him a different kind of salute, but she resisted. It still earned her a low growl and he came closer, stopping less than a foot away. She had to tilt her head back to keep looking into his eyes.

174

"I'm not in the best mood."

"I had no clue."

A brighter gold color spread through his irises, taking over the brown. The way he could do that still amazed her. His emotions caused a physical reaction in his eyes.

"What did I say?"

"Not in the best mood," she repeated.

"Sarcasm."

"It's not attractive."

"Exactly. I'm going to go upstairs and find something to wear."

"Alright."

He stepped around her, brushing his arm against hers. His skin felt a little damp and really warm where they touched. She turned her head, watching him as he began to climb the ladder. The towel wrapped around his waist didn't fall off but it did hug his ass each time he lifted his legs, reminding her that he had a nice one. A little guilt surfaced when he reached the top and moved out of sight. Part of her had wished she had seen him lose that towel.

She faced forward, stared at the door, and hoped nobody showed up in the night.

"That would be bad," she whispered.

The loft creaked. "What?"

She turned around, finding Veso standing at the top of the loft. "Nothing."

"Don't talk at all. You don't listen well."

She sealed her lips and entered the kitchen, out of his sight. A jug of bottled water sat on the counter. She found a glass and poured a little of it, drinking it all. It was a good thing she was tired. Sleep sounded good. She walked over to the only couch and took a seat. She flinched when she drew her legs up, a reminder that her thighs were tender. She lifted one, bent forward, and saw the redness there where her wet clothing had irritated her earlier while riding Veso's back. The light abrasions would fade though. It wasn't bleeding. Things could be worse.

A soft noise drew her attention and she straightened up, peering over the back of the couch. Veso just sported another pair of boxers. They looked a bit tight around his hips and she could clearly make out the outline of his cock. She twisted her head, staring at the fireplace instead of him. The mantel was wood but the fireplace was built out of small stones and what looked like cement.

Veso ate. It was so silent, she heard the slight clink every time his spoon touched the bowl. The dim room was beginning to bother her. She was in a strange place, and she didn't need Veso to remind her of what might be outside the cabin. She'd spent enough time locked inside that mine that she'd probably never feel safe again at night, now that she knew what could crash through the door. Her kidnapping flashed through her memory.

"Or come through the windows," she muttered under her breath.

"They are shuttered closed with bars across them."

Veso's soft voice made her startle and she watched as he took a seat a few feet away from her. "Don't you make a sound when you move?" She realized she'd clutched her hand to her chest. He'd given her quite a scare.

"I assumed you were talking to me." He twisted a little, staring at her.

"I talk to myself at times. That was one of them."

"You're not supposed to make any noises."

"We're almost whispering."

"And a Vamp can hear that."

"I'm nervous," she admitted.

"They will either attack us or they won't."

She adjusted her body to face him and it rubbed part of her thigh against the rough material of the couch. She flinched at the slight pain. Veso leaned closer.

"What's wrong?"

"Nothing."

"Don't lie to me. Are you hurt?" He sniffed. "I don't smell blood."

"I'm just a little tender."

"Your muscles?"

"My clothes were wet and they rubbed against my skin. It isn't bad. More like a rash."

"Let me see."

"No way." She scooted back on the couch. "It only happened on my inner thighs. That's where we rubbed together the most."

He turned his head away, staring at the door. It made her afraid, and she tensed. It was possible that he could hear something she couldn't, like a Vampire.

Long seconds passed and he stood. She glanced around for a weapon, anything to use if someone kicked in the door. Veso walked to the fireplace and gripped the mantel. He just stood there.

Glen glanced between him and the door. More time passed and she finally relaxed. "What are you doing?" she whispered as softly as she could.

"Don't ask," he rasped.

"Okay." She frowned.

He finally released the mantel and turned. His face was in the light from the other side of the cabin and his grim expression didn't bode well as he locked gazes with her. His eyes were more golden than brown again, also never a good sign. She'd figured that out after spending so much time with him. He took a few steps closer and then stopped.

"Infections are easy for humans to get. Let me see your damn thighs."

"I told you it's nothing."

"We don't need you sick. I figure by tomorrow night we'll reach VampLycan territory if you ride me again. That means you need to be well enough to hold on to me, and not in pain. Let me see. I'm able to heal you."

"How?"

"My blood."

She shook her head and grimaced. "No thanks. No more injections for me and I'm not drinking your blood." She got up. "I'm going to sleep. Do you mind if I take the bed?"

"Glenda." He frowned.

"Good night." She fled around the couch and climbed the ladder to the loft. The lamp didn't put off much light but she wanted it on. That way if

178

anything tried to break in, she wouldn't be in the dark. She was so sick of that.

The bed wasn't a big one, maybe a full, and she was pleasantly surprised when she lay down on it. It was comfortable and had some give, not overly firm. It was much better than sleeping on the ground or on that horrible cot that the Vampires had provided her with in the mine. She lay on her side, curled into a ball, and closed her eyes.

Tomorrow night she hoped they were wherever it was that Veso lived. She would be able to go home.

And then what? Shit.

She'd be on her own. Her life would need to change. She'd have to move right away. The Vampires had already taken her from her apartment once so they knew where she lived. There wasn't a lot of money in her savings account but she had good credit. She could take an emergency loan and use her credit cards to get a new place. It would probably be a good idea to give notice at her job too. They could control humans so she wouldn't even be safe during the day.

It would also mean saying goodbye to Veso.

A tightness filled her chest and she had to breathe through it. He might be happy to be rid of her, but she would miss him.

Veso paced the small living space, his gaze going up to the loft. It bothered him that Glenda wouldn't allow him to see her injuries. It was possible she was lying about the extent of them. He hadn't smelled blood and she hadn't seemed to be in pain when she'd rushed to get away from him.

He had a lot on his mind. First though, he needed to contact his father. He didn't remember his phone number. Modern technology wasn't always a good thing, the ease to place calls done by electronics storing information at a touch. He'd have to call the lodge. That number would be listed. Davis would have to relay the message or give him his dad's number.

He walked toward the backpack but then paused. His father would come. He'd ask Lavos, Garson, and Kar to join him, and he doubted his father would wait until morning. Their group would take on any Vampires who tried to stop them, and arrive within hours. It would mean assistance—but it would also put an end to his alone time with Glenda.

He bit his lip. His father would try to talk him into sending her back to the human world, despite the danger it would put her in.

He resumed pacing, battling it out inside his head. Glenda would be safer if he had the backup of his father and friends. But no way would he let her return to Oregon. The master would send his nest after her and she'd be recaptured. Once word spread that he'd kidnapped Veso, other clans would be on the alert, their members warned. It would mean the crazy bastard would try to breed her with a Lycan.

He wouldn't allow that to happen.

He stopped pacing, staring up at the loft. His father and friends would try to talk him into letting Glenda go. She wouldn't be safe yet with his clan. Some of them really hated humans. Nabby and his friends would target her, forcing Veso to fight them to defend her, and they tended to have no honor. They'd attack him in a small group instead of one on one.

Damn, damn, damn! He wasn't sure what to do yet so he put off making the call and seeking assistance getting home. It was better to focus on the night ahead. First off, that meant dealing with Glenda's injuries.

He strode over to the ladder and climbed it. She'd fight him but he didn't give a damn. Plus, it bothered him that she might be in pain.

She lay on her side as he approached the bed. Her eyes opened and she stared at him. "Is someone outside?"

"No, but they could be." He kept his voice as low as hers. "You need to remain very quiet."

"I was trying to sleep until you came up here. You told me not to talk."

"Show me your injuries."

Her mouth parted.

"I was just reminding you why you can't argue with me," he said. "Humans get infections easily, and this isn't me asking. It's an order. Show me where you're sore."

Her eyes narrowed and her mouth sealed shut. She didn't move.

He sat down on the edge of the bed, twisted, and yanked off the blanket she'd used to cover her legs. He expected her to hit him or at the very least attempt to roll away. She just stared at him with a scowl.

"Where?"

"Fine," she breathed.

She rolled onto her back and wiggled up the bed a bit, putting her head more toward the other side. He held still, watching as she gripped the hems of the boxers she wore and pulled them up, parting her legs slightly to expose her inner thighs. He looked down, seeing the red, tender skin.

181

He couldn't help but swallow hard. She had sexy thighs, and the bunched material covered her sex but not much else. The lower edges of her ass were bared.

"Happy? I told you they were fine."

He turned more to face her and gently gripped her knees. He pushed her legs farther apart and leaned in, getting a better look. There were no cuts but the skin seemed a little inflamed. "I can fix this."

"Pass."

He lifted his gaze. "I'm not hitting on you."

"I meant I'm fine. I'll pass on you forcing me to drink your blood."

"You won't have to."

He released her, slid off the bed and went to his knees, facing her again. He reached out, hooked her behind her knees with both hands and pulled her toward him. She softly gasped but didn't fight as he settled her legs on each side of him and maneuvered her so her knees were bent up. He spread her thighs and got comfortable.

"What are you doing?" She stared at his chest, lifting her head to glance lower, to his waist.

"Not fucking you, if that's what you're worried about. I know the position is intimate but keep your thighs spread."

"What are you going to do, Veso?"

He released her legs. "Keep the material out of my way. I'm going to bite my tongue and lick the sore spots. They'll heal fast. Hold still, Glenda."

"Train wreck," she muttered but threw her head back, closing her eyes. "Just reminding you of that. This is a really bad idea."

He agreed but let his fangs extend. It wasn't hard to do, staring at her thighs and her legs spread in front of him. His dick hardened but he tried to ignore it. He bit down on the tip of his tongue, the pain a welcome distraction. The coopery taste assured him he bled. He put his hands on her legs just above her knees in case she tried to get away from him and bent forward, opening his mouth.

He licked her skin, running his tongue high. Glenda sucked in a sharp breath but held still under him. He liked the way her skin tasted, as well as the softness against his tongue. He pulled back a little, licked over the same area, and moved one hand to use his thumb to clean off his red-tinged saliva. Her skin healed as he watched.

"That tingles."

"It's working. Just relax." He bit his tongue once more and began licking at her other leg, going up high on her thigh to get all the red areas. It put his nose right at the seam of her sex. The material of the boxers wasn't much of a barrier. His dick hardened even more.

Focus, he ordered himself. It was difficult to do though when all he really wanted was to tug off those boxers and place his mouth on her sex. She'd want him as much as he wanted her if he could just gain access to her clit.

He made sure to lick all the skin that looked sore, pulled back, and used his hand to clean her off again, watching her heal. Perfect, pale skin was his reward. All the irritation and redness faded fast. He looked up at her when she lifted her head, their gazes locking.

"Did it work?"

"Yes." His voice came out too deep. He cleared his throat. "You won't be in any pain now."

"Right."

"What does that mean?"

"Nothing. We should probably get some sleep."

"Yes." His gaze lowered to her thighs.

"Um, Veso?"

"What?" He let his hand caress her skin. It was so soft.

"What are you doing now?"

"I want you."

"This can't work."

"I don't care." He straightened and gripped under her knees, jerking her down the bed so her legs were parted around his hips. Then he bent again, pinning her under him, bracing his arms next to hers. He trapped her head between his hands and went for her mouth.

She gasped when he kissed her, giving him a chance to delve inside. She tasted like minty freshness, what it had said on the toothpaste she'd left out in the bathroom that he'd used too. She clutched at his arms and he expected her to claw at him, to fight, but she just clung—and kissed him back. Then her legs lifted and wrapped around his hips.

He pressed his pelvis forward, rubbing his stiff shaft along the seam of her pussy.

Her moans urged him on, not that he needed it. She ground her sex against his and he growled, jerking his face away so he could stare into her eyes. "Say yes."

"I…"

"I don't know how much longer we have together. This might be our last night left."

She licked her lips and nodded.

"Take off your clothes." He lifted up and backed away when she released him. He shoved down his shorts and watched her struggle out of the shirt. Her breasts were perfect to him. Not too big or small. Her nipples were beaded and taut. He wanted to play with them, but instead hooked his fingers in the waist of her boxers, tugging them down. She helped by lifting her hips. He threw them across the room. They sailed off the edge of the loft and disappeared below.

He lunged, pinning her to the bed and taking possession of her mouth.

Chapter Twelve

Glen couldn't think. Veso's body pressed her against the mattress, his skin hot and firm. She ran her hands up his arms and wrapped them around his neck, clutching at his back. He had fangs. Her tongue scraped against them but she didn't care. Her body felt on fire and she ached everywhere. Nothing mattered but him. Not the fact that he wasn't human or that he'd probably break her heart later.

He reached between them, his thumb rubbing against her clit. She twisted her head away from his mouth to moan louder. He stopped, ran his thumb lower, and she could feel how wet she'd become. He lifted up and moved his hand away. She hiked her legs higher around his waist, urging him closer. His hips surged forward and she wiggled frantically when his cock pressed against the opening of her pussy. He felt big and she wanted him inside her.

He snarled, the sound animalistic, and he used one of his hands to fist her hair, jerking it out of his way. His mouth found her throat and she arched, giving him access. It was possible he'd bite her but she was willing to risk it. It was all about need and wanting Veso.

He entered her slow. She sucked in a sharp breath when he paused.

"Relax. Damn, you're tight."

"You're thick."

He pushed in more, withdrew a little, then surged forward, making her take all of him. She squeezed her eyes closed and dug her nails in. He was big and extremely hard. He adjusted his body over hers, one of his huge hands grabbing her ass and lifting her a little off the mattress. He began to slowly thrust in and out, making growling noises deep within his throat. His chest vibrated against hers.

He drove in deep, thrusting faster, and pressed his pelvis tight against her clit, forcing her legs wider apart. Glen moaned louder, close to climax. A thumping sounded but she ignored it. All that existed was Veso and pleasure. He moved faster over her, his chest rubbing and vibrating against her breasts. He pulled her hair again, forcing her to turn her face toward him. He covered her mouth but didn't kiss her, probably trying to muffle some of the sounds she made.

Ecstasy exploded and she cried out. He kept fucking her fast, drawing it out, and then he tensed over her, holding still. A heartbeat later he moved slow, groaning. She felt him inside her, coming. He held still again and pulled his mouth away from hers. Both of them panted and she could feel the muscles relaxing under her hands on his back.

Glenda opened her eyes and found him watching her. His eyes were glowing that beautiful golden color. She forgot to be afraid of him trying to control her mind or that he was so different from her. She cupped his cheek.

He blinked, glanced at her mouth, and then stunned her by lowering his head and brushing his lips against hers. He stopped when she opened her mouth to deepen the kiss. He pulled back and stared down at her again, an odd expression on his face.

"What?" She was almost afraid to ask. He might already regret what they'd done, and that would hurt. Not that she'd admit it to him.

"I cut your mouth while we kissed."

"It doesn't hurt."

"It wouldn't. I cut myself too. I healed you as fast as I caused the damage."

"It's okay. No pain, no foul. Or something like that."

His lips curved upward and he actually smiled. It reminded her of how handsome he could be. But his next words where grim ones for them both.

"We exchanged more blood."

"It couldn't have been much. I didn't taste blood."

"Or you didn't notice. I was distracted and so were you. We do sex well together. You're a bit tight but you'll adjust to my body the more we do this."

"Who says we'll ever do this again?"

"We will." He turned his face a little, pressing his cheek tighter against her palm. It was a sweet thing, so unlike him, as if he liked her touch and wasn't about to hide that fact. "I knew you slept with humans with small dicks."

Glen didn't know if she should slap him or laugh. She settled on a middle ground. "You're terrible."

"I'm honest."

She felt heat spread up her neck to her face. "You don't know that for sure."

"I do. Your body resisted me at first because you've never taken someone my size."

"Well, you're abnormally large all over."

"True. I'm a VampLycan." He unfisted her hair and stroked it, spreading it out on the bed with his fingers.

They stopped talking but he didn't lift up or withdraw from her. He kept her pinned under him, their bodies intimately connected, as he played with her hair. He seemed very interested in doing that, not meeting her gaze anymore. She stroked his cheek.

"Veso?"

"What?"

"What are you thinking?"

He stilled his hand. "I'm debating about what to do."

"We should get some sleep."

He looked at her then, his eyes less bright and more brown than golden. "I'm battling logic and instinct right now. I haven't decided which one should win."

"I don't understand."

"I know. You'd be struggling to get out from under me if you did."

"What does that mean?"

"Logic tells me how bad it would be to take you as my mate. My clan hates humans. I don't know how well I could protect you there, so we'd have to flee to another clan. They might not welcome us because of who my clan leader is. Instincts are telling me to bite into you because you're my mate and drink more of your blood. You'd have to drink mine too. I'm certain you'd fight me on that but it's how mates bond. And I'd demand a deep bond with you if I took you for my mate. I don't trust that you wouldn't run away from me one day otherwise. Humans have a horrible history of disloyalty."

Glen decided she wanted to punch him but resisted. His words hurt deep. He was admitting he believed she was his mate, but he'd made it clear he didn't think much of her kind. She could see past their differences but it was still a big deal to him. He had a way of insulting her and hurting her feelings while flattering her at the same time. "I don't want to be your mate, so stop thinking about it. You really are terribly prejudiced and right now you're being a jerk."

"How so?"

"I'm human."

"I'm more than aware of your flaws."

His words were another verbal slap. She was good enough to have sex with but not to make a commitment to. "Get off me."

He scowled.

She could deny what they'd just done had meant anything to her, too, if he wanted to act that way. "We just had sex. That's all it was. We're both stressed out after all the shit we've been through. We were attracted to each other so this was bound to happen. No big deal. Not to mention, we just met. This isn't the time to make life-altering decisions. We're both exhausted and out of sorts."

"It was more than sex."

That soothed the pain a little but not by much. "You'd regret it if you mated with me, Veso." A small part of her hated saying that; she was already falling for him. But it was probably true. He'd grow to hate her one day, not able to overlook her being human. "We come from two different worlds. And we'd be a train wreck, remember?"

"I do."

"We're going to survive these stupid Vampires hunting us, get to safety, and then our lives will return to normal. We had sex because we only had each other to turn to. That's all." Keep saying it. Maybe one day I'll even believe it if I keep telling myself that.

He smiled. "Little human liar."

She had pride. Maybe his was injured because she wasn't in tears, pleading with him to mate with someone he thought of as flawed and weak. He did have a superiority complex. She refused to feed into it. "Everything I've said is the truth. What part isn't?"

"I wouldn't have fucked just any human. You mean something to me, Glenda. And you're as drawn to me as I am to you."

Damn you, Veso. Stop saying things like that. It only hurts more. Is he trying to break me? See if he can make me cry? I refuse. "It was just sex. It meant nothing."

He chuckled. "Liar."

She glanced down his body. He really had a great one. Plenty of women went to bed with guys for their looks, just to have casual sex. "You're muscular and really hot. You look like a regular guy. That's all. I forgot what you are."

"Another lie. You rode on my back after I shifted. That's not something you'd forget, even in passion. Yet you still got naked for me and accepted me inside your body." He lifted his upper body all the way up but didn't let go of her ass, holding her in place with his hips firmly pressed between her thighs. He placed his free hand on her stomach. "My sperm could be breaching one of your eggs and implanting my child inside you right now. We should mate."

Pregnant? Glen balked at the concept. Memories of something a friend went through a few years ago surfaced. May had gotten knocked up

191

by her boyfriend, they'd gotten married, and it had turned into a nightmare. John had pretended to be happy at first about the baby. Later, he'd resented the hell out of being tied down by a wife and kid. He'd slept around with countless women, taunting May with his affairs. They'd eventually divorced but she'd watched May's life spiral into pure hell. That would never be her.

She bucked her hips and grabbed at the bedding, trying to get out from under him. Veso let her go and she separated their bodies. She sat up and scooted away on the bed. "No. It was one time. I'm sure I'm not ovulating. I had a period recently."

"When?"

"I don't know!" She snagged the covers, jerking them up to her chest to cover her body.

"Lower your voice."

She'd forgotten about the danger outside, solely focused on the one indoors with her. "I lost track of time while I was being held but life couldn't be that messed up."

He stood, totally naked as he kicked off the boxers around his ankles. "So you refuse to become my mate?"

She stared into his eyes and saw anger there. "A minute ago you were debating about if you wanted me for a mate or not. Now you're asking me? What made you decide? Is it because the lowly human didn't beg you to mate? Is that what you were expecting? Get over yourself."

He turned away, showing off his muscled ass. He had a great one. She also spotted some red scratches on his upper back, realizing she must have put them there during sex. They weren't bleeding at least.

"Get some rest, Glenda. I'll be downstairs." His voice came out harsh; it was clear that she'd made him mad.

He strode over to the ladder, avoided looking at her, and climbed to the lower floor.

Glen lay down, curled into a ball, and hugged the blankets she gripped even tighter. He was angry but she felt torn up inside.

What if he was right and he'd gotten her pregnant? She'd been an idiot to say yes to a quickie with him. He was just so hot and she'd wanted him. The consequences hadn't even entered her mind.

It was his fault for licking her thighs and brushing his nose against her clit while doing it. He had turned her on and made her ache. He'd been the one to insist her thighs needed healing.

She closed her eyes and tried to focus on something else. Everything would seem better in the morning. So far no one had attacked the cabin. They might survive through the night again without being found.

She pushed away any thought of Veso and focused on her breathing. In and out.

* * * * *

Veso woke with kinks in his neck from sleeping on the too small couch. He'd dragged a chair over to the end of it and shoved a pillow on the seat to accommodate his longer legs. He stood and stretched, staring at the tiny cracks along the sides of the closest covered window. Hints of light showed through. Morning had come.

He used the bathroom and then climbed the ladder as quietly as possible. Glenda slept in the center of the bed. She lay buried in covers but one foot and hand stuck out, besides part of her face. He carefully covered her limbs to keep her warm and walked to the edge of the loft, jumping down. The human in the closet made a noise and he listened, hearing light snoring.

He walked to the front door and unbarred it, peering outside. No movement caught his eye and he inhaled, not scenting Vampire. They must have completely avoided the cabin during the night. He closed the door, barred it again, and walked over to the cell phone. It was time to call his clan. He dreaded it but he couldn't avoid it any longer. His father had to be worried. His friends were probably out searching for him. He also needed help getting Glenda back to his territory before nightfall. The Vamps wouldn't dare go after her there, now that they'd already invaded once. The clan would be on high alert.

Glenda had rejected his offer to mate her. He'd messed up by sharing his thoughts of the pros and cons of mating with her and she'd thrown them in his face. Her words replayed in head. A minute ago you were debating about if you wanted me for a mate or not. Now you're asking me? What made you decide? Is it because the lowly human didn't beg you to mate? Is that what you were expecting? Get over yourself.

He ground his teeth together and tried to cool down. He was a VampLycan. She should be flattered that he wanted her. He had so much to offer. Then again, maybe he didn't. His future with the clan would be uncertain with a human mate, as would any chance of others taking them in. She'd be in constant danger from Vampire nests and Lycan packs if they had to live in her world. He'd fight them all off but he'd be doing it alone with no backup.

"Damn." He ran his fingers through his hair and turned on the phone.

194

A few text messages waited. He read them. The human should have checked in already, begun searching for them, and the so-called king had sent threats to the human under his thrall. It was a reminder that the master would kill innocents if Veso didn't break them free and reprogram their minds, then send them somewhere safe by nightfall.

He called information, asking for the number for the lodge, then requesting it be connected. It rang four times before a familiar voice answered.

"It is good to hear your voice, Davis."

"Who is this?"

"It's Veso."

"We thought you were dead!" Excitement sounded in the VampLycan's voice. "Those damn Vampires said they killed you."

"You captured some?"

"They spoke to Kira. She's alive but the bastards attacked her too. She was bad off but she's better now. Where are you?"

"I'm not entirely sure. We made it to a cabin but I'm estimating I'm still about forty miles from home. I need you to send help. I'm being tracked by human thralls with tranquilizer darts during the day and soldier and Vamps at night. Can you trace the call?"

Silence greeted him.

"Davis?"

The VampLycan didn't answer him and he glanced at the phone. It had dropped the signal. "Damn it!" He tried calling back but it couldn't connect. He walked around, lifting the phone, searching for a stronger signal but it wasn't showing anything.

"Goddamn it," he yelled.

"What's wrong?"

Glenda's voice drew his attention toward the loft. She clutched a blanket around her body, bare shoulders revealed and her hair messy from sleep. "The signal went down."

"Why?"

"It happens sometimes if there's a storm but it was dry outside. The master must have become worried we'd captured a human since the one in the closet didn't check in a few hours ago. There were texts on his phone. That damn suckhead probably sent other humans to do something to the tower to take out cell coverage in this area."

"I thought you were going to have that guy we captured check in. We discussed this."

"I overslept!" He threw the phone. It smashed into the fireplace. "They will be coming for us. Get dressed."

"You broke another phone? What's wrong with you? Maybe we could have gotten a signal outside! Maybe it was just down for a minute or so."

"Stop wasting time arguing with me, damn it. I refuse to be drugged again. We're out of here." He stomped into the kitchen, yanking open cupboards to grab supplies.

"Crazy VampLycan," she huffed from above. "You have anger issues."

"Get dressed. We leave in five minutes."

"I am."

It had been a mistake to throw the phone but he'd needed something to take his frustration out on. Glenda was his mate. He was certain of that now. They'd shared blood when they'd kissed and he'd known.

A human wasn't supposed to be his mate, nor had he ever wanted to bind his life with any woman. Even as they fucked, he'd tried to use logic to talk himself out of claiming her. The timing was shit. His clan wouldn't accept her. They were being hunted. Then Glenda had rejected him when he'd finally settled down, ready to accept that logic didn't matter in the face of instinct.

She is my mate. She's in danger. I need to get her safe and then I'll convince her we'll be together forever. Focus on that.

He emptied the backpack the human had used, repacked it with food bars, snacks, and bottled water. He rose up and strode to the closet, jerking it open. He grabbed the man and hauled him out.

"Look at me."

The stranger's eyes snapped open.

Veso glared at him, allowing his power to flow. "King Charles has lied to you. He's evil. He'll kill you and your friends. Do you understand?"

The man paled, fear showing in every line of his face.

"You're going to go find the man and pregnant woman you told me about. Shoot the man with a dart so you can easily control the woman with care and put them on their boat. Get them the hell out of here before dark. Do you understand? Tie them up. You need to keep them safe because they won't and can't believe King Charles is evil. He'll kill you all. Keep them away for a few days. Find a safe place to hide at night. Do you understand?"

"Yes."

197

"I'm going to let you go. Stand still until I hand you the dart gun. Then you leave here and go find them, take them with you, and stay away for at least three days. You need to get as far away as you can. Understood?"

"Yes."

Veso helped the human to his feet, set him free of the restraints, then lifted the dart gun and opened the case with the darts. He removed some of the fluid inside them, not certain if the current amounts wouldn't kill a human. Small doses shouldn't harm one. He loaded the gun and handed it over to the human, along with the case.

"Run!"

The man spun, almost slammed into a wall, then got the bars off the door. He bolted once he was free, heading toward the river. Veso closed the door and decided he didn't have time to tiptoe around Glenda with his abilities. He leapt up to the loft, avoiding the ladder.

She gasped, almost falling on her ass when he landed. "Shit!"

He wanted to howl in frustration. He'd scared her—again. That was no way to convince her to be his mate. She knew he was a VampLycan but it was possible she needed more time to get used to their differences before she'd agree to drink his blood.

He'd planned to shift, have her ride his back again, but he changed his mind. He could protect her on two legs just as good as on four. They'd move slower but it was important they talk.

"You know I'm not like you," he gently reminded her. He stepped around her and dug out clothing he thought might fit him then changed. "We're leaving. Find a spare set of clothes in case we have to swim again."

He did the same for himself, fisting the extra shirt and sweats then climbing down the loft.

He located a large bag, shoved the clothing inside, and held out his hand as Glenda came down the ladder. She'd put on a man's shirt. The cargo pants she wore were baggy but she'd used a shoelace to bind the belt loops together in the front, forming an odd belt. The slippers she wore impressed him. She'd wrapped more laces around her ankles to make them stay on her feet. They'd protect her from injury better than layers of socks.

"Good job."

"Thanks." She smiled. "I'm still wearing two layers of socks but these have soles on the bottom."

"Give me the extra clothes. I'm sealing them up in case the bag gets wet."

She didn't hesitate. "You think they're coming after us right now? They'll try to shoot you with a sedative, right?"

"Yes." He closed the backpack and put it on, then lifted the shotgun. The shells for it went into the pockets of the sweats. "Stay on my ass and be quiet."

"Aren't you going to try on shoes? There's a bunch of them up in the loft. I know none of the ones in the last cabin fit you but these ones look larger." She glanced down at his bare feet.

"I don't need them."

She opened her mouth, probably to argue. He turned away fast. They needed to go.

He unbarred the door and opened it, inhaling. The only humans he scented was the one he'd sent away and Glenda. He stepped out, his gaze roaming the woods. No movement or odd sounds alerted him to intruders. The birds sang.

"What is it?" Glenda pressed up against his back, resting her hand just above his ass.

"Shush."

He continued to listen, his gaze constantly roaming, before determining it was safe. "Let's go." He took off slow for her, at a light jog.

She shut the door behind her but followed close. They made it out of the clearing and into the thicker spread of trees. Veso relaxed. An attack would have happened as they left the cabin if the master's human thralls had caught up to them.

He picked up the pace, heading in the direction of home. There was no way Glenda would make it forty miles in a day but now his people would be looking for them. He hoped they'd be found by his clan soon.

Chapter Thirteen

Glen fisted Veso's shirt and thankfully, he stopped. She panted, wanting to just drop to her knees. "I need to rest."

"Damn it." He took off the backpack and turned to face her.

"As you love to point out, I'm merely human."

"Sit."

She took a seat on the grass in the shade but it wasn't graceful by any means. Veso crouched next to her and opened the pack, handing her a bottled water. She remembered to sip it. Puking would only make her feel worse. Her sides hurt, the muscles from her ass to her ankles wanted to go on strike, and she was willing to believe once she removed the slipper booties she'd stolen from the cabin, her feet would be bloody stumps.

"We're not moving fast enough."

She studied him as she took another sip of water. "We've been running and power walking for at least two hours straight."

"You had to pee and demanded a water break."

"Sorry. Again, human here. I'm not super-scary dude with extras."

He stopped peering around and held her gaze. "Is that how you see me?"

"It wasn't meant as an insult. Really. I'm bitchy, Veso. Tired. Sweaty. Grumpy. I could go on but I won't."

"Do you want me to carry you for a while? You could wear the backpack and I could piggyback you."

It was tempting but she shook her head. He might look as if the pace wasn't wearing him down but she noticed the way his body remained tensed, his gaze constantly roaming. He also sniffed a lot. He expected them to be attacked at any second, and had since they'd left the cabin. Having her on his back might distract him. She didn't want to have to fight for her life. It was bad enough running for it.

"I'm good. Just give me a few minutes."

He pulled out a granola bar and handed it to her. "Eat."

She was grateful that he was thinking about her needs. She took a bite of the dry bar and chewed. It helped her hunger. She finished it and handed him the wrapper. He stashed it inside the backpack, offered her another drink of water, and stood.

"I know," she muttered, trying to gain the strength to get up to her feet. "Time to go."

He held out his hand and pulled her up. "We'll walk for a while but we must keep on the move."

"Thanks."

He gave a nod and took off, walking through the woods. She followed, limping behind. He glanced back and she tried to hide her soreness, forcing a smile. He went back to watching the woods around them, doing his sniffing routine.

She was slowing him down. He could shift and run. It was tempting to ask him to do that again but she didn't. While her clothes were dry this time, it didn't mean she wouldn't get thigh burns again from riding him. The last thing they needed was a repeat of the night before. He'd want to heal her with his hot tongue and she'd end up getting fucked. Literally.

Her body instantly responded to the memory. Veso had an amazing body and he knew what to do with it. He'd gotten her off in record time. A spasm gripped her belly, an ache between her thighs just imagining him inside her again. He had a great cock. It had been super hard, thick, and wonderful.

He stopped in front of her so fast she slammed into his back.

He turned his head, staring down at her with narrowed eyes. His nostrils flared and a smile curved his lips. "I do have a nice ass."

Could he smell her thinking about sex between them? It was possible. He had a nose that could pick up almost anything. "I don't know what you're talking about."

"You're getting wet."

She purposely glanced up at the sky, then back at him. "It's not raining. I thought we were in a hurry. You know, we have to keep moving, right?"

He faced forward and started walking again. "I'm going to bend you over in front of me when we're safe and fuck you."

"That's not exactly motivating me to follow you," she lied.

He snorted. "I'm going to have to teach you a lesson later. Lying to me isn't acceptable. You smell like you want to be fucked."

"Maybe it's wishful thinking on your part. All I want is to lay down for a good hour and get off my feet."

He shook his head. "You're distracting yourself by thinking about sex. I understand. I do it when my body is tired too."

Jealousy reared its ugly head. She wondered who he fantasized about. She hadn't asked him too much about his dating life. He didn't have a mate. That's all she really knew as far as the women in his life went.

"Veso?"

"What?" He kept walking.

"Um, are you seeing someone?"

He halted fast again and turned. "No. The woods are clear."

"I meant, like a girlfriend."

"I wouldn't have fucked you if I was committed to someone else. Mated VampLycans don't cheat." He turned away. "Keep moving."

"I didn't ask if you had a mate. I already knew you didn't. I want to know if there's some woman you're sleeping with." She hurried her pace since he walked faster.

"No."

"Who do you fantasize about then?"

He growled low and twisted around once more. "What?"

"Who do you think about having sex with? Are you in love with someone?"

His eyes narrowed.

She lowered hers and felt heat creep up into her cheeks. It wasn't the most comfortable conversation to have since she wouldn't exactly consider them a couple. The subject had come up though, and she really wanted to know more about Veso. He had asked her to be his mate. She had a right to ask about his personal life.

He gripped her chin and stepped closer. "This is not the time to have this discussion. We'll do it when you're safe."

He had a point but she felt as if he would probably avoid her questions later. "Is there someone in your life that you have feelings for?"

"No. I only fucked women when my body had a need I could no longer ignore and they offered. I don't take lovers. I fucked them once but never a second time. I'm also careful to never let them have my sperm."

He might not be saying it but she would never forget what he'd told her about his mother. It all made sense. Of course he'd have trust issues with women. His mother had tricked his father into getting her pregnant.

"We didn't use a condom."

"You're going to be my mate."

"I didn't agree to that."

"Keep moving, Glenda. We'll discuss this later."

She sealed her lips as he began walking again and stared at his ass. He did have a great one. It was firm, rounded, and muscular...

She just needed to keep moving. More questions filled her head that she wanted to ask. What kind of home did he have? How many other VampLycans lived with him? Did they share one big home or all have their own? Would his father have a cow over Glen being human, possibly try to kill her or something drastic?

She opened her mouth, ready to launch into another set of questions—they distracted her from her aching muscles—but Veso suddenly stopped and crouched.

She tried to do the same as gracefully as him but ended up on her hands and knees. She peered around but didn't see anything but a ton of trees.

Veso turned his head and held a finger to his lips, then motioned her to go flat. She clenched her teeth and did it, hating that she was pressed against the dirty ground. It would stick to the sweat on her but she didn't want to be shot with a dart—or worse, to have Veso shot with one.

He shrugged off the backpack and laid it down, held up his hand to tell her to stay, then crawled on his hands and knees toward some bushes.

Shit. She didn't like him leaving her there alone but she trusted him with her life.

She lay still and quiet, hoping someone wouldn't stumble upon her once Veso had gone out of sight.

Veso reached the top of a steep slope. The voices he'd heard were louder from there. He used the brush to conceal his body, peering over the edge to the creek below. Three humans were gathered on the other side of it, all wearing lightweight backpacks, and one held a dart gun.

"We have to find them," the smallest of the three stated. "King Charles is counting on us."

"I know. They probably stayed by the river. I would. It'll lead them to other cabins. I'd be looking for a phone that works, food, and weapons." The bearded man with lots of hair rubbed his jaw with one hand. "I can't think of anyone who has a land line in this area, can you, Curly?"

The third man shook his head. "Nope. We were lucky they added that tower two years ago so we could get any kind of shit reception out here. Roger paid for it himself. He'll be patrolling the river with his boat by now, looking for them. Maybe the guy'll see him and wave him down, thinking he'll help 'im."

"Maybe." The bearded man adjusted his backpack next, his body language antsy with his constant movement. "King Charles felt they'd head

206

in this direction. We've got to keep looking. The woman was kidnapped by this son of a bitch."

Veso frowned. That was the story the Vampire master had gone with? It fit though. He'd want to prey on the humans' fears to gain a sympathetic bond if they felt resistant in the least to follow his orders. Some humans could begin to think beyond the mind rape if they were away from the Vampire controlling them for a few days. A deep-seated suggestion, like they were actually trying to save a victim, might keep them following his orders longer.

"One thing's for sure," the shortest one snapped, "us standing around like this isn't finding them. Roger and his crew can handle the river. We'll spread out and keep searching over here." He reached down and touched a gun strapped to his thigh. "Shoot him with bullets in the legs if you have to. Just don't kill him. King Charles wants him alive. I don't blame him. I'd want to personally kill someone who stole my woman."

"Agreed," Curly grunted. "Just remember. This asshole is on drugs and is going to be hard to take down. Keep your weapons ready and out. He's supposed to be some skilled hunter too so watch your backs."

They broke apart and Veso backtracked to Glenda. She remained exactly where he'd left her. He hated to see the fear in her eyes. He lay down next to her, whispering, "Three of them are just ahead."

"Do they have those dart guns?"

He nodded. "Yes. They are also prepared to shoot me with bullets to cripple me."

She reached out and placed her hand on his arm, looking alarmed.

"We won't let that happen. Keep quiet and low. Follow me." He snagged the backpack but didn't put it on his back. He crawled, leading her to where he'd just been. He felt pride when he glanced back. She hadn't argued with him and did as he'd ordered. It also looked cute as hell as she belly-crawled, her ass going up in the air every time she lifted a leg to inch her lower half along the ground.

He paused where he'd watched the men and searched for signs of them. He spotted them right away. The bearded man kept by the creek but the other two had spread out, going into the woods. It meant they would only have to get past two of them. More could be out there but the area wasn't exactly high on human population. It was too remote.

King Charles might possibly have up to fifty humans total under his control. More if there were any logging camps. Veso hadn't left VampLycan territory in a while so he wasn't certain what was going on with the surrounding areas anymore. One thing was certain though, the master had set up his base and been in the area for a significant time before he'd gone after a VampLycan. He'd known the locations of all the humans.

It infuriated him. Decker had kept the clan so busy with his bullshit that Vampires had gotten within a hundred miles of their territory and set up a nest. It was just another reason to hate his clan leader.

Glenda touched his leg, her small hand lightly resting on his calf. He turned his head, peering at her.

She arched her eyebrows.

He motioned her to stay quiet and not move as he turned his head back toward the creek, watching the progress of the humans. They were moving away but were still within sight. At least she'd get some rest while they waited to move on. He once again hoped his people would find them soon.

Another thought struck, a grim one. What if Decker had already returned to the clan? It was possible no one would be sent to search for him. Nabby had been in charge when he'd been kidnapped, and that asshole also wouldn't lift a finger to help him.

But Davis would tell Bran, his father, about that call, even if Decker or Nabby ordered him not to. He could depend on three of his close friends too. Lavos, Garson, and Kar would search for him. They had formed a bond over hating the way the clan was run. All of them had been trapped by at least one parent swearing their allegiance to the clan from birth.

He glanced back to check on Glenda. Her hand remained on his leg. She'd used her other arm to tuck under her face and seemed to be using it for a pillow. Her eyes were now closed. He sniffed the air, not picking up anything that alarmed him. They'd wait it out there for a bit, she'd get a rest, then it was time to keep going. He'd get her to safety even if his friends couldn't find them. She was his mate.

The knowledge no longer irritated or angered him. A bond might have been started because of the blood share forced on them inside that mine, but an emotional one had formed since. He couldn't imagine just letting her return to her human world and never seeing her again. They'd face a lot of obstacles. One of them being her refusal to become his mate.

He smiled. That was one challenge he'd look forward to. He'd seduce her until he broke her stubbornness.

Memories of the night before struck and his dick hardened. He should have taken it slower with her but he'd waited too long to know what it felt like to have her under him, to be inside her. Once he got her home, things would be different. He'd teach her no human could compare to him. Even if he had to keep her in his bed for weeks until she agreed to become his mate.

To get Glenda to agree to mate him would be easy compared to taking over the clan and ridding it of all the rot.

He and his friends had talked about taking out Decker and making Lavos clan leader. His friend wouldn't have a problem with him taking a human mate. Kar and Garson would accept her too. They liked all females, regardless of their race. His father, Bran, might not be thrilled to see him bonded with a human, but he had faith his father would help him protect Glenda. He'd done much worse for Veso, like leaving his own clan to join one he hated to raise his son.

It would work out. It had to. One problem at a time.

Chapter Fourteen

Glen lifted her head and peered into Veso's eyes. He was watching her with a frown. He tended to be grumpier than her, even when she was exhausted and feeling like crap.

"They're out of sight. We need to get moving again. That's all the rest you can have right now. I'm sorry," he whispered. "Stay low, do not talk, and be prepared to drop flat if I motion you to."

"Okay."

She pushed up to her hands and knees, getting to her feet. Veso did too, not wasting time brushing off his clothes. He just put on the backpack and took off down the incline. She scrambled after him, struggling with her tired body and attempting not to fall on her face. They reached the creek and Veso scooped her into his arms. She didn't protest as he sloshed through the water and eased her back onto her dry feet on the other side. He let her go and continued on.

"Thanks. That was very gentlemanly. I appreciate it."

He didn't glance back. "You're my mate. I can't have you getting sick. Keep moving, Glenda. Less talking and faster walking."

She stumbled, surprised at his continued insistence. But she wasn't buying it. He hated humans too much to really want her. She was sure this was just his ego talking. "I'm not going to become your mate just because you say I am."

He spun and grabbed her so fast that she gasped, staring up at him. His hands on her hips didn't hurt but he had a good hold on her. "Let's get to safety first, then we can fight."

"Sorry." He was right. There were three men with dart guns looking for them.

He let her go, sniffed the air, and made his way through the trees again. She hurried to keep up. He had a wide stride and she almost had to jog to keep up with him.

Her mind was still stuck on him saying she was his mate. She couldn't be. Their lives were totally different. He turned into something with four legs and fur. He was also a bit of a bully and disliked her entire race. That trust issue of his with women would become a problem too. The sex was great, at least that one time, but he'd probably be impossible to live with.

Her mind brought up a host of other problems they'd face as a couple. She couldn't see Veso handling her sixty-hour workweeks well. He seemed the type to be demanding. Her job wasn't the greatest but she'd worked hard to land that manager position. It had been in the bag until she'd been kidnapped. They'd probably fired her for not showing up anyway.

Veso was probably just messing with her head about the mate thing. Anger was great motivation to survive. It also kept her distracted from thinking about being returned to that mine and becoming a breeding machine for a monster. She'd never hear anyone talk about their family history again without grimacing. Her ancestor was a maniac and mental— and also very much undead. She wished he was buried deep in some graveyard.

They reached a clearing and Veso stopped. She did too, staring up at mountains the trees had hidden. She gazed at Veso. He was grinning, looking super happy.

"You know where we are?"

"Yes. We're going over that and we'll hit VampLycan territory. We're closer than I thought."

She twisted her head again, gaping at the mountains. They were tall. Not ginormous, but the idea of climbing a few thousand feet didn't exactly excite her. "It looks kind of steep."

"We're not going around them. Don't even suggest it."

"You know we don't have rope this time, don't you?"

"We won't need it. There are a lot of trees."

"So?"

"The humans will want to avoid that."

"You're right. I want to avoid it too."

He scowled.

She turned away and spotted something glinting in the sun. "What's that?" She pointed.

Veso stepped closer, following the line of her finger. "Unbelievable."

"What is it? Should we duck? Is it those men?"

"It's a dirt bike. One of them must have driven it into this area to get here from wherever he lives."

She squinted. "You must have super eyes. All I'm seeing is a bunch of green and a tiny shiny spot."

Veso gripped her hand. "You may get your wish not to climb if it has fuel and it's not a trap. He did park it in a hidden spot. From this vantage point, just that tiny bit of it is visible to your eye. But the sun has warmed the metal so I can see it through the bushes."

"Trap?" She didn't like that idea at all but Veso tugged hard, making her follow him or trip. She kept up. He sniffed a lot again, doing his thing and glancing around. "You can see through bushes? Is that what you said?"

"I'm part Vampire, Glenda. Metal gets hot in the sun and appears near glowing to me."

She remembered then that he'd told her Vampires had the freaky ability to see heat at night. It's why they'd never traveled at night and he'd dug that hole for them to sleep in. She really hoped he was right. A dirt bike meant wheels.

"What if the person didn't leave keys?"

He snorted, continuing forward.

"What does that mean?"

"Old dirt bikes don't have keys, Glenda. Be quiet."

She sealed her lips and hurried to keep up with him. He was walking even faster, focused on the clump of bushes. As they got closer she could spot more of the bike. It was hidden behind bushes between two trees. He let go of her arm and put his finger to his lips, then motioned her to stay put. He advanced with caution, then stepped behind the bushes.

She glanced around, her heart pounding. What if whoever had left that dirt bike was lurking? She glanced at the ground and found a stick. It beat not having anything to hit someone with if they were attacked.

"Get over here," Veso whispered just loud enough for her to hear.

He was straddling the seat, the backpack on the ground. One foot braced his weight and the other was bent up a bit. He studied the woods around them again.

"What are you doing?"

"Looking for the best path to leave this area. I don't want to go the way the driver came. Wear the backpack for me. There's not much gas but it might be enough to get us home. Climb on behind me once I start it. Don't waste time. Sound will carry."

She bent, put on the backpack, and eyed the scant amount of seat left for her with dread. Veso wasn't exactly a small guy and that seat wasn't built for two people to begin with, in her estimation. It did have a guard over the back tire and an exhaust pipe. It would be just her luck if the plastic broke and she hit that tire.

"Great. Just great," she muttered.

"Hold on tight. This is going to be rough. Ready?"

He did something with his hands on the bars, then shoved his raised foot down. The engine tried to catch but didn't. He lifted his leg, then kicked again.

That time the engine started. It was incredibly loud in the quiet woods.

She moved fast, near panicked with the thought of those men with darts rushing toward them. She threw her leg over, hugging Veso in a death grip.

He slowly took off and the ass end slid a bit in the dirt.

She realized there were no foot pegs and held her feet out, terrified.

"Wrap them around me," Veso yelled, picking up speed.

He was nuts. Then again, when he took a turn to avoid a rock, her foot hit dirt. It was just a tap but she lifted both legs, trying to hook them around his waist. He was too big to really see around and what she could glimpse, only made her regret trying. He weaved through trees, rocks, and brush at a dangerous pace.

215

The dirt bike vibrated hard under her ass, her tailbone taking a beating when they bounced around on the rock-strewn ground as he picked up even more speed.

"We're going to die," she muttered. "Correction, I'm going to die. Shit."

Veso grinned. It had been a lot of years since he'd been on a dirt bike but he remembered how to handle one. He was careful not to accelerate too fast again anytime he had to slow. He didn't want to accidentally pop a wheelie. He stopped when he came to a creek, searching for the best way to cross it. It didn't appear deep. He could see the stones in the water.

He reached down and adjusted Glenda's feet so she didn't hurt him with her heels. "Hold on tight."

"Don't tell me. My eyes are closed and I'm pretending this is a ride at an amusement park."

"It's just a shallow creek. We're going to get a little wet."

"At least it's not a mountain."

He chuckled and took off slow, steering down a small embankment toward the narrowest section of water.

Movement caught his eye to the left and he saw a human running their way. He was far off but gaining ground. It was one of the men he'd seen earlier. He snarled, accelerating more. They hit the water and Glenda gasped but she clung tight to him. The back wheel spun a bit on the other side but they got clear. He turned the wheel, picking up speed.

Something sailed past out of the corner of his eye. It was a dart. The bastard was firing at them. The human could hit Glenda on the back of the

216

dirt bike. It would probably kill her if they used enough drugs to put a VampLycan down. He saw a large rock and drove toward it. He stopped hard once they were on the other side of it, leaving the engine running.

"Let go and stay here."

He tried to stand but Glenda was still wrapped around him tight. He cursed, adjusting her feet until she straddled the seat.

"Brace your legs," he said. "Hold the bike up." He climbed off, keeping it upright with his grip.

"I can't drive one of these."

"Just hold it up. Grip the handle bars but nothing else." He figured those instructions were clear enough. She did as asked.

He stepped back, leapt up onto the boulder, and peered over the top. The human was running, following the tracks from the tires. It took a few minutes for him to get within range.

Veso lunged at the running bastard. The man never even saw him until they impacted together, hitting the ground with the human under him.

Rage gripped Veso and he punched the human in the face hard. Bones broke. He didn't give a damn anymore if the human was under a Vamp's control. The stupid bastard had fired at Glenda. He'd bet his life that the master had told the idiot not to do that, knowing a full dose of drugs would likely kill her.

The human stopped moving but he still breathed. Veso leaned forward, grabbed the dart gun, and climbed to his feet. He was tempted to shoot one of those darts into the unconscious jerk. He spun away instead and pitched it out of sight.

He rounded the boulder and returned to Glenda. She looked terrified.

"It's fine." He gripped the dirt bike. "Get off so I can drive. I took care of the problem."

"You killed him?"

He shook his head as she climbed off and he threw a leg over, taking his seat. Glenda climbed on again, this time lifting her feet and wrapping her limbs around him without having to be told. He worried about her feet hitting the wheel, or worse. There was a lot of vegetation she could slam into. It wasn't very comfortable with her heels against his lap but he'd rather risk his nuts hurting than her breaking bones or losing toes.

He skirted the mountain, going around it after all. He had to slow when he found where a rainstorm had caused a landslide. The ground had long since dried but a lot of rocks had come down. Every mile they drove, though, was one they wouldn't have to walk, and each one took them closer to VampLycan territory.

They made it around the damaged section and he sped up, the grass slippery with the extra weight on the back of the dirt bike, but he recognized more landmarks. Part of his job was learning the outer territory around his clan. There was an old logging road somewhere ahead. He kept going in the direction of home and finally came across it. He headed north. It was more of a dirt trail now from years of not being maintained, but he spotted recent tire tracks as he followed it. It was probably how they'd driven him away from home.

He stopped the dirt bike, studying some of the deeper tire grooves. It hadn't rained recently; those had to have been made when the road was heavy with mud. It meant someone had been using it weeks before, when the last storm had hit. Another heavy rainstorm would have muddied the road again and erased them better.

"Damn. How long have those bastards been in this area?"

"What?" Glenda hugged him tighter.

"Nothing."

He took off slow again to avoid jarring her too much, then picked up speed, alert for an attack. It would be better to leave the logging road but he worried about Glenda. The terrain was pretty coarse and her safety came first. They wouldn't have expected him to steal a dirt bike though. It was possible they hadn't bothered to set a trap up ahead.

A few miles later, the engine sputtered and died. Veso cursed, using his bare feet to slow the coasting down to a stop. They were close to VampLycan fences. He looked up at the sky. It would be dark in a couple of hours. They might make it.

Glenda relaxed her hold on him. "Why did you stop?"

"We ran out of gas."

"Shit."

"Climb off."

She made cute little sounds as she did, groaning and then rubbing her ass with both hands. He got the urge to do it for her but resisted. He'd want to fuck her if he put his hands on her to massage out her aches and pains.

He pushed the dirt bike off the road and laid it down out of sight, then returned to her. "Give me the backpack."

She took it off. "My pleasure. I think the straps left permanent indents in my shoulders."

"We're almost home, Glenda."

That didn't seem to comfort her when she frowned, her gaze locked with his. He reached for her and touched her cheek, stepping closer. She didn't say anything though. It bothered him.

"What is it?"

"What happens when we get there? It means there's a lot of people like you, right? In other words, they probably hate humans as much as you do."

"I would never allow anyone to harm you, Glenda. I've told you this."

"Can you blame me for being nervous and leery?"

"You're smart. You fashioned a tool with your bra. You got me free despite being weak and not having claws. You've faced so much already. This will be the easy part."

"I love how you can compliment yet insult me at the same time. Nice skill there." Humor laced her voice. "You're such a dick. I also think you're full of shit, and nobody like you is going to be happy I've been your sidekick on this misadventure from hell."

He chuckled. "There's a tall fence we must climb. Dwell on that."

"Great. Fantastic. Is it barbed wire?"

She did amuse him. "No."

"There's a bright side. I won't be heavily bleeding when I meet other half-Vampire people so hopefully they won't want to eat me."

"I'm the only one who gets to do that."

Her eye widened.

He let her go and backed up, removing another bottle of water from the backpack. He let her drink first, then he finished it off. "Let's get moving. The boundary fences are ahead but we're still in for a walk before we reach home."

Chapter Fifteen

Veso suddenly stopped and Glen slammed into his back. It was irritating how often he did that and how she could never stop fast enough. She didn't have his super-fast reflexes.

"What is it now?" she whispered so he didn't grumble at her. That lesson had been learned. "The wind? Did an animal fart? You've stopped fifty times in the past hour at least."

"Shush." He cocked his head. "Someone comes."

He reached back and gave her a not so gentle shove toward a tree. She didn't need to be prompted again. She hid behind the thick trunk, immediately wondering where Veso had gone when he didn't follow. She looked around and her mouth parted in surprise. He was above her in the branches. How he'd gotten up there so fast was a mystery. She plastered herself to the rough bark and stared up at him.

He suddenly jumped and she muffled a gasp. It had to have been a fifteen-foot fall.

A snarl sounded from the other side of the tree, and then she heard a man's deep voice.

"Goddamn! You scared the shit out of me, Veso!"

"Lavos! It's so good to see you."

Glenda peaked from behind the tree. Veso and another man were hugging. That wasn't something she'd ever expected to witness. The new guy was tall, muscled, and attractive looking. They parted, Veso's back to her, and she couldn't miss the big grin on the stranger's face as he spoke.

"I thought you were dead. Don't ever do that to me again."

"I shouldn't have been taken in the first place. The fucking Vamps didn't fight fair. They buried themselves near our fence, waited until the sun went down, and then attacked. Those bastards drugged me."

"And apparently cut your hair."

Veso made a scary sound. "Don't remind me, Lavos."

"I'd be pissed too. Where were they holding you?"

"Inside a mine. We need to go back there and kill those suckheads. The master set up a nest and he has soldiers. They've been hunting us since we escaped."

Lavos slid his gaze to Glen, openly staring at her. "Want to introduce me to your friend?"

Veso turned his head. "Come here, Glenda. This is Lavos. He's a VampLycan too."

She slowly stepped around the tree. "It's just Glen. Nice to meet you, Lavos."

He sniffed, then gawked at Veso. "What is going on?"

"She's a descendant of the master who kidnapped me. The crazy bastard kidnapped her from her home, and then grabbed me to force me to breed with the human, so she could birth a girl. He wanted to make my daughter his lover one day."

Lavos's eyebrows shot up.

"My vampy relative actually considers himself a king, and he said he wants me to birth him his queen," Glen muttered. "Delusions of grandeur, if you ask me. He's bat-shit crazy."

223

"I agree." Veso nodded. "It was beyond insulting that he took me to breed."

That angered Glen. "I'm standing right here. I get it. You don't like humans." She shot a dirty look at Lavos. "And yes, he told me you're half Vampire-slash-half Lycan. I also rode his back when he had four legs." She stormed up to Veso's side and smacked his arm. "You seduced me, so cut the 'humans suck' attitude! I was obviously good enough for you to nail. It's getting old."

His eyes narrowed as they locked on her.

"You could have at least pretended that hurt."

He glanced down at his arm where she'd hit him, and then shook his head. "It was insulting that the master believed I'd give him my daughter. I wasn't talking about you."

"I still don't know what's going on but this is amusing as hell."

Glen and Veso both looked at Lavos's grinning face.

Veso spoke first. "Has Decker returned?"

Lavos's expression sobered. "No. He's never coming back. It's a long story. Shit hit the fan after you were taken."

"What happened?"

"Long story short?" Lavos sighed. "The Vampires not only attacked you, but Kira as well. One of the bastards turned her. My brother found her while she was transforming and took her to his den so the clan didn't kill her. Longer story even shorter, he fed her his blood. She's now growing claws and okay with the sunlight. His VampLycan blood seemed to activate the dormant genetics she inherited from Davis. My brother had to take over the clan in order to keep Kira safe. He's our new leader."

224

Glen lifted her gaze to Veso's face in an attempt to judge if that was a good thing or not.

Veso appeared stunned. "Lorn took the clan?"

"He had help, and the support of the other clans. Me, your father, Kar, Davis, and Garson are helping him hold it right now." Lavos kept his attention on Veso. "Lord Aveoth is hunting Decker. He's dead if he attempts to come back. Don't be surprised when you spot our neighbors flying overhead in the dark. They're patrolling with Lorn's permission, in case Decker attempts a sneak attack to take back our clan. We also think he's the one responsible for those Vamps invading our territory."

"What the hell?" Veso reached up and rubbed the back of his neck.

"Decker sent the Vampire Council after his granddaughter, Batina—who's mated with Velder's second son, Kraven—while they were in California. The fucker is working with the Vamps. We found that out recently, after Lorn talked to the other clans since the night we were attacked. We knew Decker was vindictive."

"Fuck," Veso growled. "The insane bastard."

"Always the asshole. That's Decker." Lavos lowered his gaze, staring at Glen. "So what's the story with you?"

"I just want to go home, move out of my apartment to somewhere Vampire safe, and put all this behind me," she admitted.

"You're not going anywhere. You belong at my side, where you are safe. Don't forget the master won't stop trying to recapture you until I kill him."

She pressed her lips together, regarding Veso. He was right so she couldn't argue about her crazy relative.

225

Veso stared at Lavos. "She's my mate. Or will be soon. I know she won't be welcome in our clan, so I'll stash her in my den until we take out that nest, then contact Trayis to see if he'll accept me into his clan. Can you clear that with your brother? I just want her safe until that master is dead, Lavos. That Vamp is determined to breed her with one of our kind to make for a strong female child he can raise."

"Don't be hasty," Lavos replied. "Some of our people might shit about you having a human mate, but Lorn loves Kira. He mated her. We need you to help us hold the clan. Not all of them are real happy with the change, as you can imagine."

"Lorn hates me."

"He did hate you," Lavos agreed. "I won't deny that, Veso. But I told him how we were secretly plotting to take over the clan together. He knows now that you hate everything Decker stood for. You want change as much as we do."

"The clan will pressure him to shun me for having a human mate." Veso paused. "I won't risk her life."

Glen's heart sped up. Now Veso was telling his friend she was his mate. Could he really mean it? No. He had to be messing with her. She cleared her throat. "I'll point out again I haven't agreed to that."

Veso turned his head and had the nerve to smile. "She's in denial—but she's mine."

She hit him again, slapping his arm. "You're such a bully, and so rude. I have a say in this!"

He didn't even flinch. "Does hitting me make you feel better?"

"Marginally. It would help if you acted like it hurt."

226

Lavos chuckled.

"You don't hit hard, Glenda. You're cranky and tired. Hit me if it makes you feel better but you're still my mate. You aren't returning to Oregon."

"We're in Oregon."

"We're in Alaska."

She gaped at Veso, shocked. "What?"

"Alaska," he repeated. "Not Oregon."

Lavos cleared his throat. "Um, I hate to break this up because it's weird, yet amusing, but we should start heading to the lodge. The sun is going down. That normally wouldn't be a problem but you said you're being hunted. We need to be indoors or deeper into our territory before the Vamps come out."

Veso broke eye contact with her and addressed his friend. "You didn't bring a vehicle?"

"I wasn't expecting two of you. I drove a quad. It won't seat three."

"Tell me where it is and I'll drive Glenda to my home."

Lavos shook his head. "No way, Veso. Did you hear me when I said Decker was working with Vampires? He probably told them all about our clan. They attacked a remote section to get to you and Kira, where guards were spread the thinnest. Your home is in that same area. Didn't you say that master will want to recapture her? Let's not make it easy on them. That's the first place they'll look for her come nightfall. The lodge is where we've set up headquarters. She'll be safest there. Plus, I'm not missing out on witnessing when your father and the rest of the clan gets a load of you and your human mate." The guy had the nerve to laugh. "The lodge is where we need to go."

"I'm not his mate," she muttered, annoyed. They couldn't even take her seriously, probably because she was a human.

"You are." Veso shrugged off the pack and tossed it aside. He turned swiftly and grabbed her, scooping her up into his arms. "Let's go. She walks slow and she's tired. I no longer have to worry about defending her on my own. We have humans with dart guns filled with drugs looking for us."

"Shit." Lavos sniffed the air, glancing around. "Let's move."

Glen wrapped her arms around Veso's neck. She wasn't going to complain if he wanted to carry her. She rested her head on his chest and closed her eyes. "Since you think it's fine to be bossy, I can be too. I want food. Real food. Cooked. And a bath."

"Done," Veso said. "Soon."

"Unbelievable," Lavos chuckled.

"Shut up," Veso snarled. It made his chest vibrate.

"You'd laugh too if I showed up toting a human mate, my friend."

* * * * *

It was well after dark before the lights from the lodge came into view. Veso glanced down at Glenda. She had fallen asleep in his arms over an hour before.

Lavos paused, glancing around, and sniffed the air. He turned to stare at him.

"Do you want me to go in first? I texted that we were close as soon as I got a signal on my phone. Everyone knows you've been found. I can warn them." His gaze dropped to Glenda, then back up to Veso.

228

"I don't plan to stay long once we take out that nest. I know I won't be welcome here by your brother or the rest of the clan, not with her."

"You might be surprised. Stop expecting the worst."

"Trayis has some men who mated humans in his clan. I know he'll accept me. My father was from his clan and keeps in contact with him."

"Don't count Lorn out, Veso. You've never been enemies."

"We've never been friends either. I can't see him letting me stay."

"You pretended to like Nabby and those other shits so you could warn us about the crap they planned to do in advance. We saved lives. That's because of you, my friend. Lorn knows that. I told him everything."

"Fine, but he still won't accept my mate."

"You should actually mate her."

"I plan to, but I couldn't while we were being hunted. It was too dangerous."

"Understood."

"Let's just face this. I want it over. Will Lorn support going after that nest? I need help, and I want my father to stay behind to protect Glenda. The master is a threat to her. He needs to die."

"This master sent his nest to invade our territory and they attacked Kira too. You bet your ass we're going after those bastards."

"Good." Veso paused, glancing down at Glenda. He should wake her before they faced whoever waited inside. "Glenda?"

She didn't stir in his arms.

He spoke louder. "Glenda? Wake up."

Her eyes flew open and fear instantly contorted her features.

"It's okay. I'm holding you. You're safe."

She clutched him tighter around his neck. "It's dark."

"It is, but we're deep in VampLycan territory. We're almost to the lodge. Look." He turned her in his arms so she could see the lights up the hill.

Her tense body relaxed. "Is that a hotel?"

"No. It's our clan meeting place." He gently put her on her feet. "Be brave." He took her hand. "Don't show fear. No one is going to hurt you."

"You're totally safe," Lavos added.

"Let's get this over with." Veso wasn't looking forward to meeting his new clan leader. He didn't hate Lorn, but they'd never been close. He knew Lorn hadn't liked it when he'd trained Kira to fight. They'd exchanged harsh words and Lorn had threatened to kill him if anything bad happened to her. He wondered if Lorn would blame him for Kira being attacked by Vamps.

They walked up the hill, Veso helping Glenda along. She really had trouble seeing, stumbling a few times. It was tempting to carry her but he didn't want to hurt her pride. It would bother him being carried home. She might feel the same way.

Lavos took the stairs first, throwing open the front door. Veso followed, keeping Glenda close.

The first person he saw was his father. He paced in front of the fireplace, but stopped and spun when they entered, their gazes locking.

"Veso." His father advanced in long strides, hugging him.

He had to release Glenda to wrap his arms around his father. "I'm fine. They drugged me or I wouldn't have been captured."

His father eased his tight hold and studied his face. "I thought they'd killed you."

"They had other plans. We escaped." He reached back, blindly gripped Glenda's arm and tugged her forward. He saw surprise on his father's face as he lowered his gaze, staring at her. His dad jerked his gaze back to him, one eyebrow arching.

"This is Glenda. She helped me escape…and she's going to be my mate." He braced himself, expecting a bad reaction.

His father's mouth parted, he inhaled, stared at Glenda again—and then shocked Veso by smiling. "I see. Hello, Glenda."

"Hi." She pressed against Veso's front, facing his father. "It's nice to meet you. Since you look so much like Veso, I'm guessing you're his father? He's spoken a lot about you."

"I am. My name is Bran. It's nice to meet you." His dad shot him a questioning look.

"She knows everything." Veso tried to guess where his father's thoughts may lie. "The master who kidnapped me also took Glenda. She's a relative of his. He wanted us to breed a daughter together so he could raise her to be his companion."

"He said he wanted to make her his queen," Glenda muttered. "He's crazy."

"This is a story I want to hear."

Motion and noise drew Veso's attention to the stairs. Lorn and Kira came down. He noticed immediately the changes in Kira. It wasn't just her paler complexion. There was a gracefulness to her movements that had been missing before. She smiled when she saw him. Lorn didn't.

They stopped at the bottom of the stairs and Veso pulled Glenda closer.

"Thank goodness you're alive." Kira tried to come to him but her mate snagged her arm, keeping her by his side. Kira frowned up at Lorn. "He's not a threat to me."

"That's not established yet. Your scent has changed since the last time he saw you."

"I caught him up on events." Lavos moved to the side, halfway between the couples. "He knows Kira is turning more VampLycan than Vampire."

"Who is the woman?" Lorn's frown deepened as he studied Glenda.

"My mate, or she will be soon. Don't worry. She already knows everything. And I plan to leave your clan as soon as I'm able." Veso took a deep breath and blew it out. "I'd like permission for my father to guard her while we track and take out the nest who kidnapped us. The master wants her recaptured. She won't be safe until they are all dead."

Lorn met his gaze. "Are you leaving because you have a problem with me leading the clan or because of what she is?"

"I'm glad you stepped up and took control." Lorn wasn't anything like Decker. He was a vast improvement.

"You don't want to challenge me?"

Veso shook his head. "I'm not a leader. I just want to take out the threat of that nest and keep my mate safe."

Lorn inhaled. "You haven't completed the bond."

"We've been on the run for days. It wasn't the time...but she's mine."

Lorn came closer, stopping about five feet away. "I want those bastards dusted too. Truce?"

"We're not at war, Lorn." Veso released Glenda and bowed, lowering his gaze as a sign of respect. He rose to his full height then, staring at the new clan leader. "I accept you until it's time for us to leave."

"Is it that distasteful to vow allegiance to me?"

"No."

"Then why are you planning to leave the clan?"

Veso glanced at Glenda then back at Lorn, but said nothing.

"Some won't be happy, but they're already pissed about me taking over and mating Kira." Lorn grinned. "We already have enemies here. You have a lot to fight for and defend with a human mate if you stay with us. I'd like it if you'd become one of my enforcers." His humor faded. "That doesn't mean the same thing as it once did under Decker's rule. I'm not looking for executioners or assassins. We only kill if there's no other choice. I'd like for us to finally live in peace with other clans."

"You'd let me keep Glenda?" Veso wanted it to be clear they were a package deal. He was also pleased to be asked to become an enforcer. He knew Lavos had dreamed of peace between the clans, and it was nice to know his older brother had the same goals. They were all in agreement.

Lorn gave a sharp nod. "You might want to keep her away from the clan for a while but in time, they'll come around. That's my hope. Change will be slow to take but as I said...I have hope. I'd be honored if you'd stand with us, rather than against us, Veso."

He nodded. "Done. You have my allegiance. Would you like a blood oath? I'll give it."

233

"Your word is good enough for me. The lodge is the safest place right now. Davis will defend your soon-to-be mate and my Kira when we leave. Let's go upstairs. We have a map in my office. Show me where this nest is holed up. We have bloodsuckers to hunt."

Veso waited for all of them to take the stairs, then met Glenda's gaze. She was frowning at him.

"What?"

"I didn't agree to be your mate. I have a life back home."

"You had a life until those Vampires stole you. Now you have a new one. We'll fight about this later. Every moment that master lives, you're at risk of being recaptured."

She blew out a breath and nodded. "Priorities. Got it. Let's go." She turned, heading up the stairs.

Veso followed. She might want to leave—but he wasn't letting her go. She was his mate. He'd just have to teach her that.

Chapter Sixteen

"Thank you, Perri." Glen took a seat on the couch, gripping the tray a quiet woman had handed her. It had a plate on it with a large turkey sandwich, chips, and a cold soda.

"You are welcome. I'll be downstairs with my children. Call out if you need anything."

Glen nodded. Her gaze drifted to Kira next. The other woman sat close, watching her every move. Glen was starving but didn't dig into the food, instead settling the tray on her lap. "I don't bite."

Kira grinned. "I do, but you're safe. I only sink my fangs into my mate."

Glen wasn't sure whether to be comforted by that or freaked out.

Kira chuckled. "That was a joke. I mean, it's true but your neck is safe from me."

Glen's gaze drifted to the door of the office. They were sitting in a loft area outside of it at the top of the stairs. She wished she could see Veso but couldn't from where they sat. He'd assured her she was safe. She really hoped he was telling the truth.

"Eat," Kira encouraged. "Perri wouldn't hurt you. Do you want me to take a bite of your sandwich to prove it's not drugged?"

She glanced down at her food. "Um, I never even considered it would be. Is that an issue?" She arched her eyebrows, staring at the other woman.

Kira shook her head. "Not with Perri. She's grateful my mate took the clan. Her kids were at risk."

"I don't know what that means."

"I know. This all must be so confusing for you. The man who led our clan before my mate took over killed children who showed too many Vampire traits. Perri's children were. That's the breakdown for you. Lorn won't hurt her kids. He'll protect them."

"But aren't all of you half Vampire?"

"Yes. It's complicated but Decker was a madman. He loved to kill anyone he didn't consider VampLycan enough. Being too Lycan was fine with him but being too Vampire was a death offense." Kira reached up and circled her finger next to her head. "Nuts."

"I take it he hated humans?"

Kira nodded. "My mother was human. My dad met and mated her when he wasn't living here. I don't think he ever planned to come back except my mom died. He brought me home here to keep me safe. He couldn't trust a human babysitter not to see something she shouldn't. He feared she'd hurt me if I grew claws or fur. Turns out I couldn't shift. I was persona non grata here for a long time. An outcast that Decker only put up with because of my father. He's a full VampLycan."

"Davis." Glen had met him and he'd been nice, regarding her with a warm look that hadn't scared her.

Kira nodded. "My dad is great. He fell in love with my mom like Veso fell for you."

"I don't think he's in love with me," Glen admitted softly. "I think he's mostly trying to irritate me and freak me out. He seems to like to make me mad."

Kira grinned again. "No. He verbally claimed you. That's serious for our kind. So you guys have been through hell, huh?"

"You could say that."

"Veso trained me to fight. He comes across like a dick but he's got a good heart. You could do a lot worse."

"We're so different." She regarded the other woman with a bit of suspicion. Kira was very pretty. "Did you two ever…"

It took a second for the unanswered question to sink in but then Kira shook her head. "No. Never. I've been in love with Lorn all my life. We grew up together. He just couldn't mate me until he took over the clan. It was forbidden. I even left the clan for a while to go to college. Veso was just my trainer and friend. The only VampLycan I've ever slept with is my mate."

"Oh. Good. I mean—"

"It's okay. I get it. VampLycans go into heat. Lorn used to leave, and of course I knew why, but I was still jealous."

"I don't understand."

"He couldn't have me, so he'd go hook up with other women in different clans," Kira whispered. "God, it tore me apart when he was with someone else. But Veso and I were never lovers. Hell, I don't even think he's ever slept with anyone in the clan. He's not the most social guy. He lives on the outskirts of our territory. He's not a people person, you know?"

"I could guess that about him." Glen began to eat. "He can be a bully, opinionated and pushy."

"Those are VampLycan traits. Our men are all alpha personalities, otherwise known as cavemen. He'll die to protect you though, be completely loyal, and do anything to make you happy once you're his mate. I'm familiar with humans, since I used to mostly be one and lived in that world for a bit. Mates form a link, and you being unhappy will make him unhappy. Your happiness will make him happy. It's just how it works. I know it's a bit of a stretch for you to think that way since it's not like that with humans, but he's not one."

"What about my life? I have an apartment, maybe a job still, and everything I own is in Oregon."

Kira reached out and touched her arm gently. "You'll never be safe out there, Glenda."

"It's just Glen, please. Veso refuses to shorten my name, but I got teased growing up so I hate being called that."

"It's a pretty name."

"Kids don't care about spelling. Glenda the good witch."

Kira released her and laughed. "That had to suck."

"They bought me tiaras sometimes, and wands all the way up until high school for my birthday and Christmas, thinking it was hysterical. I'm just glad you understand what I'm talking about. Veso didn't get it."

"I can't see him watching classic movies. He's more of a hunter/survival-book type of guy."

"True." Her gaze drifted to the open doorway when the men's voices rose. "What are they doing in there?"

"Plotting an attack on the nest. They need to be taken out. They shouldn't even be in this area."

"Are you going with them?"

Kira shook her head. "No. Lorn won't allow it. He'll want me to stay here to keep me safe."

Worry surfaced. "They could die, couldn't they?"

238

Kira shook her head. "VampLycans can kick Vamp ass big time. I also know my mate. He'll call in help. The other clans have offered it. He's trying to show them how different he is from Decker. He would never want assistance but Lorn isn't anything like him. Our men are coming home to us when this is over." She leaned back in her seat. "Just don't be grossed out if they're bloody and covered in dust."

"I've seen Veso take them out. Only some of them didn't dust."

"Soldiers?"

"I called them creepers."

"I can see that. They are creepy as shit. I've never seen one myself but I've heard about them all my life. They're supposed to have veins on their skin and blood in their eyes."

"They do."

"You've been through so much. I'm so sorry you were pulled into this world, Glen."

"Me too, but none of this is anyone's fault but King Charles."

Kira laughed. "That's what he's going by? Wow. He sounds like he'd deranged and full of himself."

"He totally is."

"Well, you're safe now. What can I do for you to make things better?"

"I'd kill for a shower and some clean clothes."

"I can do that. I actually lived in the lodge before Lorn mated me, and most of my things are still in my old bedroom. I'll take you to the visitor's quarters once they leave to attack that nest and get you something to wear. We're about the same size."

"Visitor's quarters?"

"There're two apartments in the basement area of the lodge. One is a two-bedroom that my father lives in, and there's a one-bedroom unit for when someone visits the clan."

"Thank you."

"We're practically family now." Kira stood. "Eat. I'm going to check on the guys. I'll be right back."

"Kira?"

The woman cocked her head, peering at her. "Yeah?"

"How does one go about mating a VampLycan?"

She sat back down. "It's not scary. I promise. Or painful."

"I'm all ears. I want to hear. Veso isn't much for talking in-depth about things."

"I bet."

* * * * *

Veso strapped on weapons. They were going after the nest—and they weren't doing it alone. A thump sounded on the roof and he tensed, staring up.

"It's just a GarLycan," Lorn said, not looking alarmed. He crossed the room and threw open the large window. He backed away and a moment later a body dropped, swinging in front of the window before entering.

The man was big, and his wings were tucked when he straightened up, standing. He wore all black leather, from his pants to his open-back shirt, a half sword strapped to his thigh, and he moved out the way as a second thump sounded up on the roof. He removed his sunglasses, revealing lively silver-colored eyes that appeared molten with the way the irises stayed in motion, as if they had a life of their own.

"I'm Chaz. That's my twin Fray you hear. We're your air support." He bowed his head at Lorn. "At your service."

A second man came through the window. They looked so much alike, the only way to tell them apart was the second one had hair a bit longer and he only wore leather pants with a black tank top. He removed his glasses too, showing the same strange silver eyes.

"Hello, VampLycans." Fray grinned. "This is going to be fun. I'm so ready to kick the ass of some bloodsuckers. Thanks for asking us to join you. It was getting a bit boring at the cliffs."

Lorn nodded. "We appreciate the assistance. Did Lord Aveoth tell you they drugged Veso?" He jerked his head to point him out.

"They used strong sedatives with dart guns," Veso explained.

"Darts don't pierce us when we're prepared." Fray's skin darkened to a grayish hue, the texture hardening.

It was the first time Veso had seen it up close. "That's a handy trait."

Fray flashed him a smile, cracks appearing in his skin from the effort. "I know. It's good to be a GarLycan. We can shell harder to reflect bullets but this is me in battle mode when I deal with suckheads. It's a mild shelling. They try to bite me like this and they'll break a fang."

"Enough." Chaz gave his twin an annoyed frown. "My brother is the outgoing one and he likes to show off sometimes. We have more air support flying above waiting to go with us. I brought eight scouts for the nest. We left another six patrolling your territory for Decker. I hope that's okay."

"Thank you." Lorn approached the men. "We appreciate this."

"The master is using some humans. He took over their minds." Veso would hate for innocents to get caught in the coming battle.

"Got it." Chaz reached up and pressed his finger against his ear. "Mind-fucked humans might be on the playground. Grab them if you see any and hold them until a VampLycan can get them straightened out." He dropped his hand. "We upgraded to have better communications. We'll bring you guys any humans we catch and you can see if you can wipe their memories."

"The new coms system is awesome. It beats yelling at each other," Flay added, his skin returning to a normal texture and color. "One of our scouts carries a signal booster on his back. We brought you guys some. Go Team Dust Vamps." He reached into a pouch attached to his belt and approached Lorn. "Just pop one in your ear and press to talk. You'll hear anyone speaking." He handed them out to the other men, including Veso.

Veso glanced at it, figured out how it worked, and put it in his ear. A deep voice instantly broadcast through the tiny speaker. "Are we flying them to the location or following from above, Chaz?"

Chaz touched his ear. "They're hooking in. Not sure yet. Stand by." He stared at Lorn, arching his eyebrows.

"I figured we'd go on motorcycles and draw out any Vamps and soldiers in the woods. They'll hear the engines and come at us."

Chaz nodded. "Good plan. We can swoop in and grab them before they get to you. This is a dust-and-destroy mission, right? Take no prisoners?"

"That's how I'd like it to go down. Will Lord Aveoth agree to that?" Lorn put on gloves.

"This is your show, Lorn." Fray grinned. "We're under your direct command. You want them all dead, you got it."

"The nest needs to die," Veso stated, staring at Lorn. "Glenda said they were holding other humans and feeding on them. They've harmed our human neighbors, possibly killed them."

Lorn held his gaze for a moment, then nodded at Chaz. "Everything with a need to feed on blood has to die."

Chaz nodded and relayed the order. "We're all set."

"Cool," Fray chuckled. "It's going to be a blood-and-dust shower. I love those."

Veso eyed the GarLycan, concerned that the man might be a little mentally challenged.

Fray winked. "Did I mention it was getting boring at the cliffs? It was. I'm so ready to kill some bad shits."

Veso could understand that. Sometimes being a guard had been tedious. He relaxed around the GarLycan.

"Let's go. This mine is eighty-two miles away and we need to drive on roads that will avoid humans but draw the attention from any hunters searching for Veso and his mate." Lorn walked to the map, trailing his finger over it. "This is the route we decided on. We'll arrive two hours before the sun comes up."

Chaz nodded. "That will work. It will give us enough time to take them on and fly home afterward. We'll be your air support while you're driving

243

there. When we hit the mine, we'll join you inside but I'll leave some of my scouts in the air to take out any who might try to flee other exits."

"Good deal." Lorn shook Chaz's hand. "Thanks again."

"Lord Aveoth doesn't like Vampires in this area either. They only have one reason to be here and that's to fuck with us all somehow."

Glenda's scent filled Veso's nose and he turned toward the door. It wasn't her though who entered the room. Kira did, carrying her clothing in her arms. It alarmed him.

Kira walked closer, shooting him a dirty look. "Give me a break. I didn't do anything to her. Glen's in the visitor's quarters taking a shower. My dad is guarding the hallway so she's not down there alone. I gave her clean clothes to wear once she's done but took her dirty ones. I thought you might like to take them with you because the Vamps might have memorized her scent to track."

Veso relaxed and accepted them. "Smart."

"You trained me well. I never had your keen sense of smell, but you could always track me wherever I went until I caught on about how you were able to do it."

"Thank you, Kira." He accepted Glenda's clothing, balling them up and shoving them under his arm.

"You're welcome. Do you know what would be better though? If I wore Glen's clothes and rode behind Veso. They might mistake me for her."

"No way in hell," Lorn snapped. "You're staying here, Kira."

She sighed. "Fine. I'm not going to fight with you, especially in front of the GarLycans." She smiled at Lord Aveoth's two enforcers. "It makes him look bad when I win and he totally spoils me," she whispered.

"Kira," Lorn warned.

"Fine. Be careful, everyone. We'll be waiting here. Doing nothing."

Veso felt a little envious as he watched Lorn kiss and hug his mate goodbye. Glenda was showering. He wouldn't be able to see her before they left. Time was of the essence if they wanted to attack the nest during the night. And they needed to do that so no humans spotted their winged allies in the sky over territory that didn't belong to the clans.

"Let's get going. Garson and Kar will have gassed the motorcycles and have them waiting outside for us." Lorn led the way.

Lavos walked next to Veso. "You up for this? You could stay here."

"You need me. I've been in that mine and the master wasn't there when I left. I think he's holed up somewhere close to the mine."

"You should probably tell our winged friends that."

Veso reached up, pushed on the earpiece, and relayed that information to everyone. He couldn't wait to get his hands on the master responsible for kidnapping him and threatening Glenda's future.

Chapter Seventeen

Movement caught Veso's attention from the right side of the road as he drove. He glanced that way, seeing the source. One of the GarLycans had swooped down and grabbed hold of someone. Judging by the high-pitched shrieks, it was either a Vampire or a soldier. It flailed its arms and legs, being flown higher into the sky and above the treetops by the scout. A second scout flew closer and as he passed the first one, the three shapes became two. They'd dusted the thing in the air.

He had to appreciate the way the GarLycans worked as a team. They'd located at least four enemies already, dispatching them in the same manner. There might not be too many Vamps or soldiers left alive to fight when they reached the mine if the bastards kept coming at them while they drove in that direction.

"Nice job." Lorn's voice sounded in the earpiece.

"Soldier," one of the scouts responded. "That's all we've killed so far. Duster, look to eleven o'clock. Spot it on the ridge? You're closest."

"Got it," a gruff voice replied.

Veso glanced up, seeing one of the GarLycans break away from the group overhead and fly toward a hill. Veso couldn't see anything up there since his main focus was on the road, but he kept glancing that way and saw when the scout grabbed another body, taking it up in the air. A second scout flew toward Duster, they crossed close together, and this time the third body didn't disappear. It fell from the sky in one big piece and a smaller one.

"Shit. New soldier," Duster shared over the coms. "I'll fly down and make sure the body and head are exposed to the sun."

"Thanks." Chaz paused. "Watch him, Flay. Work in teams of two. That one was easy to spot since it was running but I don't want anyone attacked if there's a smart one being very still so we can't see them."

"On it," Flay responded. "I've got you covered, Duster."

Veso reached up and pressed against his ear when he saw the first cabin he and Glenda had reached after leaving the mine. "We're close."

"VampLycans lead the charge," Chaz ordered. "We have the air and we'll flank you from behind."

Veso sped up, driving in front of Lorn and Lavos, knowing exactly where to go. He stopped right in front of the mine. The truck was parked there. He turned off the motorcycle and removed Glenda's clothing from under his shirt, laying it on the bike seat.

"The master is here," he announced to everyone.

Lorn stepped up next to him. "He's all yours. Anyone find him, let Veso be the one to kill this bastard. He's owed that."

"Thanks." Veso flashed him a grateful look.

"I didn't get to kill the one who attacked my Kira but I sure wanted to take his head." Lorn shrugged. "Let's go wipe out a nest."

Four GarLycans landed behind them. "Are we plotting more are just going in?" Flay drew his short sword.

"We're going in." Veso unleashed his claws and fangs, storming toward the mine opening.

Two soldiers rushed at their group about fifty feet inside. Lorn took out one while Veso beheaded the second. He inhaled, searching for the scent of the master. It was one he remembered well. The blond bastard wasn't going to get away. He smelled him and turned left at the first split in the wide shaft. The teams divided in half. Lorn glanced back, seeing Lavos, Flay, another GarLycan scout, and Kar with him.

Another soldier came streaking out of the dark. Veso lunged forward, right at it, and ripped his claws through its throat. It dusted an instant later and he kept on going.

"You could save a few for us," Flay called out.

Veso nodded just as three more soldier came running at him from ahead. He obligingly shoved past them that time, letting the rest of his team dispatch them. He had the scent of the master and it was getting stronger. He also picked up fresh human blood, a lot of it. He snarled and rushed forward, not carrying if the others kept up.

The tunnels split again and he turned right, tracking the master and the blood. He came to a doorway with some light spilling through the side cracks. Veso lifted his foot, kicking in the ill-fitting wood that had been placed over it for privacy since it didn't have an exterior lock. It went flying inward and he winced over the well-lit scene that waited.

Candles were lit in the rounded cavern that made up a room. A human was tied down on the hard-packed earth, her blood saturating the floor and her body.

The master had been drinking from her chest but he jerked his head up at the sound of Veso's violent entry. Shock widened the master's eyes.

He must not have heard them coming, too focused on gorging from his victim.

Veso snarled, glaring at him. "I'm back, you bastard."

The master leapt up, rushing for a dart gun placed on the floor behind him. Veso moved just as fast and caught him by the back of his shirt, impaling the Vampire with his claws at the same time. The master hissed in pain.

Veso wasn't done. He spun, slamming the bastard face first into the rock wall, then did it a second time just to hear bones break. He flung him down and dropped on his back.

"No more drugs," Veso growled. Grabbing the Vampire by his hair to keep him in place, he turned, staring at the human on the floor. Her eyes were open, staring back at him. No fear showed but she looked pretty out of it and close to death.

Sound by the door had him glancing that way. Lavos and Flay entered, both of them grimacing over the woman.

"She's still alive. Get her out of here," Veso ordered.

It was Lavos who pulled off his shirt, removed it, and covered the woman. Flay slashed at the bonds tied to the stakes to free her wrists and ankles. Lavos lifted the woman, cursing. "She's lost a lot of blood."

"I can fly her to a hospital," Flay offered, opening his arms.

"I don't think she'll make it." Lavos shook his head.

Another scout entered the room. He had jet-black hair, very tan skin, and dark eyes. "Give her to me." His gruff voice revealed his identity. It was Duster. "I can save her."

"She's too far gone," Lavos whispered.

249

Duster approached and just tore the woman out of Lavos's arms. "I can save her, VampLycan." He turned, striding out of the room fast.

Lavos went to follow but Flay caught his arm. "Don't. He's right. He has a chance of getting her to a hospital in time. He can fly faster than any of us. There's a twenty-four-hour emergency clinic about twenty miles from here. We know where all of them are located since sometimes humans trespass and the bears get to them before we do."

The master began to fight Veso, bucking to get free. He focused on him as he leaned in, snarling. "I have something to say to you, Charles."

"I am King Charles!"

"You're an asshole. Glenda will never birth anything for you. She's safe, and you'll never cause her harm." Veso dug his claws into the master's scalp, drawing blood.

Charles screamed and shrieked. Veso wrapped his other hand around the bastard's throat and used his claws to slowly cut into him. The Vamp didn't deserve a fast, merciful death. He wanted him to suffer and know he was about to die.

"Glenda is mine. Not yours. You should never have come after a VampLycan. We're wiping out your entire fucking nest."

"Hold on!" Lorn rushed into the room.

Veso snarled, glaring at him. "He's mine to kill."

Lorn came to a halt and nodded. "I just want to ask him one thing first."

Veso eased his grip on the master's throat. He was choking, bleeding. He dug his claws into the bastard's back instead, hurting him more. "Fine." He lifted up, yanking the Vampire to his feet with him. He held him up with his claws dug into his back.

250

Lorn came closer, staring at the master. "Where is Decker Filmore?"

"Fuck you," the master choked, blood running out of his mouth.

Lorn shifted his gaze to Veso. He understood the importance and nodded, twisting his claws and causing the master to shriek from the pain. He gripped him by his arm with his free hand, squeezed hard, and bone broke. "Answer him."

The master screamed again but then went silent.

"Answer him," Veso snarled. "Otherwise we'll tear your limbs from your body and wait for you to heal enough to wake up before we start again."

"That sounds fun." Flay grinned. "I call right leg."

"I'll take the left," Lavos offered.

"Answer him," Veso hissed. "You're going to die but I'll make it faster. Your choice."

"With the council in Chicago," the master wheezed. "They'll make you pay for this! I was under orders to come here from them. You have to let me go!"

"What were your orders?"

The Vampire glared but answered. "They wanted someone to come here and kill some VampLycans. We were to set fire to your homes and cause as much damage as possible."

"Why?" Lorn's voice deepened, his anger growing.

"I didn't ask," the master hissed. "I saw an opportunity."

"To drug one and breed me to Glenda?" Veso dug his claws in a little deeper.

251

The master screamed, "Yes!"

"That's all I needed." Lorn backed up. "Verification. Decker is working with these bastards. He's the reason they are here. End him."

"With pleasure." Veso leaned in, snarling next to the master's ear. "Be a king in hell."

He released Charles's arm and grabbed his throat again, slowly ripping into the soft flesh in front. The Vamp tried to scream but choked on his own blood. It took a few adjustments with his hand but he beheaded the bastard, his body turning to dust. Veso backed away, wiping the blood from both hands on his pants.

"Bet that felt good." Flay spun. "Let's go hunting. I'm sure there are more of them down here."

"Fucking Decker," Lorn rasped, fury in his tone. "I'm sure he sent them to punish us for not fighting to keep him here and agreeing to slaughter the other clans."

"It doesn't matter, my sometimes-furry friends. We'll kill them all," Fray called out as he left the room.

Veso followed them out. They wouldn't stop until everyone in the nest had been disposed of.

* * * * *

Glen woke, startled by the door opening. She'd fallen asleep on the couch in the small living room of the guest apartment.

Bran stepped inside, carrying a brown bag and a mug with a lid.

"Sorry if I woke you. I figured you might be hungry."

"Thank you." She sat up straighter. "Have you heard anything yet?"

He shook his head and placed the bag and mug on the coffee table in front of her. "Do you mind if I open the windows and let in some sunlight? It's so gloomy in this basement."

"Sure. Go ahead. It's morning already?"

"It is."

He crossed the room to the high windows along one wall, pulling back heavy drapes. Light came in from the outside, brightening the room a lot. She leaned over and turned off the lamp on the table.

Bran turned, staring at her. He didn't move to leave so she figured he might want to say something to her or maybe get to know her. Veso had stated he wanted to mate her. As his father, Bran might have questions. She could totally understand that.

She hadn't been alone with Veso's father until that moment. Kira had told her he'd stayed behind though at the lodge to help protect them. He'd avoided her all night. Now, his face didn't give away any of his emotions as he silently regarded her. She noticed again how young he looked. If she hadn't known he was Veso's dad, she'd have sworn they were brothers, only a few years apart.

"Do I frighten you? There's no need for that."

"I'm sorry. Am I staring? You look so much like Veso, only with longer hair. Too much so."

"I don't understand."

"You don't look old enough to be anyone's father unless they are really young."

He chuckled. "Ah. I guess my son didn't tell you everything. We age very slowly. I assure you, I'm much older than I look."

253

She wasn't about to ask for the year he was born. It seemed rude. That also reminded her of her manners. "Would you like to have a seat?"

He came closer and sat in a chair on the other side of the coffee table. "Thank you, Glenda."

"It's just Glen, please."

"My son calls you Glenda."

"I'm aware. He seems to have a problem with shortened names, unfortunately. Veso told me about you." She glanced down at the mug, smelling coffee. She looked back at him. "How you left your clan to care for him when he was just a boy. He loves you a lot."

His expression softened. "He shared that with you?"

"Yes. He told me about his mother too. She sounds like she was pretty terrible to you both."

Bran's mouth compressed into a tight line.

"I'm sorry. I didn't mean to upset you. Veso told me about how you built a cabin for him, and you sacrificed a lot to raise him."

"It was a privilege, not a hardship. He's my son." Bran suddenly leaned forward, his eyes growing brighter. "I want you to tell me the truth."

She lowered her gaze fast, staring at the coffee. "Please don't try to control me."

He sat back in the chair. "My son told you about our gifts."

"He did." She glanced up to find Bran's eyes had returned to their normal color, the unnatural brightness gone. "I won't lie to you. Just ask me whatever you want to know."

254

"Why are you refusing to be my son's mate? Is it because he's a VampLycan?"

"I didn't know anything about you until I was kidnapped. The world was round and the scary things in life were diseases and killer criminals. Human ones. I have a life I built and worked hard for. Staying here would mean giving all that up. Plus, I don't know him all that well. It's kind of nuts to know a person for less than a week and then promise to spend the rest of your life with them."

"The world is still round. Disease and human killers remain frightening for you. That hasn't changed. Your knowledge has just been expanded, Glen."

"That's true."

"The world you lived in will never be the same. You'll look at pale humans at night now, wondering if they just avoid the sun or if they are Vampires. Do you know what they would do if they believed you knew what they were? They'd come after you. Knowledge is a dangerous thing to them. You'd be seen as a threat, the enemy, and treated as such. You spent time with Vampires. Did you have fun?"

"No." She knew where he was going. "I can't just stay with Veso out of fear though, and because I know he'd keep me safe from them."

"Do you feel anything for my son?"

She bit her lip, not sure how to answer that.

"Are you confused?"

She nodded.

"It's in your human nature to question things, to be wary of being hurt. Have you had your heart broken by someone in the past?"

255

"Everyone has."

"Not everyone, but I know the pain that comes with trying to love someone who is incapable of returning those feelings. I wanted to mate Veso's mother. She birthed my child. It was only right that we join together and become a family. She didn't agree. It deeply hurt me for a while. It isn't natural to have a child the way we did. She tricked me."

"Veso told me."

Bran placed his arms on the sides of the chair, curling his fingers into fists. "He never wanted a mate. We've discussed it many times. His mother made him believe he wasn't worthy of being loved by a woman. I always hoped he'd meet some VampLycan who would change his mind. Instead, he brought you home. I don't care that you're human, Glen. It wouldn't even matter to me if you were a Vampire. My son wants to make you his mate, and I hope you agree. You'd be a fool if you say no."

She wasn't sure how to respond to that but obviously Veso got his attitude from his father.

"No human will protect and care for you as well as my son would. I know about your world. He won't have an affair or abandon you one day. A mate is for life."

"We haven't known each other all that long."

"Stop acting so shortsightedly human. You're more than that now." Bran leaned forward again but this time he didn't do that funky thing with his eyes. "Try listening to your heart and your instincts. That's what VampLycans do. We feel deep emotions and go with our gut. My son has chosen you because his instincts, his feelings, his gut tells him you're the right one for him. You're compatible with my son in ways that no one else has ever been. He was dead set against it. Think about that. He's willing to take the biggest risk of his life with you. Won't you do the same for him?"

Bran stood. "Eat. Think long and hard while you do, Glen. My son's heart hangs on your decision when he returns." He crossed the room to the door and peered back at her. "If he returns. We do die, you know. His mother did. He hasn't felt much since then—until you. That matters a hell of a lot to me. I hope it does to you too. Your life that you knew will never be the same after all of this. Stop dwelling on that and think of your future. You could have a good one with my son."

Glen watched the door close and she sighed, reaching for the coffee. She tugged off the lid and blew, taking a sip. He'd put sugar and milk in it so it wasn't bitter.

Bran had given her a lot to think about. That wasn't how she had imagined their conversation would go down. She was pretty sure he'd want her to leave the territory as soon as possible. Veso had a problem with her being human, but his father didn't. He just wanted his son to be happy.

What if Veso never came back? The thought made her chest hurt. "Damn."

Chapter Eighteen

Veso just wanted to go find Glenda but he had to stay at the meeting. Lorn had insisted everyone who'd taken part during the mission be in his office for the debriefing in case there were questions. His new clan leader had them all on a conference call with the three other VampLycan and the GarLycan leaders.

"We took out a total of seventeen soldiers, counting the ones Veso told us about when he first escaped the nest. We found the secondary location where the master was sleeping during the day. It was a dugout where the mine used to store explosives. Three sleeping bags were there." Lorn paused. "The master confirmed for us that Decker Filmore was working with the Vampire Council in Chicago."

"I'll send scouts that way." Lord Aveoth sounded furious. "Why do you think there were so many soldiers? Were they expecting us to attack them?"

"Doubtful." Veso spoke up. "The master wanted to be called a king. He was a pretentious prick and probably loved having those things at his beck and call."

Velder's voice came out of the speakerphone. "Are you certain you got them all?"

"Pretty sure." Chaz glanced around. "The new soldiers were being kept inside the mine and most of the ones in the woods hunting were damn near rabid. Those ones ran at anything that made sound or moved. The motorcycles worked like a charm to draw their attention. We could patrol the skies around that area at night for the next week if you think it's needed."

"Do that," Aveoth growled. "Those bastard Vampires have harmed enough humans in that area. It's already going to draw attention, since someone is bound to report those turned or killed as missing persons. What about Vamps?"

"I killed one when I escaped with Glenda. I killed the master tonight." Veso had taken him out faster than he'd intended but it was done.

"I killed a third one." Lorn adjusted in his seat. "He was hiding with the dead bodies of the victims they'd bled out, probably hoping the decay would hide his scent. It didn't."

"Great joint venture," Velder praised. "Thank you."

Veso gazed at Fray and Chaz, nodding toward them. The other scouts were on the roof, waiting for the twin brothers before flying home to the cliffs. They'd made it out of the human territory before the sun rose. They could fly over VampLycan territory home without being spotted by anyone except clan.

"This is how the clans should work together." Lord Aveoth paused. "Thank you for inviting us to the hunt, Lorn."

"Thank you for offering your scouts. They were amazing."

Veso was done listening to the political bullshit and backed up until he reached the door. He spun then, ignoring his father's frown, and fled. He had heard enough. The clans were getting along. Lorn would be a good leader. He wanted to go see Glenda.

"Veso!"

259

He'd made it halfway down the stairs when his father's low voice stopped him. He gripped the railing and twisted, glaring up at him. "I want to see Glenda, not listen to them pay tribute to each other for not fighting about what needed to be done. That nest was a threat to us all."

Bran walked down the stairs to him and gripped his shoulder. "I understand but I wanted to speak to you first."

"You aren't talking me out of taking Glenda as my mate. Get over her being human."

His father's grip tightened painfully but Veso didn't flinch away. "Don't insult me." His fingers eased and released. "I am glad you found a woman you want to share your life with. I was just going to suggest you take things slow for her. She is human, after all. They don't trust their instincts, if they even have any. The time you've spent together has been stressful. Perhaps she'd agree if you showed her a less violent side of yourself."

"She's getting me for a mate. This is who I am."

"It's not an insult but she's not a VampLycan. Her world was much softer than the one we live in. I'm positive that the bloodshed she's witnessed has traumatized her."

"She's tougher than you believe, Father."

"Really?"

"Yes. I expected tears, for her to break down or even start screaming when I had to kill in front of her. She could have tried to run away from me but she didn't. Glenda is brave and strong inside. Even when I showed my temper she stood up to me. She saw what I was capable of, yet held her ground."

"She's losing a lot if she stays here with you. Have you considered that? I'm certain she has."

"We both know she'll never be safe returning to the life she had. What if that master told his council about his plan to breed her with a VampLycan? He only had two Vampires with him—that we know of. And I'm betting he left a nest behind somewhere in order to come here short term. I can't see that asshole not growing a large one to make them adore his stupid ass. They may know her name and go after her to seek vengeance for his death."

"How did she react to that theory?"

"I haven't mentioned it to her."

"Why not? It might help her agree to be your mate."

"She's mine regardless of what she wants." Veso turned and quickly went down the stairs and headed toward the kitchen, where the basement stairs were located. He heard his father coming after him again and spun, halting fast, and growled. "What now?"

"You can't just mate her against her will. She'd grow to hate you," Bran argued.

"Let me handle Glenda. It won't be by force once I sink my fangs into her and share my blood."

"I think you should give her more time."

"I didn't ask for your advice."

"Do you think I wasn't tempted to bite into your mother and make her take my blood to form a bond? I was. She had my son, yet refused to allow me to take you out of this hellish clan. It was my worst nightmare. She pledged you to Decker to be raised as one of his assassins. I figured she'd

261

at least share my misery at what she'd done if she had to feel it through our link. I didn't though. It's wrong to force a mating, regardless of the circumstances."

"Glenda and I are meant to be mates. I was resistant at first but she's mine. She'll realize we belong together once she stops being stubborn."

Bran shook his head. "It will be a mistake."

"It's mine to make."

"You're my son, damn it! I've seen you miserable enough for too many years. Take her home today, spend time with her, and allow her to get to know you when you aren't being chased or hunted. Give her a few days. As your mate, she deserves your best effort to make her happy. It's not just about you, Veso."

He took a deep breath and blew it out, thinking. His father had always been too wise. "I would do anything for her."

"Then give her a few days. Don't force this on her. Seduce her, charm her, and wait for her to agree."

"Fine. I'll take her to my den. Will you trail us to make certain there are no issues? I don't want to have to kill anyone else in front of her if they decide to be rude to my human."

"Not your den. Take her to your home."

"It's safer there."

"You're still in the mindset that Decker rules this clan, but he doesn't. There's no need to hide your human. Word will spread or Lorn will announce it at some point. I'll guard your home so no one can attack without getting through me first. It's best to learn who your enemies are.

Let them strike if they plan to. We'll take them out. That's what Lorn has done."

Veso considered it. "She'd be more comfortable in my home than the den."

"That's very true. Just be patient with your Glenda." He paused. "She also enjoys being called Glen."

"It's a man's name. I refuse."

"It's the name she chooses. Respect that."

Veso growled and spun, resuming his walk to the stairwell of the basement. His father didn't follow him that time.

Davis sat in a chair in the hallway with a book. He smiled when he saw him, standing.

"You're back. I'll let Kira know and go upstairs with her. Is Lorn in his office?"

"Yes. He's filling in the other clans. Thank you for guarding Glenda."

"It's been quiet. The most aggressive ones have already challenged Lorn, if they were unhappy about him mating Kira and taking over the clan, so it's the sneaky ones we have to watch out for."

"I expect they'll have issues with me taking a human mate. At least Kira was raised with us." Veso just didn't give a damn. He'd rip anyone apart who tried to hurt Glenda.

"No one at the lodge would gossip so I doubt many are aware that she's here. You might want to speak to Lorn about announcing it to the clan at once, so you can see who reacts badly to it and we can watch them."

"That's what my father spoke of. Right now, I just plan on taking her to my place and resting."

"Of course. We're just glad you're not dead. We thought you were for a while."

"I'm grateful to be home." Veso passed Davis and entered the one-bedroom guest quarters. He paused inside the door, meeting Glenda's stare from the small kitchen. She was doing dishes.

She turned off the water, rounded the small island, and rushed at him.

"You're okay!"

It pleased and surprised him when she threw herself against him, hugging his waist. He grinned, holding her close. "You're happy to see me."

She lifted her chin. "Of course I am. I was worried."

"You do care."

She tried to back up and let him go. He hugged her tighter.

Glen had been so worried that she'd just reacted instinctually when Veso had walked in. Happy didn't cover what she felt, knowing he was alive and well. Elated, overjoyed, and relieved were words that came to mind. One glance at his expression though had her pulling it together. "Do you have to look so smug? They had dart guns and you went in at night, when those creeper things weren't lying on the floor half out of it. I imagined the worst."

"We had plenty of support. I'm an excellent fighter. There was no doubt that I would survive."

"Well, I wasn't so sure." She realized he had dried blood on him and cringed. "Ewww. Let me go."

He finally released her and allowed her to back up. She studied his clothes. He'd changed them before he'd left, since he wasn't wearing what he had been the last time she'd seen him. The fact that they were covered in blood, some ashy soot, and other things meant he'd gone after the nest in what he now wore.

"You should take a shower. Are you hungry? Davis brought some groceries over. I could make you something."

"That's a caring chore a mate would do." He grinned. "Worrying about me, wanting to feed me."

He might be amused but she wasn't. "Go shower. I'll fix you something."

"I want to take you to my place right now."

"The den you told Lavos you wanted to stash me in? I have to admit I'm so tired of dirt and rock, being below ground in that mine for as long as I was."

"I've changed my mind about taking you there. I have a cabin. It's something I built. You'll like it."

"Am I no longer in danger?" She'd felt welcome at the lodge.

"Possibly. It's complicated." He held out his hand. "Come with me. I want to leave the lodge."

She trusted him. He'd kept her safe so far. "Okay. I think you should shower first."

"I will when I get us home. My clothes are there." He led her out into the hallway. Davis was gone. They exited a stairwell that led upward and to the back of the building. Veso kept hold of her hand and led her into the woods. She spotted some homes but they didn't go close to any of them, keeping off the trails.

"How far out do you live?"

"Far. Do you want me to carry you?"

"No. I was just curious." She saw fewer homes as they walked deeper into the woods. He kept at a fast pace that she struggled to keep up with. "How big is your, um, territory?"

"Big."

"Don't you guys have ATVs or something?"

"We do but they are annoying. We have enhanced hearing and the noises from the engines tend to grate on our nerves. They are only used if we have to bring something extremely heavy or large to homes."

"So you just walk everywhere?"

"You're so human." He grinned.

"I am." She didn't feel sorry about that, but she glanced at Veso's body. No wonder he was so in shape. Just traveling from the lodge to his cabin was giving her a workout. Her calf and ass muscles were feeling the burn.

"We're almost there."

"Good." She was a little out of breath and her throat was dry. "Next time I'll bring some water for the long hike."

Veso halted and made her gasp when he just scooped her up in his arms. She hesitated but wrapped her arms around his neck. They passed a stream, then he carried her up a small hill. He stopped and put her on her feet at the top.

"There it is."

She turned her head and stared at the cute A-frame cabin. It looked like something out of a magazine, only without a garage, driveway, or sidewalk. The trees had been cut back around the structure to make a clearing where the cabin sat in the middle. "You built this?"

"My father helped."

"It's impressive." She peered at him.

His features showed his uncertainty and he frowned.

"I'm serious. It's beautiful." She turned her head, staring at his home again. "It looks as if a professional built it."

He grumbled low.

She met his gaze. "What?"

"We don't hire construction crews like you do in your world to build homes. We do it ourselves."

"To keep humans away?"

"We just don't need them."

She sealed her lips and nodded. Sometimes when he acted sweet, she forgot about how much he held a grudge against her kind. He began to walk again so she followed him to the front door. He just gripped the handle and pushed it open.

"You don't lock your doors?"

"I wasn't home. There was no reason to do so. VampLycans don't steal from each other." He moved out of the way and jerked his head, his gaze scanning the area. "Go inside."

She stepped into his living room and openly admired the log beams overhead. She glanced down. "Hardwood floors. Don't tell me you made those too?"

He snorted, closing the doors. "I installed them but no, I didn't make them. I ordered them online and we picked them up from the lodge. We do buy things from your world. I didn't make the glass for the windows either."

The room was open from the living room to the kitchen. The fireplace was large, all gray stones. "Those look real." She pointed.

"They are. I handpicked each rock from the creek. Are we going to discuss every feature of my cabin?"

She faced him. "I'm nervous."

"Why?"

Yeah, why, Glen? She swallowed hard. They were alone inside his home and it was nicer than she'd imagined. She could even picture herself living there. She could also imagine how much it would break her heart if Veso talked her into staying, then one day regretted it. Love would turn to hate. "Go shower."

He titled his head, his eyes narrowing as he studied her. "Are you trying to be rid of me?"

"No. You're covered in...whatever that is. You should wash it off and put on clean clothes." She glanced down at herself. "Luckily it's dry since it's not on me too."

"Blood and ash doesn't make you nervous. You've seen both on me before."

That was true. He'd killed to get them out of that mine. She lifted her gaze to his. "Fine. We're alone."

"So?"

"We're not running for our lives anymore. I remember the last time we were in a cabin together and what happened between us. Are you going to try to seduce me again?"

He nodded, not denying it.

"That's why I'm nervous. Go shower. I'd like a little time."

"To do what?"

"I don't know. I just want some space and time to think."

"You're my mate. This is where you belong. I'll be in the bedroom. You could join me in the shower."

"Time," she repeated softly, hoping he'd take the hint.

Irritation flashed over his features but he turned, stomping toward the back of the cabin. "Lock the door and don't go outside."

"Okay."

He gazed back at her with a scow, hesitating.

"I'm not going to run outdoors. I'd never find my way back to the lodge, and besides, I'm human. I understand that's not exactly a good thing to be here."

"No one would dare harm you. I'd kill them."

He disappeared and she walked over to his front door. It did have a few locks. She twisted them, tested to make certain they worked, then slowly let herself glance at every inch of the room. It wasn't a big home but it was comfortable. A stairwell led up to a loft over the kitchen.

She just stood there instead of exploring what lay out of sight though.

Veso had made it clear he planned to make her his mate. Just how far will he go? That unanswered question had her biting her lip and hugging her waist, worried.

He might say he was certain they should mate but what if he was wrong? All the things he'd said about humans replayed through her head. Would he always see her as weak? Less than? Inferior to a VampLycan? She paced, deep in thought. She couldn't do all the nifty things he could. She'd just be plain old human.

Trust your instincts.

She held still, just breathing, and closed her eyes. Her heart wanted to stay with Veso. She was falling in love with him. The idea of sleeping with him every night and being with him every day was something she desperately wanted. Her head warned her that it would be the worst mistake she could ever make. They were so different. The gap might be too wide to bridge.

"Shit," she rasped. "I don't know what to do."

Chapter Nineteen

"I didn't know you were evil."

Veso arched his eyebrows, looking confused.

Glen cut another bite off the steak and slowly chewed. Veso had taken his shower, thawed out a few steaks from his freezer, and then proceeded to fry them up in cast iron skillets. He'd made side dishes too. They now sat across from each other at his dining room table tucked to the side of the kitchen.

"You're an excellent cook. It was a joke," she explained.

"I don't see the humor in that kind of accusation."

"You're not going to play fair to get your way, are you?"

He said nothing, just cutting a bite off his own steak and shoving it into his mouth.

"This is the best steak I've ever had," she admitted.

He swallowed, taking a sip of his soda. "Thank you. I'm better in the bedroom than I am in the kitchen."

She gaped at him, surprised that he'd boasted that. He was so cocky.

"Stop fighting me, Glen. We're meant to be together."

It took her a second to respond. "You didn't call me Glenda for once."

"I'm aware. I still believe it's a man's name but you like it. I can compromise. I want you to be happy."

"Who are you and have you done with the real Veso?"

He chuckled. "I have you inside my home and you're safe. This is me relaxed."

"Now you're purposely trying to freak me out, aren't you?"

He put his silverware down. "I'm trying to show you I can be a good mate to you, Glen. I want you to stay with me."

"I got that."

"I'll protect you, make certain you're happy, and we can add more bedrooms onto my cabin. It only has two bedrooms but we can build them as needed."

"For what?"

"Our children."

Her mouth hung open.

"What? Was that the wrong thing to say? You can't control your ovaries the way a Lycan does. It means I'll probably get you pregnant. I never wanted to be a father but I'm willing to face that to be with you."

She stood, getting out of her chair. The urge to flee to the door was strong but she just stared at him. "What kind of game are you playing?"

He slowly rose to his feet. "No games."

"You hate humans."

"Not you. I've stated that many times. Don't you believe me?"

"You'll regret it if we do this mate thing."

"I won't."

"You can't be sure of that. People get married and divorced all the time."

"I'm VampLycan. We don't divorce." He looked and sounded insulted by the very prospect.

"So you're saying every VampLycan relationship works out?"

"I wish I could say that but it wouldn't be true. Though it's rare for mates to want to end their bonds."

She'd have scoffed at him for saying something like that but the world as she'd known it wasn't the same anymore. "How rare?"

"I've only seen bad matings when emotions weren't part of the reason for the mating."

"Can you say that in a way I'd understand?"

"Sometimes matings have been arranged to forge alliances. The couple has no emotional attachment to each other and it never grows between them. That isn't going to happen with us. We have feelings for each other."

Her heart sped up and she stepped closer to him, watching his eyes. "Lust isn't enough to be the glue to keep a relationship together."

"Is that all you think I feel?"

"We don't really know each other."

"I've learned enough about you to be certain you're my mate."

"Like what? I'm less annoying to you than other humans?"

He stepped around the table and came even closer, stopping when they almost bumped into each other. "You're brave, smart, and make me laugh."

"Yeah. That's so you. Always laughing."

He smiled. "Your sarcasm is noted."

"Which if I remember correctly, you don't find attractive."

"It is on you." He lifted his hand and gently brushed her hair back from her face. "I don't want to let you go. I look forward to arguing with you and I find our differences fun."

"I find you irritating."

"Do you?"

"Yes. You're a bully, Veso."

"It's not such a bad thing."

She opened her mouth to protest but he lowered his face, kissing her.

Glen closed her eyes and leaned into him. He was a bully, but he was also sexy and had an amazing mouth. His tongue swept between her lips and he wrapped his arm around her, lifting her off her feet.

She wrapped her arms and legs around him, clinging. He made it impossible to think when he devoured her mouth as if their very lives depended upon it. The soft growls coming from him turned her on more. She barely noticed he was walking until he stopped, lowering her. Their mouths parted, both of them breathing hard, and she realized she lay on his bed.

He lifted up and she released him, letting him go. He tore off his shirt, stepped back, and unfastened his pants.

"Get those clothes off."

She glanced around his bedroom. It wasn't the biggest master bedroom she'd ever seen but it was large enough to accommodate his bed. "King-sized? Why am I not surprised?"

"Don't ever mention the word 'king' while we're about to have sex." He grimaced, shoving down his pants. He didn't wear underwear, and he was aroused. She openly admired his cock. That part of him seemed to be growing as she watched.

"Right. Sorry. Good plan."

"Glenda?" He cleared his throat. "Glen, take off the clothes."

She sat up and edged off the bed, stripping fast. Her gaze traveled to the doorway he'd carried her through but she didn't feel like running. She wanted Veso. It was probably a big mistake to do this with him again but life, she knew, was too short. If there was anyone she was willing to take a chance with, it would be him.

Veso stretched out on the bed naked as she hurried to climb on there with him, her gaze traveling over every tan, muscled inch. She swallowed hard. "Have I ever told you that you're incredibly hot?"

"So are you."

"You must want to get laid badly."

He scooted across the bed when she joined him. He grabbed her by her wrist and yanked. It didn't hurt but it left her gasping, falling on top of him. Veso rolled, pinning her under him. She knew he was being careful not to squish her with his big body. He had to weigh twice what she did.

"Don't ever put yourself down."

"I wasn't."

"I watch your human films and shows. It gets boring here in the winters. Your body does this to mine." He adjusted over her, pressing his erection against her thigh. There was no missing the feel of that. "Spread your thighs wider."

She did, liking the way his voice deepened. "I turn you on too."

"You drive me insane. I like it." He scooted down a bit, cupping her breast with one hand. "Now it's my turn."

"To do what?"

He just smiled, then lowered his head. She moaned when his hot, wet mouth clamped onto the breast he wasn't using his fingers to torment.

She understood. He planned to drive her insane.

She grabbed hold of his broad shoulders, closed her eyes, and threw her head back. He wasn't gentle but it didn't hurt when he sucked hard on her nipple, using his teeth to lightly nip the tip. It just made her quiver and a longing surfaced to have him inside her.

"Veso!"

He released her breasts with his hand and mouth. The bed moved when he shifted his weight. She thought he'd climb back up her but he never did anything she guessed he'd do. He slid his big hands under her thighs and shoved them up, apart. She jerked her eyes open and lifted her head, just in time to see him bury his face. That mouth of his latched onto her clit. She moaned, then did lose her mind as the pleasure hit.

"That's not fair," she got out.

He began to growl, adding vibrations to his tongue tormenting her clit. She clawed at the bedding. It didn't take long before the orgasm tore through her and she cried out his name. She panted, eyes closed.

Veso rose up and closed her legs. He then rolled her over onto her stomach. Glen opened her eyes when he let her legs go, sliding his hands under her hips. He pulled her up to her knees, held her there, and she flipped her hair out of the way to stare at him over her shoulder. He moved behind her and spread his legs to make their hips line up.

"You're mine," he snarled.

She moaned as entered her from behind. She braced her arms, enjoying the feel of him taking her. His cock was so hard and thick, breaching her slow. He felt amazing.

"My mate." His voice deepened. "I'm never letting you go."

She wasn't about to argue with him when he began to withdraw, then thrust forward. That would have implied she could talk.

He moved faster, adjusted his hips a little, and she moaned louder.

"My Glen," he snarled.

He came down over her, wrapping his front along her back. He eased his hold on her waist to pull her hair of the way, and then his mouth was on her neck. He nibbled, licked, and nipped at her skin.

"Oh God!"

He fucked her harder, faster. The second climax built, then slammed through her. She didn't cry out that time, too breathless from her heavy breathing. Veso groaned and ground his hips against her ass, slowing his movements. She swore she could feel him coming inside her.

The pain when he bit her actually felt good, had her arms shaking, almost collapsing.

Veso slid his arm under her before she face-planted onto his bedding and held her up. It was so hard to think but she knew what he was doing. Kira had told her all about the mating habits of VampLycans.

He groaned again and kept pumping his hips, his cock still hard inside her. His body trembled over hers and he suddenly threw himself to the left, taking her with him, since he had his arm locked around her chest. They hit the mattress on their sides.

Veso let go of her throat, licking the throbbing area he'd bitten. "You're mine. Mate me. Say yes." He reached up and she turned her head, unable to see his face since he lay flat on his side. He suddenly shoved his arm in front of her and she gawked at the bloody bite on his inner arm, almost at his wrist.

"Drink my blood, Glen," he urged.

She hesitated. It would mate them for life if they exchanged blood during sex. He was buried inside her pussy still. That technically had to count, despite both of them just getting off. She moaned when he used the arm wrapped around her, trapped under her ribs, to cup one of her breasts, playing with it. Her nipples were sensitive, and she shivered.

"Drink. Mate me."

Blood from his arm dripped onto the bed inches in front of her face.

"Please, Glenda…"

It was the pleading in his voice that did it. He really wanted to make her his.

She squeezed her eyes closed and leaned forward a little. Wet warmth touched her lips as she pressed them against his arm.

Blood.

She couldn't look.

Veso adjusted his body on the bed, pressing his arm more firmly against her open mouth.

"Drink," he gasped, starting to slowly fuck her again. His voice deepened to an inhuman tone and he breathed on her throat. "Swallow for me."

He was great at distracting her from the fact that she had a mouthful of blood. She almost expected to gag as she drank some down, but didn't. He lifted a leg, pinning her on her side better, and drove his cock into her deeper.

He bit her again, in the same spot. It felt even better that time, and a new sensation filled her. Heat began in her throat, spreading down to her stomach and quickly to her sex. Her clit throbbed and she moaned, sucking on his skin to get more blood. Whatever weird thing was happening to her body, she suddenly wanted more.

Veso thrust slowly, in and out, and she rolled her hips, desperately wanting to come. He understood and fucked her faster. A third climax struck so suddenly that she jerked in his hold. He pulled his arm away from her mouth and hugged her as he snarled. His body tensed along her back and he released her shoulder.

"Mine!"

His arms around her eased a little but not by much. She opened her eyes, staring at the wall across the room. Her lips were coated with his blood, the iron taste of it in her mouth as she tried to catch her breath. Her body felt way too warm, as if she were running a fever.

She'd just mated Veso.

He cleared his throat. "Say something."

She blinked, trying not to panic. They were mated. He'd seduced her into it. No, she couldn't totally blame that on him. He hadn't been fucking her when he'd asked her to drink his blood. She's the one who'd opened her mouth and shoved it against his arm.

"Glen?" He lifted his head and she turned hers.

The sight of blood on his mouth too, his chin, knowing it was hers... "You bit me," she got out.

"Twice. I'd have let you bite me but you don't have these." He curled his upper lip, revealing his fangs.

"So we're officially mated now?" She needed him to verbally confirm it, to hear the words.

His features softened. "We're mates. That's a wonderful thing."

He wiggled a little and she lifted up, freeing his trapped arm under her ribs. He bent that arm after planting it on the bed, holding his head up but firmly wrapping his other one around her waist to keep them intimately linked. The fact that his leg still pinned hers wasn't lost on her too. He probably figured she'd try to make a run for it. She was his though. They were mates. Excitement and fear clashed inside her all at once. There was no going back, no changing her mind.

"Breathe."

"I am."

"Too rapidly. Slow it down, Glen. There's no need to panic."

She was. Her heart was racing and her lungs were working too fast. She swallowed, reminded of the blood she'd drank since she could still taste it. It was smeared on her lips, probably her face too. It was on his.

He leaned in, holding her gaze. "I love you."

She searched his eyes, stunned. He looked sincere. He'd actually dropped the L bomb on her.

"I do. You're strong, Glenda. Stop looking as if you're about to faint."

"Glen. You said you'd call me that."

He had the nerve to smile. "You want to argue now? I just told you that you're the owner of my heart and always will be. I'm laying myself bare to you. This is where you're supposed to tell me that you love me too."

"I..."

"I love you. It's not so hard to share your feelings, Glen. That was my second time uttering those words. You can say them too."

Please don't break my heart one day. "I love you, Veso. I'm just still a bit scared," she admitted.

"We're mates. Love is natural between us. I know it's not easy to accept. I fought my instincts to mate you at first, not trusting them because of the blood injected into us at the mine. We've had time since then for it to have worn off. You just drank my blood because you know inside that you're my mate. Try to imagine a life without me. I'll give you a minute to think on it. I've done that...and I didn't like what I pictured."

He made it sound so simple. Life never was.

"Just close your eyes and think ahead five years if I let you return to your world alone."

It wasn't all that much to ask and it beat staring at him, because the blood on his face still made her feel slightly disturbed, reminding her of how she must look too. She closed her eyes, putting herself back inside her apartment. She'd rarely be there because she worked at least six days a week, ten- to twelve-hour shifts she didn't even get all the overtime pay for. It had been lonely. All those meals she ate in front of her TV and the nights she slept alone. Her life had been sad and kind of pathetic.

He cuddled her tighter against his body, putting his lips close to her ear. "I'll always be here for you. We'll share everything together. You have a mate. Accept that and cherish it. I do."

She parted her eyelids, staring at him. "You are evil."

"Why? Because I make sense?"

"No, because you don't play fair."

He smiled. "I'm a VampLycan. I'll do whatever it takes to get what I want."

He was honest. She'd always give him credit for that. And blunt. She should be too. "We're so different. Doesn't that worry you?"

"I've heard that opposites attract. We're proof that's true."

"Do you have an answer for everything?"

"I think so."

"Fine. What about all my belongings in Oregon? I don't even own clothes anymore, just ones Kira leant me. She'll want them back at some point. I don't want to write off my stuff. How will I support myself? I have a car. My lease isn't up for another four months on my apartment. I have some savings but not enough to pay off—"

"That's all easy to take care of."

"Really? Tell me the wonders of the world, oh great know-it-all."

He snorted, smiling again. "I'll send my father to pack the belongings you want and have them shipped here. I have money, which makes it yours too. He can pay off your car and sell it for you. I'm certain your city vehicle wouldn't survive one winter here." He frowned. "I'll drive you anywhere you need to go that a vehicle is required. You won't need one of your own."

"That sounds so sexist."

He grinned. "It's not. We had to walk to our cabin, remember? No roads."

"I'll want to go grocery shopping and stuff. That means I need a car to get to a town at some point."

"Never without me at your side. Humans don't like us, Glen. It wouldn't be safe. They distrust anyone from a VampLycan town. They believe we're some kind of religious cult."

"Why?"

"We keep separate from them except mail and supply runs. It's always been that way."

"To keep your secret," she guessed.

"Yes."

"I can't have your dad packing my underwear. Not to mention, he won't want to do that."

"He'll do it because you're my mate and your safety comes first. I won't allow you to return to your home. The master is no longer a threat but that doesn't mean other Vampires won't be hunting for you. He was working with their council. It's possible he shared your name and his plans with them. At some point, they are going to realize he's dead."

"I don't have keys to my place, which means I have to get another set from the landlord. I have to pay off my lease and give notice that I'm moving." He had no idea how the real world worked. That was obvious. "Your father isn't me, so they aren't going to let him do any of that."

"You forget what we can do." His eyes began to glow.

283

"Mind control."

The yellow of them faded to the natural color. "Yes. My father can gain access to your home, pack whatever you want sent here, and do so safely. He'll go in during the day and can handle any humans he needs to deal with on your behalf."

"You make it sound so easy."

"It is, Glen."

"What about my mom? I still call her every so often."

"We do have phones in Alaska. Just don't tell her where you are. The Vamps could use your family to track you."

It made her go still inside. "They're in danger?"

"Doubtful, especially if they have no information on where to find you. To kill a human in a city draws too much attention so they tend to avoid doing that."

"What do I tell her?"

"That you met the man of your dreams." He grinned. "I swept you off your feet and I'm incredibly handsome. Any mother would love to hear that."

He was impossible—and all hers.

It hit hard. He really was hers.

He chuckled. "Breathe, mate. Don't faint on me."

"Fuck you. You're so bossy!"

"I can do that." He kissed her.

Chapter Twenty

Veso chuckled, watching Glen dust his mantel. She turned her head, shooting him a dirty look.

She amused him. He was mostly grateful that she wasn't attempting to sneak out of the cabin to escape. He worried she'd change her mind about being his mate. Her muscles were probably sore though, since he'd celebrated their mating with lots of sex.

"Dust isn't funny. There's layers of it. Don't you sneeze a lot?"

"It's one chore I hate. The house is clean."

"Except for your shelves and the surfaces above the floor and counters."

"You did want a job." He grinned, enjoying riling her. She was really attractive when she got mad.

"Ha ha ha. Bite me."

He rounded the counter, stalking toward her.

She completely turned and held up the dust rag, pointing a finger at him. "Stop. I didn't mean that in the literal sense. You have big fangs."

"I've got big everything." He stopped a few feet from her and glanced at her upheld hand. "I'm just trying to show you I'm a good mate by doing what you demand." He let his fangs extend, showing them off. He ran his tongue over the tips.

"You're so not funny."

"I disagree." A sudden sound outside had him tensing, moving quickly for the door. "Stay here."

He unlocked it and exited fast, his claws extending too. The sight of his father made him relax. "What's wrong?"

"Lorn has decided to announce your human is part of our clan. He wants you and Glen at the back of the lodge within the hour."

"That's not a good idea." Veso wanted his mate to be safe. The thought of putting her in the midst of a full clan meeting didn't sit well with him.

"I agree," Glen said from behind him.

He turned, growling low when he saw her standing in the open doorway. "I told you to stay inside."

"I heard your father's voice." She stepped farther out onto the porch and stood next to him, waving. "Hi, Bran."

His father's gaze ran over Glen and he smiled. "I see your bite mark. You mated her."

He glanced at Glen to see her reaction. She wore one of his shirts; it was loose around her neck and revealing parts of her shoulders. His mark couldn't be missed. He'd licked it to heal the bite but a bruise remained. She blushed a little, reached up to adjust the shirt, but smiled. It looked a little forced.

He wondered if she was rethinking her decision to mate with him. He'd kept her busy all night, between sex and the naps they'd taken. The shared shower earlier that morning had been nice, and he'd fixed breakfast for them both, then washed the dishes while she'd started to clean. They hadn't done much talking.

Then he noticed the color high in her cheeks and breathed easier. It wasn't regret he saw but embarrassment. She was so human.

"You can't disobey an order from our clan leader. Lorn knows what he's doing." His father came up the porch steps. "We're changing things. It will be safe for her."

He debated it.

Bran scowled. "Do you think we'd allow anything to happen? That I would? She's your mate. I'd kill for her. Lorn and his enforcers will squash any trouble if it arises."

"Fine." To not show up would be disrespectful to Lorn. He didn't want to have to move to another clan and build a new home for his mate. It would take time, and she wasn't made for outdoor living. Winter would come before it was finished. "I just hope Lorn understands I'll rip apart anyone who goes after my Glen."

"He does."

He reached out and placed his hand on her lower back. "Put on shoes. We're going to the lodge."

"Great." She turned and reentered his cabin. "I'm changing my clothes too since I'm dressed for comfort right now, but I'll hurry."

Veso wasn't sure what that meant. She had put on one of his shirts and a pair of Kira's leggings. Her outfit seemed fine to him.

"It's going to be fine, son."

"It better be. She's had to watch me kill enough times this week."

"She needs to learn that life here can be harsher."

"I'm attempting to downplay that a little. She's still adjusting to me."

"Did you get her permission to bond? She doesn't appear agitated."

"I didn't force the mating."

"Good. I'm proud of you."

"I do listen to your advice. I need a favor though."

"Name it."

"Someone needs to clean up Glen's human life. It seems to bother her, not having her own clothing. She rents an apartment in Oregon."

"Say no more. Just tell me when you want me to go."

"Perhaps next week or the one after it. I want to make sure we don't have any problems here before you leave. Thank you for patrolling last night. It gave me the ability to just focus on my mate."

"I'll do the same tonight. This is an important time for your bonding to grow."

"Did you manage to get any sleep?"

"I took a nap once I saw movement inside your home, until Lorn called. I'll get more later."

"Thank you."

"I'd do anything for you."

Veso surprised his father by giving him a hug. "Thank you. You could have been difficult about Glen being human."

Bran patted his back. "I see you're using the name she likes."

Veso chuckled, pulling away. "She corrects me every time I slip. I'm a faster learner and it pleases her."

"Mates will do that." A sadness crept into his father's eyes.

"You should try to find one."

"Some of us aren't meant to have a mate."

"I believed that too. I was wrong."

288

"The only additions to our family I'm expecting are when your mate gives you sons and daughters."

That thought scared Veso.

His father grinned, seeming to guess where his mind had gone. "Fatherhood comes naturally. It's instinctual. You'll be an excellent father. I do admit I'm a bit grateful I wasn't aware of your existence until after you were born."

"Why?"

"It would have driven me insane to watch a woman suffer the pain of birthing my child. That's one thing we can't protect them from."

"Fuck." Veso hadn't thought of that.

His father laughed. "You're not obsessing over this upcoming meeting anymore."

"That's not amusing. I can't get Glen pregnant. She's human. What if she's too weak to birth one of my children? I can't lose her."

"Feed her your blood often. It will strengthen her. She won't turn into one of us but it will boost her immune system and her ability to heal. And we have a doctor."

"One I don't trust."

"I'd trust the one with Trayis's clan. We'll visit there when the time comes. My old cabin still stands. She'd be comfortable there late in a pregnancy."

"Trayis would allow it?"

"He's a friend. Yes, he would."

It was one less worry. Veso sighed. Mating a human was difficult but Glen was worth it.

* * * * *

I'm probably heading right into my own death. Glen glanced at the two men she walked between. Veso looked furious and his father seemed tense. Their gazes constantly roamed the woods. It was as if they expected someone to attack them at any moment. That didn't help alleviate the pit of dread building in her stomach.

Humans are the enemy here. That means me. She wanted to snort aloud, knowing she was probably the most harmless thing in the woods. The hill came into sight and so did the lodge. It perched on the top of it, looming as grimly as the house in that scary movie about Norman. Only these people wouldn't be gripping butcher knives. They had claws.

All the better to slash me with. Shit!

Veso took her hand. "I'll keep you safe."

She peered up at him. "Who is going to keep you safe?"

"I will," Bran stated matter-of-factly. "And Lorn will have his enforcers ready to take out any threats. Hide your fear, Glen. You're the mate of a VampLycan. Shoulders back, keep your breathing steady, and think of something that makes you angry if you get the urge to run. Hold your ground no matter what happens. We're predators. You don't want to incite anyone to attempt to hunt you."

"You would make such a bad motivational speaker. Your son gets that from you. Don't quit your day job."

Bran frowned at her but Veso chuckled. "I got that joke."

"I wasn't kidding," she muttered. "I understood the gist of it though. Act like they're mean dogs. Stare them down, don't turn my back on them, and act bigger than they are if they look like they might attack me."

"Who gave you that advice?"

"I don't know. I think I saw it in a movie," she admitted.

"Just stay at my side and follow my orders." Veso squeezed her hand.

"Be submissive like a good little mate. Got it."

"That's not what I meant. If I say get behind me, be at my back. If I say duck to avoid being splattered with blood, then you—"

"Try not to puke. I remember when you got creeper blood on me. Trust me, I'll duck. I also don't want to be hit with a flying body part. I remember your fighting motto."

"My son has one?"

She met Bran's curious stare. "Off with their heads."

He chuckled. "That's good."

"I thought you'd like it. Do you enjoy ripping heads off too?"

"It depends on whose."

"Good answer." She sealed her lips, grateful her father-in-mate seemed to like her. She wanted to keep her head on her shoulders.

The uphill climb didn't do wonders for her already aching leg muscles. She managed to avoid limping though or grimacing in pain when they reached the top. One thing was for sure. She'd get plenty of exercise living with Veso. All of them were so in shape for a reason.

The sight of a large group of people distracted her from her discomfort. Oh boy. Here we go. Veso and his father came to a halt at the line of trees, keeping them there.

Lorn stood on the back porch, easy to spot. He turned his head, looking in their direction. His voice rang out across the clearing. "I called this meeting for a few reasons. I've invited representatives from the other clans to visit us. I'm not certain of the exact date yet since it's going to take time to plan, but I'll accept suggestions for amusing our guests while they're here. I want everyone to feel a part of this."

One man loudly cleared his throat. "Why would you do that?"

Lorn turned his head to the right. "Because we are mending relationships with the other clans. You have your friends over for dinner. That's exactly what we're going to do."

"They could attack us," a woman called out.

"They didn't start shit with us. Decker caused the friction," Lorn snapped. "He's no longer your leader. I am. I refuse to live with the threat of war always shadowing us. No more! If you have a problem with that, challenge me."

Kira stepped from the sidelines and approached Lorn. She stopped a few feet behind him. He reached back and pulled her forward, his mouth moving but the words too low for Glen to hear. Kira nodded, then let her gaze travel over the gathered crowd.

Kira's voice rose loud and clear. "How many of you have lost children? Brothers? Fathers? Mates? And for what? So Decker alone could gain power. How did that make your lives better? Most of you have family ties to the other clans and have worried about their fates. War between

VampLycans serves no purpose but to cause more grief. Peace with the other clans is best for all of us."

"I know I'd love to be able to visit other clans without their women acting as if I'm rabid. None the ones here are my mate, and damn it, winters are long," a man yelled.

Some of the crowd laughed.

"I don't get it," Glen murmured.

"I'll explain later," Veso mumbled.

She nodded.

"I will make peace with the other clans. That's how it's going to be." Lorn waited a few seconds before he spoke again. "The laws we were once forced to follow are archaic. Garson made an excellent point. It's been difficult for some of you to find mates if they weren't born in this clan. Decker's actions made us unwelcome to visit other clans. Not only will peace with the other VampLycans make them less leery of us, but we need to adapt to modern times. Veso has found his mate and we are going to welcome her into our clan. She's human, and her name is Glen."

There were some growls and gasps from the crowd.

Veso gripped her hand and pulled her away from the trees, striding into the clearing. A few men near the back turned, either hearing or sensing them approach. Glen's heart pounded but she felt safer knowing her mate and his father stayed on each side of her. They stopped about ten feet from the back of the group. More heads turned and Glen became the center of attention.

"No!" A woman shoved through the group. She was pretty, probably in her thirties, and the death glare she sent Glen made her shiver.

293

One of the men in the back stepped in her path, blocking her from getting any closer. "Don't, Brista," he hissed.

The woman turned her glower on Veso. "You wouldn't even test a mating with me but you bit a human? You fucked her?" She spat on the ground. "Traitor!"

Veso snarled. "Don't use that tone when talking about my mate." He released Glen's hand. "I'll kill anyone who tries to touch her."

"Glen is a part of our clan now," Lorn announced. "That's final. Veso isn't a traitor because he found his true mate. Glen was kidnapped by the Vampires, and they escaped together. I'd welcome any mate you found as well, Brista. It's time to let old prejudices go."

"Of course you'd say that," a blond man shouted. "You always had it bad for Kira when she was still human. You're going to ruin this clan by encouraging the sexual deviants! What's next? Allowing our men to fuck humans from the nearby towns? It's sick! You're sanctioning him to breed with that thing."

Veso stormed toward the blond. Glen tried to grab his arm but Bran jerked her to his side, leashing her wrist with his firm grip. All she could do was watch as people, including Brista, scampered out of his path. The blond man shoved a few of the ones nearest him and met Veso.

Lorn was there suddenly, getting between them. "Stop!"

"He called my mate a thing!" Veso's voice came out gruff and Glen didn't have to see his face to know he'd gone a bit hairy. She spotted it spreading down his bare arms. It looked as if he was about to shift forms.

"He fucked and plans to breed with a human," the blond sneered.

Lorn turned his back on Veso, facing the blond. "Bow your fucking head and apologize, or I'll let him kill you. I know change is difficult but you'd better get your head out of your ass."

"He's weak!" the blond accused. "A sexual deviant who likes to fuck even weaker things. I demand to fight him. And you made Veso an enforcer? You're unfit to lead us!"

Lorn shook his head. "You always were an idiot, Bobel. You've got no place in this clan with that kind of archaic thinking. You pick who you want to fight. Me for leadership, or Veso? Decide."

"Veso. I challenge him for his weakling. Then I'll kill her and rid our clan of her stench."

Lorn glanced back at Veso. "You have my permission." He got out of the way.

Glen wanted to turn away, hating to see her guy fight, but she didn't. The blond wasn't as big as Veso but he looked pretty tough still. The jerk's words penetrated her worried brain and she glanced up at Bran.

"Does challenging for me mean what I think it does? You can fight to win a woman here?"

Bran gave a sharp nod and shushed her. "My son will win."

"Skin or fur?"

Glen whipped her head forward at the sound of Veso's snarled question. They were about to fight for her. Actually fight. For. Her. She had to lock her knees. It was barbaric and horrifying.

She came to a quick realization though—she did love Veso. He could die.

"Skin. This won't take long." The blond shot her a disgusted look. "Enjoy your last breaths, soon-to-be-widow of Veso."

The urge to flip him off surfaced but she resisted. It would look childish. These were the kind of people who wouldn't appreciate hand gestures. "Is it rude to encourage my man to win by cheering for him?" She kept her voice low.

"Don't distract him," Bran warned.

She took that for a no.

The fight began the second the blond swung one of his hands toward Veso's throat. He had claws.

Veso jerked out of the way, the razor-sharp points missing him by inches. He punched, striking the blond in the face. It snapped his head back and blood flew. Bile rose when she saw it wasn't just from the force of her mate's fist. He had claws too, ones that had ripped open Bobel's face.

"That's so gross," she whispered.

"Quiet," Bran breathed.

Glen clenched her teeth.

The blond shook his head, stumbling forward, and tried to slash at Veso with his claws again. He probably couldn't see so good with all that blood on his face. Veso dodged both of Bobel's hands, grabbed his wrist and jerked him forward, twisting him in his arms.

"Do you know what my fighting motto is?"

She closed her eyes when she heard Veso's shouted words, pretty sure he was warning her.

"Death to anyone who talks shit about my mate or threatens her."

296

There was a thud, as if something had hit the dirt. Glen peeked.

Veso still had his back to her, the blond in front of him so she couldn't see his body. It was what lay on the ground near their feet that caught her attention. She quickly averted her gaze.

"Off with their heads," she whispered.

"That's my son," Bran boasted. "A quick, efficient killer."

"You make him sound like a serial killer. That guy was an asshole," she whispered. "He needed to die."

Bran released her wrist and patted her back. "You'll make him an excellent mate."

"Just tell me when I can look at Veso again without seeing the dead guy's head or body. I'll hurl. That will make me not cool, right?"

Bran chuckled. "Just glare at the ones staring at you."

"That I can do. Especially the bitch who hates me. Please tell me her and Veso weren't lovers. She sounded like a jealous ex-girlfriend."

"He never touched her."

She felt relief. "Good. We have enough stacked against us without an ex with a grudge."

Chapter Twenty-One

Glen paced the living room as she waited for Veso to come out. He'd had to shower again. It once would have sent her screaming if a man in her life had a penchant for getting blood on his clothes the way he did. Of course, her exes had been human.

Motion from the hallway had her stopping to stare at him.

He only wore a towel around his waist, his hair wet, and drops of water drew her attention to his muscled chest. Her guy was super-hot, albeit a bit unhappy, judging by the scowl on his handsome face.

"What's wrong?" She stepped closer to him.

"I'm trying to show you my less violent side but I keep having to kill idiots. Are you plotting to run away from me?"

"No. I didn't like that bobble man. He was rude, and he made your dislike of humans seem tame in comparison. I wasn't exactly fond of the whole challenge thing. I'm a person, not a poker chip to gamble with."

"His name was Bobel, and the rules are different here."

"So any asshat can challenge a man for his mate?"

"It rarely happens."

"It shouldn't ever. Don't women have the right to choose who they want to be with?"

"They do. It's more of a Lycan tradition than a VampLycan one. Sometimes attractive women are something men fight over. You are very appealing, Glen. I hope his death hasn't upset you."

"I'm not too broken up. He wanted to kill me because I'm a lowly human."

"But? You've looked pensive and have been too quiet since we started home."

"I've just been doing a lot of thinking."

"I won't let you go. I'll fight for you every time, Glen."

"I'm more than aware." She placed her hand on his chest. "I might be a bit freaked and still on the fence about whether mating you this fast was a bright idea, but it's a done deal. I don't regret it. I'm just reeling a bit."

"This is a lot for you to assimilate."

"You have that right, but a few things are clear."

"Such as?"

She sucked in a deep breath, peering into his eyes. "I have fallen in love with you. It sounds crazy to feel this way so fast but I'm listening to my gut."

"You should always trust your instincts."

"Plus, you're really good in bed, can cook, you built a log cabin. I mean, that is so over-the-top masculine. Who could resist all that? The only down sides are you live in Alaska, people die a lot here, and you must have a lot of experience at getting blood out of your clothes. Or maybe you just buy a lot of them."

"I usually don't have to kill this many people in such a short amount of time."

"That's oddly comforting." She chuckled. "Am I losing my mind?"

"No. You've handled everything extremely well."

"For a human." She couldn't help but tease him a bit.

He grinned.

"I'm not going to run from you. We're practically married. I take vows seriously."

"Do you need a church ceremony?"

"I understand that mating is rock solid. I'm not exactly a huge fan of weddings anyway."

"I'm glad. I would hate to wear a suit. They look uncomfortable." He surprised her by leaning in, brushing his lips over hers. "But I would do it to make you happy."

"Thank you."

"Your happiness is my happiness. That's how this works."

"In that case, why don't we go in the bedroom?" She smiled. "I'll forgo the wedding but I insist on the honeymoon."

He wrapped his arms around her waist, pulling her close. A low growl came from him and his eyes sparked with arousal, glowing a little. "That means sex."

She ignored his wet towel and body, not caring. "Lots of sex."

He scooped her up, making her laugh, and carried her toward the bedroom. "I should convince you that I'm the best mate you could ever have until you no longer have any doubt."

"I like that plan so I'll pretend you need to."

He stopped next to the bed. "I'm going to love you, Glen."

"Even though I'm human?"

"Because you're human. I wouldn't change a thing about you."

"I think you're pretty sexy, VampLycan. I wouldn't change anything about you either."

"This is going to work." Sincerity sounded in his voice.

"We'll make sure of it."

Epilogue

Eight days later

Lorn rubbed the back of his neck after he hung up the phone, meeting his brother's gaze across from his desk. Lavos had just walked into his office and plopped down.

"Shit."

"What is it?" Lavos frowned.

"That was a woman who lives in Colorado. I guess she mistook our lodge for a hotel. It's listed as such in the phone directory. She's been asking the state troopers to make a trip to Kegslee but they won't do it yet. They won't even file a missing person's report until someone is out of contact up here for a few weeks, since it's hunting season. The woman who called hasn't been able to contact her son or his family. She was crying, begging me to send someone out that way."

"The phone lines go down sometimes."

"That's what I told her. She sounded old and upset though. She wouldn't calm, and honestly, I felt bad for her. I promised her I'd send someone to her family with a message." He lifted a pad he'd written on. "This is the address. Get Veso to go. Tell him to let the human know his mother is in tears and to find a damn phone that works to call her."

"I can't believe you're sending anyone to do this."

Lorn sighed. "I'm worried they may have been turned into soldiers for that damn nest we took out. This woman deserves closure if her family is dead."

"Veso's on his honeymoon still." Lavos held out his hand. "I'll go."

Lorn passed the paper over. "Thanks."

"No problem. You're right. Any of the humans turned were innocents pulled into that mess. It's the least we can do."

"I'm hoping their phone is just down."

Lavos walked toward the door. "Me too. I'll take Garson and Kar with me. You're welcome."

"Why is that doing me any favors?"

Lavos spun at the door to face him. "We've got a couple female visitors from Crocker's clan. Specifically, trouble-seeking sisters."

"Goddamn it," Lorn spat. "I hate those two."

"Yeah. They love to mess with my friends until they're fighting each other to show off who's strongest. Not this time. Good thing you made them enforcers and I can order them around. See you later," Lavos called, leaving.

Lorn got up, walked to the map on the wall. He located Kegslee. It wasn't too far from their territory. It would only take a few hours for his brother to reach it using the main roads. He studied the area, spotting Pick nearby. That was the abandoned mining town hooked to that mine where they took out the nest.

He had a bad feeling they'd just find an empty home where the family used to live. That town was directly in the path of where the Vampires would have traveled.

Want to read the first chapter of the next book?

Lavos - VLG #5

by Laurann Dohner

Chapter One

Jadee unlocked the RV and stepped inside. "Dad?"

The silence seemed ominous but the lights were on. She entered and did a quick search of the interior. He wasn't there but his bed had been made. She paused in the kitchen area, studying the gun sitting on the surface of the table. He usually kept his weapons locked up. The security shutters were all down, blocking out the exterior light. It was odd. A prick of apprehension stabbed at her.

She turned, going to the open door to peer out at the woods. It was late afternoon and the sun was going down fast. There was no sign of her dad or his car. She closed the door and locked it. There could be bears or other wildlife she didn't want to meet up close and personal.

She walked to the front and sat down in the driver's seat. The bad feeling increased tenfold as she stared at the metal over the windshield and side doors. Why were they down? She turned on the CB and made sure it was on the channel her father usually used.

"Dad? Come back. It's Jadee."

She waited, hoping he was within range. The mountains were rugged and she doubted the antenna on top of this mobile tank would reach far.

304

He might have gone to pick up supplies, but he'd been expecting her. Something was off.

"Jadee? Is that you, hon?"

The voice didn't belong to her dad. Irritation rose. She identified that southern accent. "Mark?"

"Where are you?"

"Dad's RV. Where is he?"

"Lock the doors. Do it now."

"Don't give me orders." She leaned back as bitter memories of her childhood flashed through her mind. She always had that reaction to her father's research partner. "Where is my dad? Is he with you?"

"Listen to me, damn it! Lock the doors—and are the shutters down? Please tell me you didn't open them. You're in danger."

"I locked the door after I came inside."

"Are the shutters still down?"

She stared at the thick metal. "Yes."

"Good. We didn't know your father's code to get inside. We'd hoped you would go there first and reach our camp before the sun went down."

Mark's droning voice grated on her nerves. "Where is my dad?"

"Um..." Mark grew silent.

She tensed. "What is going on?"

"They got your father," he stated softly.

"Stop playing games. What are you talking about?" A list of reasons why she hated Mark Tarnet filled her head, beginning with the way he could never just spit something out. He seemed to take pleasure from annoying others. "Who has my father? Was he arrested? What for this time? Did he trespass on private property again?"

"Do you see his tablet? Open it and let's do this live."

"Just tell me what the hell is going on and where my dad is!"

The silence was on purpose. He refused to answer.

She cursed, hanging up the CB and rising from the seat. The tablet was on the kitchen counter and she turned it on. Within seconds, an incoming request came for video chat. She clicked it on and glared at her father's research partner.

His appearance stunned her. His hair was wild and his usually rounded face looked gaunt. He sat in what appeared to be a metal room, and she saw two people crouched behind him. Peggy didn't appear as if she'd brushed her hair in a good while and Brent's normally clean-shaven face had days of growth. The siblings both seemed exhausted.

"You look like hell." Jadee lifted the tablet, making sure the plug wasn't pulled, and took a seat at the table in front of the gun. She used it to help prop up the device. "I take it that's the interior of that new trailer my dad told me about? It looks industrial."

"What did your father tell you about why we're here?" Mark leaned in closer.

Jadee wasn't in a mood to play games. "The same crap he always says. He thought he was finally going to have proof about his theories. I only came because he was so worked up. He's already had one heart attack. Someone needed to talk some sense into him. I would have called to ask how to find him faster but my cell couldn't pick up a signal. Speaking of, how come we can get the internet here?"

"It's a short-distance signal we set up." Peggy bent lower, peering at the camera over Mark's shoulder. "Are you sure the doors are locked and the shutters are still down? It's important."

"Let me guess. It's getting dark and you're expecting visitors." Jadee became more annoyed. "I'll tell you the same thing I told my dad. Nobody in their right mind would want to live out here—including Vampires. They theoretically would stick to large cities with lots of people since they're supposed to drink human blood. This was a bullshit trip you made. There isn't even a hospital near here. What are you geniuses going to do if my dad gets sick again? Somebody has to look out for him since none of you will."

Brent leaned forward, hogging the screen. "I'm so sorry, Jadee. We believe your dad is dead."

The shock felt as if she'd been punched in the gut. Denial was instant. "What do you mean you think? What are you talking about?"

Mark shoved him aside, intently peering at her. "We found damaged night walkers."

Jadee was about to lose her temper—big time. "I don't want to hear this crap! Is he lost in the woods or something? Did you call in search and rescue?"

"It's true," Brent swore. "We were contacted by a reliable source via our website about a sighting of Vampires. He also said some people he knew had disappeared. He was certain the Vampires were taking them."

Jadee resisted rolling her eyes. "Oh, someone from your website said so? It must have been true. How do you know he was reliable?"

Brent hesitated. "Well, he sounded sincere and he had good details, so we packed up and headed here. We lost contact with him after that though and were worried that something happened to him. We arrived five days ago and set our trap. We caught four of them."

"They're Vampires," Peggy whispered shakily. "Real ones."

"They were more animalistic than we expected," Mark added. "They seemed mentally unstable too but they're allergic to sunlight. It burns them. That's why you've got to make sure you're locked in and the shutters are down. It's too late to reach you. It's already getting dark. You're going to have to stay there until morning."

"The Vampires escaped," Peggy blurted. "Your dad had already called you and you said you were flying here. We weren't sure when you'd arrive And we can't get cell service, so we weren't able to warn you to stay away. We didn't even know they'd escaped at first until Victor disappeared last night. They were too strong to handle at night so we were only running tests on them when the sun came up."

"We'd locked ourselves inside at night, thankfully. Otherwise we'd all be dead." Mark paused. "I'm so sorry, Jadee. They got him."

"His car is gone. He must have driven to get groceries." Jadee wondered if the extreme isolation had made them jump to the worst conclusions possible.

"They pushed it into a ravine," Peggy whimpered. "They've done that to all our cars, and we found tracks where they pushed the big rig that hauls this trailer into the river. They've stranded us."

"Right." She was fed up. "This guy who contacted you probably has friends and they're messing with you."

"No. It's all true!" Peggy swore. "This isn't a hoax."

"The RV is fine." She glanced around.

308

"The engine isn't. We checked it during the day once we realized we were trapped. The RV's impossible for them to move. There were signs that they'd crawled under it so we took a peek. Your father had activated the emergency pillars on the motor home. They are six footings that flatten to the ground. It's a precaution for high winds and bad storms. The wheels won't roll. We have the same setup here. It's why they haven't managed to kill us yet."

Jadee was fed up. Their paranoid delusions had finally gotten the best of them. Her father ran for supplies often and his hunk-of-junk tow car had probably just broken down again. He refused to spend money on it. "The RV has power. Notice the lights on?"

"It's the solar panels. I'm telling you, we looked under it and they ripped out the oil pan on the motor home. It wasn't shielded as well as the hood is with the reinforced steel." Mark shook his head. "We're stranded. They've taken out all our vehicles."

Jadee clenched her jaw, ready to start screaming at the idiots. They were so gullible. "Have you guys been smoking pot? Been adding a little LSD to it again? Is that it? Or have you just totally lost your damn minds? Dad probably went to a major town because he needed his car repaired. Remember New Mexico? You called to tell me you thought he'd been kidnapped by an army of ghosts. Instead, he was waiting on a new transmission to be installed in some out-of-the-way repair shop."

"Wait until darkness falls," Mark warned. "They tried to break into our trailer a few times last night."

Peggy leaned in, her face close to the screen. "Do not let them in! I know you don't believe us but damn it, we found Vampires, hon. These are real Vampires. They kill their victims by tearing out their throats and drinking the blood."

"Show her the evidence," Brent urged. "We found a few bodies of the locals. They decapitated them postmortem. We believe it's so they won't turn, if legend is accurate about their bites transmitting the Vampire disease. Maybe we should ask her to rush outside and make a run for it in her rental car. She could come back in the morning to rescue us."

Jadee frowned. "I rented a truck from the airport, not a car. Dad said I'd need one to get to your camp."

"It's too late," Peggy moaned. "It's miles to the main highway. You've seen how fast those things run. They'd catch up to her and attack. Hell, they would probably be on her before she made it ten feet out the door. Look at the cameras. The sun is too far down. It's already dark enough for them to be awake and moving around in the shade of all the trees."

"They have us cut off," Mark agreed. "She'd never get out of here in time and escape."

A bad feeling settled in the pit of Jadee's stomach but she didn't want to believe what they had to say. Her father and his team had never found anything real. They sure weren't going to locate a nest of Vampires in the middle of the Alaskan woods. "Hey, loco researchers," Jadee interrupted. "I'm done playing this game. Where the hell is my father, really?"

"Maybe they won't go to the motor home since they already took Victor." Mark ignored her to instead stare at Peggy. "It's possible they

310

won't find her rental if we make a lot of noise and keep them occupied. At first light, we can make it out together."

"That means they'll attack us again." Peggy backed up and bumped against the wall. The terror on her face appeared genuine enough as she frantically looked around. "Can the exterior take it?"

Mark stood, approaching her with his hands outstretched to grip her by the shoulders. "The trailer shell has two inches of steel. We're safe. Stay calm. We built it to withstand a Sasquatch attack. They're supposedly bigger and stronger than night walkers. We made it last night, didn't we?"

Jadee rolled her eyes. "Sasquatch?"

Brent dropped into Mark's empty seat. "We were on Bigfoot's trail and your dad had designed this trailer after hearing about how the creatures were breaking into cabins. He wanted us to be safe. It's a nine- by twenty-five-foot container with all our monitoring equipment. We even have a toilet and two pull-down bunks for taking naps."

"Oh my God. Does it have windows? Maybe you guys are experiencing carbon monoxide poisoning or something. Open a door and let in fresh air. How long have you been locked in there?" Jadee wondered if that was the reason they'd lost their minds.

A loud thump sounded over the speakers and all three of the people on the screen looked upward toward the roof of the metal container they were inside. Brent's eyes widened as he gasped, "They're back!"

Peggy began to sob.

Mark hugged her against his chest. "Quiet!"

"Where's the trailer?" Jadee stood. "I'm coming over there just to prove that you guys are nuts. Or your so-called source is just some asshole having fun at your expense. You've lost it. You need to open the doors and I'll take you to a nice hospital where they'll treat you for whatever the hell is wrong with you."

"Hook her into the outside monitors," Mark hissed. "Show her what we're seeing."

"Did you hear me?" Jadee's frustration rose. "Tell me where you guys set up in relation to the RV and I'll come there."

Brent twisted to the side and suddenly her view changed to a dark screen. She could tell by the gray-toned images that they were using the night-vision cameras. The trees were clearly outlined and they seemed to be set up in a small clearing without any signs of civilization. The image switched, going to another camera angle.

A man stood on top of what appeared to be a shipping trailer, the kind usually hooked to a big rig. It was a view from the top of the roof looking down the length. Jadee frowned, staring at the back of the person. He wore slacks and a ripped-up dark shirt. His hair was shoulder length and scraggly. He turned, facing the camera as he jumped once, seeming to test the roof of the trailer. The night camera made him look really pale, and his eyes appeared black to her as he scanned the top of the roof.

She gasped when a second figure suddenly seemed to drop from the sky next to the first man. The sound was loud when he landed and it happened so fast, she hadn't expected it. It was another man, his hair almost as stark white as his skin. He wore a dark t-shirt and jeans.

Jadee gripped the tablet with both hands and sank back into the seat.

The camera view changed to one showing the back of the trailer. It had double doors, just like any other big-rig trailer she'd ever seen, and a woman in a long black dress was trying to pry them apart with her bare hands. Her hair was dark, down to her ass in a ratty mess. The angle was from above, and she looked up, almost peering into the lens. Her mouth opened, revealing some gnarly, sharp-looking fangs.

"Holy fuck," Jadee whispered. Shock kept her gaze glued to the screen.

The woman resembled something right out of a horror movie with that scary open mouth. It got worse when she bent, suddenly jumping. Her body passed the camera at least twelve feet above her, her clothes a blur. She was gone from view in a flash.

The camera feed switched back to the top of the trailer, showing all three of them on the roof. They jumped around, the sounds noisy. Their erratic, weird movements reminded Jadee of marionette dolls being jerked upright, only they didn't have strings attached to them to leap that high. They fell hard enough that it made her wince when their feet hit metal. It should have hurt them, possible even broken their bones.

The feed changed, showing Brent's face very close to the camera. "Did you see them? Make a run for it," he hissed. "While they're here."

"Don't! There's only three of them here. The fourth one might be close to her." Mark was suddenly there, tearing the other tablet out of Brent's hands. "They run fast, damn it! It's too quiet without the wind blowing and they might hear your engine start. Sound carries in these mountains. Just stay there until the sun rises. You're the only hope we have."

"Shut up!" Peggy hissed. "Listen. They stopped."

Mark turned his head, staring at something to the side of the camera. His mouth parted. "They're gone. I don't see them on any of the cameras." He looked at Jadee. "You're locked in, right? You didn't open the shutters?"

"You think they heard us talking to her?" Brent cursed. "Fuck!"

She abandoned the tablet on the table. Pure fear coursed through Jadee and it helped launch her to her feet, moving fast to the side door. She reached it and threw the bolts and bars that helped secure the door in place. She glanced at the windows, making certain all the security shutters were down. They were.

"Jadee!"

She returned to the table and picked up the forgotten tablet. "What?"

Brent's eyes were wide and his gaze locked on her. "Are you locked in with the shutters down?"

"Yes."

"Keep quiet and turn off the lights. You don't want to draw their attention if they don't know you're there," he whispered.

"She said the shutters are down. They can't see inside if the lights are on or not," Peggy whispered. "Just be quiet."

Jadee didn't move. No way was she going to turn off the lights and sit in the dark to startle at every sound. She remembered the camping trip on her twelfth birthday, when they'd told her Werewolves were coming, and her father's team had played some recorded wolf howls. She'd damn near peed herself sitting in front of the campfire until they'd laughed, pointing out the speakers.

Then there was the time they'd left fake gold coins around her bed when she'd been eight, telling her leprechauns had visited while she slept. Saying how luck she'd been not to be carried off by them. She'd believed it until she'd realized the coins were made of chocolate, covered with foil. Other pranks they'd pulled flashed through her mind, too many. It made her think this had to be another joke. They could have put footage together of the so-called Vampires and staged the entire thing.

It had sucked being Victor Trollis's daughter at times, thanks to her father and his team of researchers dragging her all over the world hunting for mythical creatures. It had only stopped after she'd demanded to live with her grandmother to have some semblance of normalcy.

She got a grip on her hammering heart and glared at the camera. "You guys suck. Put my dad on now. Is this payback for not driving to Arizona for his birthday two months ago? Some of us have to work real jobs instead of living off my dad's trust fund, pursuing crazy notions of myths. How did that last trip work out for you guys, anyway? Did you find a Chupacabra? No? Big surprise!"

Something landed on the roof of the RV hard enough to make it rock. Jadee lifted her gaze, her mouth parting.

"Be quiet," Brent breathed.

Heavy tread stomped from the kitchen area above her to the back, toward her father's bedroom. She put the tablet down, ignoring it, and grabbed her dad's gun.

The handle of the door she'd used to get inside rattled but the lock held. Something smashed into it, sounding very much like a fist. A deep hiss followed.

"Fuck me," Jadee muttered. She stood, only glancing down to make sure the safety was off on the gun. "Dad? Not funny."

The stomping ceased for a second. Whoever was up there turned around, walking back. Each footstep was loud enough for her to track despite not being able to see up there. She slid out the gun's clip and

315

checked the ammunition. It was loaded with real bullets, not blanks. She'd been raised around enough guns to know the difference by sight. She slid the clip back in and checked the chamber, seeing a round already loaded.

Something smashed into the glass behind one of the shutters. The sound assured her it did enough damage to probably web the safety glass. That was either a baseball bat or something equally destructive. Her father wouldn't harm his precious Road Warrior—the title he'd dubbed his RV— for a joke. It had cost him hundreds of thousands of dollars to specially outfit it the way he'd wanted.

"Shut up!" Mark demanded, his voice coming from the forgotten tablet on the table.

She turned, glancing down to see all three of her father's team staring at her, huddled around their camera. She reached over and found the volume, muting them as she stood in the middle of the aisle, tense.

A loud boom came from the top of the roof. In seconds, it repeated, and in her mind, she could almost imagine one of those things doing the same thing to her father's RV that they'd done to the trailer, those freaky, weird leaps into the air only to slam down moments later. A third and fourth loud boom assured her one of them seemed to be testing the strength of the roof.

Jadee looked at the gun in her hand. The Glock 19 suddenly didn't make her feel safe. She kept hold of it and inched down the hallway, going directly under the loud thumps from above to reach the hallway closet. She yanked it open, shoving coats aside to get to the hidden back panel. The six-digit code had always been her birthday. She opened the safe and reached for the thigh holster. It took about a minute to secure it on and snuggly slip the handgun into the cradle, the weight of it comforting. She felt a little safer gripping the Bushmaster ACR rifle. It only took seconds to slide in a clip.

Her hands trembled as she shoved another clip down the front of her shirt. She kicked the closet door shut, hugging the weapon close.

"I'm loaded for bear," she yelled. "Break in and I'll open fire on you. I don't give a shit what the hell you are. Having holes ripping through your body is going to ruin your fun! I've got enough rounds to turn your ass into Swiss cheese."

A female scream coming from outside made Jadee jerk, shoving her back against the closet. She was afraid she might fire out of pure fear and pressed her finger down along the underside of the weapon. She used her left hand to chamber a round so it was ready to go if that door gave way.

A second set of footsteps stormed closer from above and suddenly what sounded like a heavy body dropped flat. She winced, swearing she heard something scratching the roof.

"Do you hear me?" she yelled louder. "I have live ammunition and I will shoot you!"

Something slammed against the door but the locks held. There wasn't a window there, and the closed shutters next to it didn't give her a view of outside. She braced her legs, worried her knees might collapse under her otherwise. The last thing she wanted to do was fall over from fright.

Another loud thump came from up top, near the back. That made three she could count, since the scratching sounds didn't stop and the person on the other side of the door continued to batter it with what sounded like a heavy object.

"Assholes!" Jadee shouted. "Enough. I'm not screwing around. I have an arsenal at my back and I'm gripping an assault rifle. My dad is a paranoid gun fanatic who made me learn how to fire anything that took bullets or shells from the time I could walk. I won't miss, and I'll keep firing. I can reload faster than you can say 'oh shit'. Take your freaky circus act somewhere else!"

Silence reigned. It was eerie and sudden.

Jadee sucked in a deep breath, blowing it out slowly. It was possible her threats had made them reconsider making her a target. She bit her bottom lip, relaxing her grip on the rifle. The weight of the handgun against her outer thigh seemed suddenly heavy.

"Goddamn," she rasped. Her dad and his geek squad had actually found a nest of Vampires. What are they doing in the middle of Nowhere, Alaska? It didn't make sense.

"Come out," a man's creepy voice crooned.

Jadee stopped breathing, trapping air inside her lungs. It sounded as if a nail slid across metal above, from where the voice had originated.

"We want to play," a female voice called out from the other side of the door.

"And make you bleed." Another man laughed above her.

"And scream!" the female added.

Jadee forced herself to breathe and tightened her grip on the rifle, sliding her finger over the trigger. A chill ran down her spine. They sounded deranged. She was tempted to tell them to break in and find out who did the bleeding, but she remained mute, waiting to see what they'd do next.

The RV was a tank on wheels. Her father had designed it to withstand anything he hunted.

She moved fast toward the front cab area, reaching up to the control panel that was mounted on the ceiling right before the driver's section. She read each button and hovered her finger over the one labeled Panic.

She hesitated. The siren blasting might scare them off. She debated pressing it. Another scenario popped into her head.

Someone might hear it and come. Like the cops.

* * * * *

"What are we doing out here?" Kar jerked his coat tighter around his body. "It's a Friday night."

"We have to go check on a human family and relay a message to them. Lorn wants us to do it and he's our leader, so here we are. A human called the lodge because she can't reach her family." Lavos nonchalantly shrugged. "Besides, it's not as if you had anything else to do."

"Fuck you."

Lavos grinned. "No thanks. You're not my type."

His friend flipped him off but grinned. "As if you could get that lucky."

"Not even in jest, man. Although, you do have big tits."

"I don't have man boobies."

"Yeah, you do. You get any bigger and we're going to have to special order your shirts with built-in bras."

"Shut up," Garson demanded from the backseat of the open Jeep. "The Tab sisters are visiting and I could be pounding Ginna if I hadn't been assigned this bullshit task. I don't want to hear anything about sex or tits."

319

Kar snorted. "The only pounding you'd have been doing is with your fist when you watched Ginna walk off with me. Everyone knows she only visits our clan because I'm there. And who knows? Maybe Kinna's given up her preference for men over sixty and would have bedded me too. I bet they're crying right now because I'm out on this stupid drive."

"I want a mate. You just like fucking. I'm a better choice than you, and I would have told Ginna so. She would have come home with me."

Kar snorted and shot Garson an amused grin. "Your place is a mess. You ever take a woman there and they'd be convinced you're looking for a maid instead."

"It's not that bad. I'm just not a neat freak. Why did you pick us to go with you?" Garson asked. "What about Veso? Couldn't you have called him, Lavos?"

"He's bonding with his new mate."

"A human one." Kar chuckled. "I never saw that coming in a million years. I almost feel sorry for her. He's a grumpy bastard."

"I couldn't believe Lorn was so great about accepting her into our clan. Does Veso have blackmail on your older brother the way Davis had on Decker?"

Sometimes Lavos's friends annoyed him. "No. Of course not, Garson. We wanted change in the clan."

"That's a big one," Kar sighed. "Human-huge."

"Lorn is very smart," Lavos said. "We talked about it afterward. He figured some of the clan probably hoped Veso would challenge him for leadership once he showed up alive. They believed until then that he was loyal to Decker."

"So Lorn accepted his mate as a thank you for not making him fight and have to kill another one of our clan members? I get that." Kar nodded.

"Wrong. My brother knew Veso had already made enemies who might come after him. Veso pledged loyalty to him, so Lorn did the same. Only a dick like Decker would deny a man his mate."

"So that means we can start testing matings with humans?" Garson sounded excited. "That's going to be awesome! I'm so getting me a mate."

"Wrong again. Keep your hands off women in the nearby towns."

"That's not fair," Garson snarled. "I could rock a human chick's world."

"Maybe if you ever learned mind control," Kar muttered. "And told her to pretend she was experiencing an earthquake."

"I heard that." Garson reached between the seats and punched him in the arm. "I'm great in bed."

Lavos gripped the wheel and turned off onto a dirt road, slowing the Jeep. "The house is just ahead. Knock off the banter before they overhear your conversation. We're here on official business."

"Who bitched because someone else had better things to do than answer their phone? I'm sure that's it." Garson cleared his throat. "They were probably avoiding talking to them."

Lavos slowed even more, on alert as he glanced all around, mindful of his surroundings. "It's the man's mother. He didn't call her when he should have. I'm not going into the full story but she's worried. Lorn said to check on them and give them the message. That's what we're doing."

"Why is this our problem?" Garson leaned forward between the seats. "Bullshit, I tell you."

"You're supposed to be an enforcer, not a whiner," Kar muttered. "Can you at least act like you take your duty seriously? And the task probably is bullshit but we still need to check it out. I'm sure the lines are just down because of that storm that blew through and it will get fixed eventually. It's normal, but people who don't live in this area wouldn't know that."

"I'm hungry," Garson muttered.

"Shut up." Lavos frowned as the darkened house came into view. No lights shone in any of the windows of the two-story home set back into the woods. A truck was parked by the front door and a sat car next to it. "You should have eaten before we left."

Lavos hit the brakes and stopped behind the truck. He didn't bother to wear a seat belt so he just slid out the driver's seat and quickly approached the front door. He was three steps up the porch before he came to an abrupt halt.

Kar bumped into his back. "Why'd you stop?"

Lavos sniffed again. "Smell."

His friend inhaled and suddenly moved to his side. "Shit."

"That stinks," Garson whispered. "What the hell died?"

Lavos took a few steps closer, his vision adjusting to the darkness. The door was closed but upon closer inspection, he saw the splintered wood near the handle and lock. He kicked out, slamming his boot against the door to send it inward. He entered the house first, knowing his friends followed close behind. The stench greatly intensified now that there wasn't a barrier between them and the interior.

The dining room table lay in pieces with glass fragments all around it. Lavos reached out and flipped on the lights. They instantly came on, and

322

more destruction awaited, with the couch in the living room on its back. Dry red stains were smeared all over it.

"Blood," Kar confirmed. "A lot of it."

"Shit," Garson muttered from another room. "It looks like someone was slaughtered in the kitchen. There's enough splatter in here on the walls and ceiling to assure me they didn't survive."

Lavos spun, following the source of the putrid stench of death, tracking it up the stairs. Dark stains on the carpet revealed more blood. He located all three bodies in the master bedroom. He hesitated inside the room, his gaze traveling over the horror of what remained of the family that had lived in the house.

"What the hell did this?" Kar inched around him. "They're in pieces. I don't pick up any traces of gunpowder. This sure wasn't a murder/suicide of someone going on a bender and losing their shit."

"It wasn't an animal," Garson announced. "It would have eaten them where they were killed instead of obviously carrying them upstairs to dump them in this room."

"No shit," Kar muttered. "Animals wouldn't have closed the front door either after they were gone."

Lavos approached the body closest to him and crouched, studying it. "They've been dead for at least five days, and you're right. This was done with intent." He reached out and dreaded touching the head but had no choice as he pressed his fingers against the back of blood-matted hair. He studied the way they'd been torn apart and cursed. "This wasn't done by an animal or one of ours. I'm thinking Vampire."

Garson walked around the carnage, studying the other two corpses. "How the hell can you tell?"

Lavos sighed. "They'd be even more shredded if a Lycan had done this."

"This wasn't a feeding," Kar spat. "Too much blood was spilled. This was outright cruel and vicious. It had to be a human."

"No." Lavos examined the remains. "See this? The bones were snapped and this person's arm was ripped off. A Lycan would have used his claws. We'd see a lot more shredding of the skin. A human wouldn't have been strong enough to do this without a weapon. I'm not seeing any sharp instrument marks on the exposed bones."

"GarLycan? Gargoyle?" Kar inched closer.

Lavos shook his head. "They would have disposed of the bodies. They're anal about that. Whatever did this was stronger than a human but not a shifter. There's no animal hair in this mess. Look at the hand over there." He pointed. "They grabbed some long hair from whoever killed them. It looks human and it's black. Notice these people have light brown to blonde hair? It came from whoever attacked them."

"Fucking crazy Vamps," Garson cursed. "Why are they screwing with us so much recently? Who wants to make the call?"

Lavos rose up. "There's no cell signal this far out and I didn't bring a satellite phone. I wasn't expecting to find trouble."

Kar grimly stared at Lavos. "Are you thinking what I am? They must have intentionally taken out a pole somewhere so these people couldn't call for help. How many Vamps do you think did this? A nest of bloodsuckers or just one sick bastard?"

"I'm guessing it wasn't a full nest. They wouldn't have allowed that much blood to go to waste. The stink of death is too strong to detect how many were here," Lavos stated. "We'd better check the neighbors."

"Shit. You think there could be more victims?" Kar didn't wait for an answer. "What are we going to do with these three to hide their murder? The state troopers can't find this shit. Burn the house down?"

"It's too close to the woods. We'd risk it spreading despite all that rain that came down in this area a week ago," Lavos decided. He shot a look at Garson. "Tag, you're it."

"Fuck no." The other man shook his head. "No way."

"I'm sure they have a shovel in the shed," Kar snickered. "You said you wanted to pound something. Try earth while you bury them deep, and make sure it's far enough away from the house that they aren't found."

"What about all the blood?"

Lavos felt a headache coming on. "We'll handle that later, once we call for reinforcements. Maybe Davis can set a few bombs along the foundation and bring it down without causing a fire. He might be able to make it look like a propane accident. Nobody is going to want to waste the resources to rummage through the rubble if there's no smell of death. They like to bring in cadaver dogs for that shit. No bodies here means no digging. Get rid of every piece of those poor victims. Wrap them up in the destroyed carpets and bury them far from here. We're going to go check out the nearby houses."

"You guys suck ass!" Garson stomped toward the door.

Kar snickered, following Lavos. "That's what you get for bitching so much in the Jeep."

325

"Shut up," Lavos warned. "Or you can do the digging."

Kar frowned but didn't make another comment.

Lavos hurried down the stairs and walked outside. He bypassed the Jeep and his gaze roamed the landscape. "That way." He pointed.

"You picked up the scent of the prick who did this?"

"Nope. I see a faint light coming from that hill over there."

"Why not drive?"

"It's faster to run, and quieter." Lavos took a deep breath. "Race you." He rushed forward before his friend could respond.

Ten minutes later they walked out of the second cabin. Lavos fought his rage. "Two people lived there, and they didn't leave on their own."

"No shit. It looks like someone put up a fight. Why did they take these ones away when they just left the bodies of the other family? Do you think these are victims of that nest that attacked us? Those soldiers had to come from somewhere."

Lavos shook his head. "Those bodies in the other house aren't more than maybe five days old. We'd taken that nest out before then."

"Shit. More Vampires in this area?"

Lavos glanced up at the night sky. "I'm hoping they didn't turn them. What if they're starting a new nest in the area? That first family could have been slaughtered by a newbie group if they put up too much of a fight. You know how nuts they are right after they change."

"Fuck." Kar lifted a hand and ran it through his hair. "Why would they do that?"

"Decker already sent some of these assholes to cause trouble. I'm sure he's heard from someone that Lorn took the clan and we extinguished Borrow's nest. Payback. To be a prick. Should I go on?"

"Nope. Do you want me to take the Jeep and drive until I get a cell signal to call in reinforcements? We could be dealing with a blanket effect in this area if they've decided to take it over. How many residents do you think live within town limits?"

"Maybe twenty-five tops. That's a lot of Vampires to support in a nest, and it still doesn't account for why the master allowed the waste of that family of three. You saw all the blood spilled. Every drop would be precious, unless they're killing the wildlife to feed from."

"This is all kinds of fucked up. But this town is close enough to launch an attack against us."

Lavos blew out a breath. "Exactly. Stick close. Let's go check out more homes. We need to discover what we're dealing with before we ask more of our people to come here to clean up this mess. I don't want them walking into a trap."

"What about us?" Kar frowned. "I don't want to end up facing down a few dozen Vamps."

"You were bitching about no excitement on a Friday evening. Feeling bored now?"

"Sometimes I hate you."

Lavos grinned. "You don't mean that."

"How can you smile? We might end up tangling with a nest of suckheads. It's just two of us," Kar reminded him. "Three if we go back and grab Garson."

Lavos lifted his hand, concentrating until claws slid out of his fingertips. The deadly tips were a menacing sight. "Decapitate the fuckers. We can handle some Vamps."

"You're crazy."

"I'm pissed," Lavos admitted. "Lorn's got enough shit to deal with right now. He doesn't need this on top of it all. Stay close and keep alert."

"Fuck." Kar allowed his own claws to slide out. "I liked these clothes. I got dressed up for the Tab twins because I figured we wouldn't be gone long. Blood is a bitch to wash out."

"This is more important."

They went north, jogging through the woods. Lavos came to a halt and cocked his head. "Do you hear that?"

"It sounds like someone's car alarm."

"The battery would have died if it had been going for more than a few hours. That means the scene will be fresh. Let's go." He zoned in on the direction of the sound.

www.ingramcontent.com/pod-product-compliance
Lightning Source LLC
Chambersburg PA
CBHW030603180626
46816CB00005B/1652